SCIENCE FICTION?
OCCULT TRUTHS?
MEANINGFUL ALLEGORIES?
PSYCHOLOGICAL INSIGHTS?

E Pluribus Unicorn is *all* of these and
more. Theodore Sturgeon's imagination
stretches beyond the limits to encompass
strange movements backward and forward
in time, bizarre contractions of space,
psychic probings and fusions, powerful
dreams, terrifying foresight, and huge un-
derworlds of hidden instincts and primitive
desires.

Books by Theodore Sturgeon

The Cosmic Rape
E Pluribus Unicorn
Sturgeon Is Alive and Well . . .

Published by POCKET BOOKS

E Pluribus Unicorn
Theodore Sturgeon

With an introduction by

Groff Conklin

PUBLISHED BY POCKET BOOKS NEW YORK

ACKNOWLEDGMENTS

"The Silken-Swift . . . ," copyright 1953 by Fantasy House; "The Professor's Teddy-Bear," copyright 1948 by Weird Tales; "Bianca's Hands," copyright 1947 by Consolidated Press, copyright 1951 by Permabooks for use in Groff Conklins *In the Grip of Terror*; "A Saucer of Loneliness," copyright 1953 by Galaxy Publishing Corp.; "The World Well Lost," copyright 1953 by Bell Publications, Inc.; "It Wasn't Syzygy," copyright 1948 by Weird Tales; "Scars" was originally titled "The Deadly Ratio," copyright 1949 by Theodore Sturgeon; "Fluffy," copyright 1947 by Weird Tales; "The Sex Opposite," copyright 1952 by Ziff-Davis Publishing Co.; "Cellmate" was originally titled "Fluke," copyright 1949 by Popular Publications, Inc.; "Die, Maestro, Die," copyright 1947 by Weird Tales; "A Way of Thinking," copyright 1953 by Ziff-Davis Publishing Co.

POCKET BOOKS, a Simon & Schuster division of
GULF & WESTERN CORPORATION
1230 Avenue of the Americas, New York, N.Y. 10020

To Marion

My book and I may say,
since with her we are crowned,

"I have my full content,
wherever I am bound."

Contents

Essay on Sturgeon

I HAVE *traveled far and seen much in modern imaginative fiction, but never have I met the likes of this man Sturgeon. Particularly have I never met the Sturgeon you will discover in this extraordinary collection of Love Letters to the Spirit of the Unicorn. (There are some Hate Letters, too.) Most of us modern escapists hang around the stage door of the science fictioneers, handing out bouquets to the inventors of new and better supergadgets. To discover that Sturgeon, the man of "Killdozer" and "Mewhu's Jet" and "The Chromium Helmet" is also a master of the weird, the supernatural, the horrible, the uncompromisingly fantastic, may come as something of a shock to those who have not peeked into his first collection.* Without Sorcery, *where there was a mixed bag of fowl, both science fictional and pure Shottle Boppian, or magical.*

This slight and bearded satyr, with his wholly uncontrollable imagination and his completely enchanting black-banged wife, is wilful, disobedient, lyrical, cruel, tender, taunting, haunting, and (I suspect) a bit "tetched in the haid." No one could write so explodingly if he were not. Certainly no living writer has quite Sturgeon's grasp on horror and hilarity nor knows quite so many kinds of people as well. You don't read these stories: they happen to you. When you meet some of their characters, you will wish you hadn't—and that's a warning. But once you've met them you'll never forget them —and that's a promise!

This is no place to try and parse the compleat Sturgeon. I suppose I should at least take off a day or so and try to analyze the stories in this book for their content, their meaning and their influence, but to hell with it. I'm too sulphurously busy wiping the sweat of terror out of my eyes to be able to concentrate on such arcanities. (New word; Mr. S. always makes me want to invent a new vocabulary to describe him, and I always fail.)

The point is that in the thirteen items in this book you will find everything you need to set you beside yourself, send you into jet-propelled shivers, and generally termite your placidity. For this faun-headed gent does not believe in being placid. He believes it is his mission to upset your neat little apple carts. He loves to conduct you politely by the hand into regions of roiling emotion and tenebrous imagination where you wouldn't think of going by yourself as long as you had a shred of common sense left about you.

That, actually, is the key that will unlock this book for you. Just go quietly mad (or not so quietly) before you start reading it: it's the only way you can thoroughly enjoy this stuff. Forget you are a Modern Man, a Rationalist, an Agnostic, a Scientific-Minded Bloke, before you go any further. Let loose your most hidden instincts, your most primitive desires; unbutton the waistband of your proprieties and uninhibit your super ego; let everything go as you start into this collection; otherwise you'll be shocked, and who would like that?

But don't let me frighten you too much. Not too much— just enough to get you started. As a matter of fact, there are lovely and tender tales in this book, as well as delightfully repulsive ones. I don't know which I like best! And if you have any regard for writing with the scintillation of sheer poetry in it, you too won't know which type you go for most, either. All I know is that in the present volume you will find practically everything your little Unconscious desires, from shocking bloodiness and sudden death to the softest kind of ethereal loveliness—often in one and the same story, too. For Sturgeon is a man who covers the waterfront of the Impossible—and does it with distinction, individuality, and a special brand of marvelling on which only he has a patent.

Perhaps a word of explanation should be offered as to why the present volume has not completely occupied itself with traditional science fiction. The trouble is that Sturgeon cannot keep up with the anthologies. Practically every piece of short science fiction he has ever written has been anthologized or is about to be, except for those longer items which have been turned into novels.

But enough of this. Get on to the lovely (and lusty) fable of the Unicorn, and read on through to the ghoulish little affair of the wax-doll-in-reverse that ends this book. Approach with strong heart and strong stomach, friends, for you are about to read of mysteries and monsters never heretofore imagined by man!

GROFF CONKLIN

THERE'S a village by the Bogs, and in the village is a Great House. In the Great House lived a squire who had land and treasures and, for a daughter, Rita.

In the village lived Del, whose voice was a thunder in the inn when he drank there; whose corded, cabled body was golden-skinned, and whose hair flung challenges back to the sun.

Deep in the Bogs, which were brackish, there was a pool of purest water, shaded by willows and wide-wondering aspen, cupped by banks of a moss most marvellously blue. Here grew mandrake, and there were strange pipings in mid-summer. No one ever heard them but a quiet girl whose beauty was so very contained that none of it showed. Her name was Barbara.

There was a green evening, breathless with growth, when Del took his usual way down the lane beside the manor and saw a white shadow adrift inside the tall iron pickets. He stopped, and the shadow approached, and became Rita. "Slip around to the gate," she said, "and I'll open it for you."

She wore a gown like a cloud and a silver circlet round her head. Night was caught in her hair, moonlight in her face, and in her great eyes, secrets swam.

Del said, "I have no business with the squire."

"He's gone," she said. "I've sent the servants away. Come to the gate."

"I need no gate." He leaped and caught the top bar of the fence, and in a continuous fluid motion went high and across and down beside her. She looked at his arms, one, the other; then up at his hair. She pressed her small hands tight together and made a little laugh, and then she was gone through the tailored trees, lightly, swiftly, not looking back. He followed, one step for three of hers, keeping pace with a new pounding in the sides of his neck. They crossed a flower bed and a wide marble terrace. There was an open door, and when he passed through it he stopped, for she was nowhere in sight. Then the door clicked shut behind him and he whirled. She was there, her back to the panel, laughing up at him in the dim-ness. He thought she would come to him then, but instead she twisted by, close, her eyes on his. She smelt of violets and

1

sandalwood. He followed her into a great hall, quite dark but full of the subdued lights of polished wood, cloisonné, tooled leather and gold-threaded tapestry. She flung open another door, and they were in a small room with a carpet made of rosy silences, and a candle-lit table. Two places were set, each with five different crystal glasses and old silver as prodigally used as the iron pickets outside. Six teakwood steps rose to a great oval window. "The moon," she said, "will rise for us there."

She motioned him to a chair and crossed to a sideboard, where there was a rack of decanters—ruby wine and white; one with a strange brown bead; pink, and amber. She took down the first and poured. Then she lifted the silver domes from the salvers on the table, and a magic of fragrance filled the air. There were smoking sweets and savories, rare seafood and slivers of fowl, and morsels of strange meat wrapped in flower petals, spitted with foreign fruits and tiny soft seashells. All about were spices, each like a separate voice in the distant murmur of a crowd: saffron and sesame, cumin and marjoram and mace.

And all the while Del watched her in wonder, seeing how the candles left the moonlight in her face, and how completely she trusted her hands, which did such deftness without supervision—so composed she was, for all the silent secret laughter that tugged at her lips, for all the bright dark mysteries that swirled and swam within her.

They ate, and the oval window yellowed and darkened while the candlelight grew bright. She poured another wine, and another, and with the courses of the meal they were as May to the crocus and as frost to the apple.

Del knew it was alchemy and he yielded to it without question. That which was purposely over-sweet would be piquantly cut; this induced thirst would, with exquisite timing, be quenched. He knew she was watching him; he knew she was aware of the heat in his cheeks and the tingle at his fingertips. His wonder grew, but he was not afraid.

In all this time she spoke hardly a word; but at last the feast was over and they rose. She touched a silken rope on the wall, and panelling slid aside. The table rolled silently into some ingenious recess and the panel returned. She waved him to an L-shaped couch in one corner, and as he sat close to her, she turned and took down the lute which hung on the wall behind her. He had his moment of confusion; his arms were

2

ready for her, but not for the instrument as well. Her eyes sparkled, but her composure was unshaken.

Now she spoke, while her fingers strolled and danced on the lute, and her words marched and wandered in and about the music. She had a thousand voices, so that he wondered which of them was truly hers. Sometimes she sang; sometimes it was a wordless crooning. She seemed at times remote from him, puzzled at the turn the music was taking, and at other times she seemed to hear the pulsing roar in his eardrums, and she played laughing syncopations to it. She sang words which he almost understood:

> *Bee to blossom, honey dew,*
> *Claw to mouse, and rain to tree,*
> *Moon to midnight, I to you;*
> *Sun to starlight, you to me . . .*

and she sang something wordless:

> *Ake ya rundefle, rundefle fye,*
> *Orel ya rundefle kown,*
> *En yea, en yea, ya bunderbee bye*
> *En sor, en see, en sown.*

which he also almost understood.

In still another voice she told him the story of a great hairy spider and a little pink girl who found it between the leaves of a half-open book; and at first he was all fright and pity for the girl, but then she went on to tell of what the spider suffered, with his home disrupted by this yawping giant, and so vividly did she tell of it that at the end he was laughing at himself and all but crying for the poor spider.

So the hours slipped by, and suddenly, between songs, she was in his arms; and in the instant she had twisted up and away from him, leaving him gasping. She said, in still a new voice, sober and low, "No, Del. We must wait for the moon."

His thighs ached and he realized that he had half-risen, arms out, hands clutching and feeling the extraordinary fabric of her gown though it was gone from them; and he sank back to the couch with an odd, faint sound that was wrong for the room. He flexed his fingers and, reluctantly, the sensation of white gossamer left them. At last he looked across at her and she laughed and leapt high lightly, and it was as if she stopped

3

in midair to stretch for a moment before she alighted beside him, bent and kissed his mouth, and leapt away.

The roaring in his ears was greater, and at this it seemed to acquire a tangible weight. His head bowed; he tucked his knuckles into the upper curve of his eye sockets and rested his elbows on his knees. He could hear the sweet sussurrus of Rita's gown as she moved about the room; he could sense the violets and sandalwood. She was dancing, immersed in the joy of movement and of his nearness. She made her own music, humming, sometimes whispering to the melodies in her mind.

And at length he became aware that she had stopped; he could hear nothing, though he knew she was still near. Heavily he raised his head. She was in the center of the room, balanced like a huge white moth, her eyes quite dark now with their secrets quiet. She was staring at the window, poised, waiting.

He followed her gaze. The big oval was black no longer, but dusted over with silver light. Del rose slowly. The dust was a mist, a loom, and then, at one edge, there was a shard of the moon itself creeping and growing.

Because Del stopped breathing, he could hear her breathe; it was rapid and so deep it faintly strummed her versatile vocal cords.

"Rita . . ."

Without answering she ran to the sideboard and filled two small glasses. She gave him one, then, "Wait," she breathed, "oh, wait!"

Spellbound, he waited while the white stain crept across the window. He understood suddenly that he must be still until the great oval was completely filled with direct moonlight, and this helped him, because it set a foreseeable limit to his waiting; and it hurt him, because nothing in life, he thought, had ever moved so slowly. He had a moment of rebellion, in which he damned himself for falling in with her complex pacing; but with it he realized that now the darker silver was wasting away, now it was a finger's breadth, and now a thread, and now, and *now*—.

She made a brittle feline cry and sprang up the dark steps to the window. So bright was the light that her body was a jet cameo against it. So delicately wrought was her gown that he could see the epaulettes of silver light the moon gave her. She was so beautiful his eyes stung.

"Drink," she whispered. "Drink with me, darling, darling . . ."

4

For an instant he did not understand her at all, and only gradually did he become aware of the little glass he held. He raised it toward her and drank. And of all the twists and titillations of taste he had had this night, this was the most startling; for it had no taste at all, almost no substance, and a temperature almost exactly that of blood. He looked stupidly down at the glass and back up at the girl. He thought that she had turned about and was watching him, though he could not be sure, since her silhouette was the same.

And then he had his second of unbearable shock, for the light went out.

The moon was gone, the window, the room, Rita was gone.

For a stunned instant he stood tautly, stretching his eyes wide. He made a sound that was not a word. He dropped the glass and pressed his palms to his eyes, feeling them blink, feeling the stiff silk of his lashes against them. Then he snatched the hands away, and it was still dark, and more than dark; this was not a blackness. This was like trying to see with an elbow or with a tongue; it was not black, it was *Nothingness*.

He fell to his knees.

Rita laughed.

An odd, alert part of his mind seized on the laugh and understood it, and horror and fury spread through his whole being; for this was the laugh which had been tugging at her lips all evening, and it was a hard, cruel, self-assured laugh. And at the same time, because of the anger or in spite of it, desire exploded whitely within him. He moved toward the sound, groping, mouthing. There was a quick, faint series of rustling sounds from the steps, and then a light, strong web fell around him. He struck out at it, and recognized it for the unforgettable thing it was—her robe. He caught at it, ripped it, stamped upon it. He heard her bare feet run lightly down and past him, and lunged, and caught nothing. He stood, gasping painfully.

She laughed again.

"I'm blind," he said hoarsely. "Rita, I'm blind!"

"I know," she said coolly, close beside him. And again she laughed.

"What have you done to me?"

"I've watched you be a dirty animal of a man," she said.

He grunted and lunged again. His knees struck something —a chair, a cabinet—and he fell heavily. He thought he touched her foot.

5

"Here, lover, here!" she taunted.

He fumbled about for the thing which had tripped him, found it, used it to help him upright again. He peered uselessly about.

"Here, lover!"

He leaped, and crashed into the door jamb: cheekbone, collarbone, hip-bone, ankle were one straight blaze of pain. He clung to the polished wood.

After a time he said, in agony, "Why?"

"No man has ever touched me and none ever will," she sang. Her breath was on his cheek. He reached and touched nothing, and then he heard her leap from her perch on a statue's pedestal by the door, where she had stood high and leaned over to speak.

No pain, no blindness, not even the understanding that it was her witch's brew working in him could quell the wild desire he felt at her nearness. Nothing could tame the fury that shook him as she laughed. He staggered after her, bellowing.

She danced around him, laughing. Once she pushed him into a clattering rack of fire-irons. Once she caught his elbow from behind and spun him. And once, incredibly, she sprang past him and, in midair, kissed him again on the mouth.

He descended into Hell, surrounded by the small, sure patter of bare feet and sweet cool laughter. He rushed and crashed, he crouched and bled and whimpered like a hound. His roaring and blundering took an echo, and that must have been the great hall. Then there were walls that seemed more than unyielding; they struck back. And there were panels to lean against, gasping, which became opening doors as he leaned. And always the black nothingness, the writhing temptation of the pat-pat of firm flesh on smooth stones, and the ravening fury.

It was cooler, and there was no echo. He became aware of the whisper of the wind through trees. The balcony, he thought; and then, right in his ear, so that he felt her warm breath, "Come, lover . . ." and he sprang. He sprang and missed, and instead of sprawling on the terrace, there was nothing, and nothing, and nothing, and then, when he least expected it, a shower of cruel thumps as he rolled down the marble steps.

He must have had a shred of consciousness left, for he was vaguely aware of the approach of her bare feet, and of the small, cautious hand that touched his shoulder and moved to

6

his mouth, and then his chest. Then it was withdrawn, and either she laughed or the sound was still in his mind.

Deep in the Bogs, which were brackish, there was a pool of purest water, shaded by willows and wide-wondering aspens, cupped by banks of a moss most marvellously blue. Here grew mandrake, and there were strange pipings in mid-summer. No one ever heard them but a quiet girl whose beauty was so very contained that none of it showed. Her name was Barbara.

No one noticed Barbara, no one lived with her, no one cared. And Barbara's life was very full, for she was born to receive. Others are born wishing to receive, so they wear bright masks and make attractive sounds like cicadas and operettas, so others will be forced, one way or another, to give to them. But Barbara's receptors were wide open, and always had been, so that she needed no substitute for sunlight through a tulip petal, or the sound of morning-glories climbing, or the tangy sweet smell of formic acid which is the only death cry possible to an ant, or any other of the thousand things overlooked by folk who can only wish to receive. Barbara had a garden and an orchard, and took things in to market when she cared to, and the rest of the time she spent in taking what was given. Weeds grew in her garden, but since they were welcomed, they grew only where they could keep the watermelons from being sunburned. The rabbits were welcome, so they kept to the two rows of carrots, the one of lettuce, and the one of tomato vines which were planted for them, and they left the rest alone. Goldenrod shot up beside the bean hills to lend a hand upward, and the birds ate only the figs and peaches from the waviest top branches, and in return patrolled the lower ones for caterpillars and egg-laying flies. And if a fruit stayed green for two weeks longer until Barbara had time to go to market, or if a mole could channel moisture to the roots of the corn, why it was the least they could do.

For a brace of years Barbara had wandered more and more, impelled by a thing she could not name—if indeed she was aware of it at all. She knew only that over-the-rise was a strange and friendly place, and that it was a fine thing on arriving there to find another rise to go over. It may very well be that she now needed someone to love, for loving is a most receiving thing, as anyone can attest who has been loved without returning it. It is the one who is loved who must give and give. And she found her love, not in her wandering, but at the market. The shape of her love, his colors and sounds, were so much with her that when she saw him first it was without surprise; and thereafter, for a very long while, it was quite enough that he lived. He gave to her by being alive, by setting the air athrum with his mighty voice, by his stride, which was, for a man afoot, the exact analog of what the horseman calls a "perfect seat."

After seeing him, of course, she received twice and twice again as much as ever before. A tree was straight and tall for the magnificent sake of being straight and tall, but wasn't straightness a part of him, and being tall? The oriole gave more now than song, and the hawk more than walking the wind, for had they not hearts like his, warm blood and his same striving to keep it so for tomorrow? And more and more, over-the-rise was the place for her, for only there could there be more and still more things like him.

But when she found the pure pool in the brackish Bogs, there was no more over-the-rise for her. It was a place without hardness or hate, where the aspens trembled only for wonder, and where all contentment was rewarded. Every single rabbit there was *the* champion nose-twinkler, and every waterbird could stand on one leg the longest, and proud of it. Shelf-fungi hung to the willow-trunks, making that certain, single purple of which the sunset is incapable, and a tanager and a cardinal gravely granted one another his definition of "red."

Here Barbara brought a heart light with happiness, large with love, and set it down on the blue moss. And since the loving heart can receive more than anything else, so it is most needed, and Barbara took the best bird songs, and the richest colors, and the deepest peace, and all the other things which are most worth giving. The chipmunks brought her nuts when she was hungry and the prettiest stones when she was not. A green snake explained to her, in pantomime, how a river of jewels may flow uphill, and three mad otters described how a bundle of joy may slip and slide down and down and be all the more joyful for it. And there was the magic moment when a midge hovered, and then a honeybee, and then a bumblebee, and at last a hummingbird; and there they hung, playing a chord in A sharp minor.

Then one day the pool fell silent, and Barbara learned why the water was pure.

The aspens stopped trembling.

The rabbits all came out of the thicket and clustered on the blue bank, backs straight, ears up, and all their noses as still as coral.

The waterbirds stepped backwards, like courtiers, and stopped on the brink with their heads turned sidewise, one eye closed, the better to see with the other.

The chipmunks respectfully emptied their cheek pouches, scrubbed their paws together and tucked them out of sight; then stood still as tent pegs.

The pressure of growth around the pool ceased: the very grass waited.

The last sound of all to be heard—and by then it was very quiet—was the soft *whick!* of an owl's eyelids as it awoke to watch.

He came like a cloud, the earth cupping itself to take each of his golden hooves. He stopped on the bank and lowered his head, and for a brief moment his eyes met Barbara's, and she looked into a second universe of wisdom and compassion. Then there was the arch of the magnificent neck, the blinding flash of his golden horn.

And he drank, and he was gone. Everyone knows the water is pure, where the unicorn drinks.

How long had he been there? How long gone? Did time wait too, like the grass?

"And couldn't he stay?" she wept. "Couldn't he stay?"

To have seen the unicorn is a sad thing; one might never see him more. But then—to have seen the unicorn!

She began to make a song.

It was late when Barbara came in from the Bogs, so late the mood was bleached with cold and fleeing to the horizon. She struck the highroad just below the Great House and turned to pass it and go out to her garden house.

Near the locked main gate an animal was barking. A sick animal, a big animal. . . .

Barbara could see in the dark better than most, and soon saw the creature clinging to the gate, climbing, uttering that coughing moan as it went. At the top it slipped, fell outward, dangled; then there was a ripping sound, and it fell heavily to the ground and lay still and quiet.

She ran to it, and it began to make the sound again. It was a man, and he was weeping.

It was her love, her love, who was tall and straight and so very alive—her love, battered and bleeding, puffy, broken, his clothes torn, crying.

9

Now of all times was the time for a lover to receive, to take from the loved one his pain, his trouble, his fear. "Oh, hush, hush," she whispered, her hands touching his bruised face like swift feathers. "It's all over now. It's all over."

She turned him over on his back and knelt to bring him up sitting. She lifted one of his thick arms around her shoulder. He was very heavy, but she was very strong. When he was upright, gasping weakly, she looked up and down the road in the waning moonlight. Nothing, no one. The Great House was dark. Across the road, though, was a meadow with high hedgerows which might break the wind a little.

"Come, my love, my dear love," she whispered. He trembled violently.

All but carrying him, she got him across the road, over the shallow ditch, and through a gap in the hedge. She almost fell with him there. She gritted her teeth and set him down gently. She let him lean against the hedge, and then ran and swept up great armfuls of sweet broom. She made a tight springy bundle of it and set it on the ground beside him, and put a corner of her cloak over it, and gently lowered his head until it was pillowed. She folded the rest of the cloak about him. He was very cold.

There was no water near, and she dared not leave him. With her kerchief she cleaned some of the blood from his face. He was still very cold. He said, "You devil. You rotten little devil."

"Shh." She crept in beside him and cradled his head. "You'll be warm in a minute."

"Stand still," he growled. "Keep running away."

"I won't run away," she whispered. "Oh, my darling, you've been hurt, so hurt. I won't leave you. I promise I won't leave you."

He lay very still. He made the growling sound again.

"I'll tell you a lovely thing," she said softly. "Listen to me, think about the lovely thing," she crooned.

"There's a place in the bog, a pool of pure water, where the trees live beautifully, willow and aspen and birch, where everything is peaceful, my darling, and the flowers grow without tearing their petals. The moss is blue and the water is like diamonds."

"You tell me stories in a thousand voices," he muttered.

"Shh. Listen, my darling. This isn't a story, it's a real place. Four miles north and a little west, and you can see the trees

10

from the ridge with the two dwarf oaks. And I know why the water is pure!" she cried gladly. "I know why!"

He said nothing. He took a deep breath and it hurt him, for he shuddered painfully.

"The unicorn drinks there," she whispered. "I *saw* him!"

Still he said nothing. She said, "I made a song about it. Listen, this is the song I made:

> *And He—suddenly gleamed! My dazzled eyes*
> *Coming from outer sunshine to this green*
> *And secret gloaming, met without surprise*
> *The vision. Only after, when the sheen*
> *And splendor of his going fled away,*
> *I knew amazement, wonder and despair,*
> *That he should come—and pass—and would not stay,*
> *The Silken-swift—the gloriously Fair!*
> *That he should come—and pass—and would not stay,*
> *So that, forever after, I must go,*
> *Take the long road that mounts against the day,*
> *Travelling in the hope that I shall know*
> *Again that lifted moment, high and sweet,*
> *Somewhere—on purple moor or windy hill—*
> *Remembering still his wild and delicate feet,*
> *The magic and the dream—remembering still!*

His breathing was more regular. She said, "I truly *saw* him!"

"I'm blind," he said. "Blind, I'm blind."

"Oh, my dear . . ."

He fumbled for her hand, found it. For a long moment he held it. Then, slowly, he brought up his other hand and with them both he felt her hand, turned it about, squeezed it. Suddenly he grunted, half sitting. "You're here!"

"Of course, darling. Of course I'm here."

"Why?" he shouted. "Why? *Why?* Why all of this? Why blind me?" He sat up, mouthing, and put his great hand on her throat. "Why do all that if . . ." The words ran together into an animal noise. Wine and witchery, anger and agony boiled in his veins.

Once she cried out.

Once she sobbed.

"Now," he said, "you'll catch no unicorns. Get away from me." He cuffed her.

11

"You're mad. You're sick," she cried.

"Get away," he said ominously.

Terrified, she rose. He took the cloak and hurled it after her. It almost toppled her as she ran away, crying silently.

After a long time, from behind the hedge, the sick, coughing sobs began again.

Three weeks later Rita was in the market when a hard hand took her upper arm and pressed her into the angle of a cottage wall. She did not start. She flashed her eyes upward and recognized him, and then said composedly, "Don't touch me."

"I need you to tell me something," he said. "And tell me you *will!*" His voice was as hard as his hand.

"I'll tell you anything you like," she said. "But don't touch me."

He hesitated, then released her. She turned to him casually. "What is it?" Her gaze darted across his face and its almost-healed scars. The small smile tugged at one corner of her mouth.

His eyes were slits. "I have to know this: why did you make up all that . . . prettiness, that food, that poison . . . just for me? You could have had me for less."

She smiled. "Just for you? It was your turn, that's all."

He was genuinely surprised. "It's happened before?"

She nodded. "Whenever it's the full of the moon—and the squire's away."

"You're lying!"

"You forget yourself!" she said sharply. Then, smiling, "It is the truth, though."

"I'd've heard talk—"

"Would you now? And tell me—how many of your friends know about your humiliating adventure?"

He hung his head.

She nodded. "You see? They go away until they're healed, and they come back and say nothing. And they always will."

"You're a devil . . . why do you do it Why?"

"I told you," she said openly. "I'm a woman and I act like a woman in my own way. No man will ever touch me, though. I am virgin and shall remain so."

"You're *what?*" he roared.

She held up a restraining, ladylike glove. "Please," she said, pained.

"Listen," he said, quietly now, but with such intensity that for once she stepped back a pace. He closed his eyes, thinking hard. "You told me—the pool, the pool of the unicorn, and a song, wait. 'The Silken-swift, the gloriously Fair . . .' Remember? And then I—I saw to it that *you'd* never catch a unicorn!"

She shook her head, complete candor in her face. "I like that, 'the Silken-swift.' Pretty. But believe me—no! That isn't mine."

He put his face close to hers, and though it was barely a whisper, it came out like bullets. "Liar! Liar! I couldn't forget. I was sick, I was hurt, I was poisoned, but I know what I did!" He turned on his heel and strode away.

She put the thumb of her glove against her upper teeth for a second, then ran after him. "Del!"

He stopped but, rudely, would not turn. She rounded him, faced him. "I'll not have you believing that of me—it's the one thing I have left," she said tremulously.

He made no attempt to conceal his surprise. She controlled her expression with a visible effort, and said, "Please. Tell me a little more—just about the pool, the song, whatever it was."

"You don't remember?"

"I don't *know!*" she flashed. She was deeply agitated.

He said with mock patience, "You told me of a unicorn pool out on the Bogs. You said you had seen *him* drink there. You made a song about it. And then I—"

"Where? Where was this?"

"You forget so soon?"

"Where? Where did it happen?"

"In the meadow, across the road from your gate, where you followed me," he said. "Where my sight came back to me, when the sun came up."

She looked at him blankly, and slowly her face changed. First the imprisoned smile struggling to be free, and then—she was herself again, and she laughed. She laughed a great ringing peal of the laughter that had plagued him so, and she did not stop until he put one hand behind his back, then the other, and she saw his shoulders swell with the effort to keep from striking her dead.

"You animal!" she said, goodhumoredly. "Do you know what you've done? Oh, you . . . you *animal!*" She glanced around to see that there were no ears to hear her. "I left you at the foot of the terrace steps," she told him.

13

Her eyes sparkled. "Inside the gates, you understand? And you . . ."

"Don't laugh," he said quietly.

She did not laugh. "That was someone else out there. Who, I can't imagine. But it wasn't I."

He paled. "You followed me out."

"On my soul I did not," she said soberly. Then she quelled another laugh.

"That can't be," he said. "I couldn't have . . ."

"But you were blind, blind and crazy, Del-my-lover!"

"Squire's daughter, take care," he hissed. Then he pulled his big hand through his hair. "It can't be. It's three weeks; I'd have been accused . . ."

"There are those who wouldn't," she smiled. "Or—perhaps she will, in time."

"There has never been a woman so foul," he said evenly, looking her straight in the eye. "You're lying—you know you're lying."

"What must I do to prove it—aside from that which I'll have no man do?"

His lip curled. "Catch the unicorn," he said.

"If I did, you'd believe I was virgin?"

"I must," he admitted. He turned away, then said, over his shoulder, "But—*you*?"

She watched him thoughtfully until he left the marketplace. Her eyes sparkled; then she walked briskly to the goldsmith's, where she ordered a bridle of woven gold.

If the unicorn pool lay in the Bogs nearby, Rita reasoned, someone who was familiar with that brakish wasteland must know of it. And when she made a list in her mind of those few who travelled the Bogs, she knew whom to ask. With that, the other deduction came readily. Her laughter drew stares as she moved through the marketplace.

By the vegetable stall she stopped. The girl looked up patiently.

Rita stood swinging one expensive glove against the other wrist, half-smiling. "So you're the one." She studied the plain, inward-turning, peaceful face until Barbara had to turn her eyes away. Rita said, without further preamble, "I want you to show me the unicorn pool in two weeks."

Barbara looked up again, and now it was Rita who dropped

14

her eyes. Rita said, "I can have someone else find it, of course. If you'd rather not." She spoke very clearly, and people turned to listen. They looked from Barbara to Rita and back again, and they waited.

"I don't mind," said Barbara faintly. As soon as Rita had left, smiling, she packed up her things and went silently back to her house.

The goldsmith, of course, made no secret of such an extraordinary commission; and that, plus the gossips who had overheard Rita talking to Barbara, made the expedition into a cavalcade. The whole village turned out to see; the boys kept firmly in check so that Rita might lead the way; the young bloods ranged behind her (some a little less carefree then they might be) and others snickering behind their hands. Behind them the girls, one or two a little pale, others eager as cats to see the squire's daughter fail, and perhaps even . . . but then, only she had the golden bridle.

She carried it casually, but casualness could not hide it, for it was not wrapped, and it swung and blazed in the sun. She wore a flowing white robe, trimmed a little short so that she might negotiate the rough bogland; she had on a golden girdle and little gold sandals, and a gold chain bound her head and hair like a coronet.

Barbara walked quietly a little behind Rita, closed in with her own thoughts. Not once did she look at Del, who strode somberly by himself.

Rita halted a moment and let Barbara catch up, then walked beside her. "Tell me," she said quietly, "why did you come? It needn't have been you."

"I'm his friend," Barbara said. She quickly touched the bridle with her finger. "The unicorn."

"Oh," said Rita. "The unicorn." She looked archly at the other girl. "You wouldn't betray all your friends, would you?"

Barbara looked at her thoughtfully, without anger. "If—when you catch the unicorn," she said carefully, "what will you do with him?"

"What an amazing question! I shall keep him, of course!"

"I thought I might persuade you to let him go."

Rita smiled, and hung the bridle on her other arm. "You could never do that."

15

"I know," said Barbara. "But I thought I might, so that's why I came." And before Rita could answer, she dropped behind again.

The last ridge, the one which overlooked the unicorn pool, saw a series of gasps as the ranks of villagers topped it, one after the other, and saw what lay below; and it was indeed beautiful.

Surprisingly, it was Del who took it upon himself to call out, in his great voice, "Everyone wait here!" And everyone did; the top of the ridge filled slowly, from one side to the other, with craning, murmuring people. And then Del bounded after Rita and Barbara.

Barbara said, "I'll stop here."

"Wait," said Rita, imperiously. Of Del she demanded, "What are you coming for?"

"To see fair play," he growled. "The little I know of witchcraft makes me like none of it."

"Very well," she said calmly. Then she smiled her very own smile. "Since you insist, I'd rather enjoy Barbara's company too."

Barbara hesitated. "Come, he won't hurt you, girl," said Rita. "He doesn't know you exist."

"Oh," said Barbara, wonderingly.

Del said gruffly, "I do so. She has the vegetable stall."

Rita smiled at Barbara, the secrets bright in her eyes. Barbara said nothing, but came with them.

"You should go back, you know," Rita said silkily to Del, when she could. "Haven't you been humiliated enough yet?"

He did not answer.

She said, "Stubborn animal! Do you think I'd have come this far if I weren't sure?"

"Yes," said Del, "I think perhaps you would."

They reached the blue moss. Rita shuffled it about with her feet and then sank gracefully down to it. Barbara stood alone in the shadows of the willow grove. Del thumped gently at an aspen with his fist. Rita, smiling, arranged the bridle to cast, and laid it across her lap.

The rabbits stayed hid. There was an uneasiness about the grove. Barbara sank to her knees, and put out her hand. A chipmunk ran to nestle in it.

This time there was a difference. This time it was not the slow silencing of living things that warned of his approach, but a sudden babble from the people on the ridge.

16

Rita gathered her legs under her like a sprinter, and held the bridle poised. Her eyes were round and bright, and the tip of her tongue showed between her white teeth. Barbara was a statue. Del put his back against his tree, and became as still as Barbara.

Then from the ridge came a single, simultaneous intake of breath, and silence. One knew without looking that some stared speechless, that some buried their faces or threw an arm over their eyes.

He came.

He came slowly this time, his golden hooves choosing his paces like so many embroidery needles. He held his splendid head high. He regarded the three on the bank gravely, and then turned to look at the ridge for a moment. At last he turned, and came round the pond by the willow grove. Just on the blue moss, he stopped to look down into the pond. It seemed that he drew one deep clear breath. He bent his head then, and drank, and lifted his head to shake away the shining drops.

He turned toward the three spellbound humans and looked at them each in turn. And it was not Rita he went to, at last, nor Barbara. He came to Del, and he drank of Del's eyes with his own just as he had partaken of the pool—deeply and at leisure. The beauty and wisdom were there, and the compassion, and what looked like a bright white point of anger. Del knew that the creature had read everything then, and that he knew all three of them in ways unknown to human beings.

There was a majestic sadness in the way he turned then, and dropped his shining head, and stepped daintily to Rita. She sighed, and rose up a little, lifting the bridle. The unicorn lowered his horn to receive it—

—and tossed his head, tore the bridle out of her grasp, sent the golden thing high in the air. It turned there in the sun, and fell into the pond.

And the instant it touched the water, the pond was a bog and the birds rose mourning from the trees. The unicorn looked up at them, and shook himself. Then he trotted to Barbara and knelt, and put his smooth, stainless head in her lap.

Barbara's hands stayed on the ground by her sides. Her gaze roved over the warm white beauty, up to the tip of the golden horn and back.

The scream was frightening. Rita's hands were up like claws,

17

and she had bitten her tongue; there was blood on her mouth. She screamed again. She threw herself off the now withered moss toward the unicorn and Barbara. "She can't be!" Rita shrieked. She collided with Del's broad right hand. "It's wrong, I tell you, she, you, I. . . ."

"I'm satisfied," said Del, low in his throat. "Keep away, squire's daughter."

She recoiled from him, made as if to try to circle him. He stepped forward. She ground her chin into one shoulder, then the other, in a gesture of sheer frustration, turned suddenly and ran toward the ridge. "It's mine, it's mine," she screamed. "I tell you it can't be hers, don't you understand? I never once, I never did, but she, but she—"

She slowed and stopped, then, and fell silent at the sound that rose from the ridge. It began like the first patter of rain on oak leaves, and it gathered voice until it was a rumble and then a roar. She stood looking up, her face working, the sound washing over her. She shrank from it.

It was laughter.

She turned once, a pleading just beginning to form on her face. Del regarded her stonily. She faced the ridge then, and squared her shoulders, and walked up the hill, to go into the laughter, to go through it, to have it follow her all the way home and all the days of her life.

Del turned to Barbara just as she bent over the beautiful head. She said, "Silken-swift . . . go free."

The unicorn raised its head and looked up at Del. Del's mouth opened. He took a clumsy step forward, stopped again. "You!"

Barbara's face was wet. "You weren't to know," she choked. "You weren't ever to know . . . I was so glad you were blind, because I thought you'd never know."

He fell on his knees beside her. And when he did, the unicorn touched her face with his satin nose, and all the girl's pent-up beauty flooded outward. The unicorn rose from his kneeling, and whickered softly. Del looked at her, and only the unicorn was more beautiful. He put out his hand to the shining neck, and for a moment felt the incredible silk of the mane flowing across his fingers. The unicorn reared then, and wheeled, and in a great leap was across the bog, and in two more was on the crest of the farther ridge. He paused there briefly, with the sun on him, and then was gone.

Barbara said, "For us, he lost his pool, his beautiful pool."

18

And Del said, "He will get another. He must." With difficulty he added, "He couldn't be . . . punished . . . for being so gloriously Fair."

"Sleep," said the monster. It spoke with its ear, with little lips writhing deep within the folds of flesh, because its mouth was full of blood.

"I don't want to sleep now. I'm having a dream," said Jeremy. "When I sleep, all my dreams go away. Or they're just pretend dreams. I'm having a real dream now."

"What are you dreaming now?" asked the monster.

"I am dreaming that I'm grown up—"

"Seven feet tall and very fat," said the monster.

"You're silly," said Jeremy. "I will be five feet, six and three-eighth inches tall. I will be bald on top and will wear eye-glasses like little thick ashtrays. I will give lectures to young things about human destiny and the metempsychosis of Plato."

"What's a metempsychosis?" asked the monster hungrily.

Jeremy was four and could afford to be patient. "A metempsychosis is a thing that happens when a person moves from one house to another."

"Like when your daddy moved here from Monroe Street?"

"Sort of. But not that kind of a house, with shingles and sewers and things. *This* kind of a house," he said, and smote his little chest.

"Oh," said the monster. It moved up and crouched on Jeremy's throat, looking more like a teddy bear than ever. "Now?" it begged. It was not very heavy.

"Not now," said Jeremy petulantly. "It'll make me sleep. I want to watch my dream some more. There's a girl who's not listening to my lecture. She's thinking about her hair."

"What about her hair?" asked the monster.

"It's brown," said Jeremy. "It's shiny, too. She wishes it were golden."

"Why?"

"Somebody named Bert likes golden hair."

"Go ahead and make it golden then."

"I can't! What would the other young ones say?"

"Does that matter?"

"Maybe not. Could I make her hair golden?"

"Who is she?" countered the monster.

"She is a girl who will be born here in about twenty years," said Jeremy.

The monster snuggled closer to his neck.

"If she is to be born here, then of course you can change her hair. Hurry and do it and go to sleep."

Jeremy laughed delightedly.

"What happened?" asked the monster.

"I changed it," said Jeremy. "The girl behind her squeaked like the mouse with its leg caught. Then she jumped up. It's a big lecture-room, you know, built up and away from the speaker-place. It has steep aisles. Her foot slipped on the hard step.

He burst into joyous laughter.

"Now what?"

"She broke her neck. She's dead."

The monster sniggered. "That's a very funny dream. Now change the other girl's hair back again. Nobody else saw it, except you?"

"Nobody else saw," said Jeremy. "There! It's changed back again. She never even knew she had golden hair for a little while."

"That's fine. Does that end the dream?"

"I s'pose it does," said Jeremy regretfully. "It ends the lecture, anyhow. The young people are all crowding around the girl with the broken neck. The young men all have sweat under their noses. The girls are all trying to put their fists into their mouths. You can go ahead."

The monster made a happy sound and pressed its mouth hard against Jeremy's neck. Jeremy closed his eyes.

The door opened. "Jeremy, darling," said Mummy. She had a tired, soft face and smiling eyes. "I heard you laugh."

Jeremy opened his eyes slowly. His lashes were so long that when they swung up, there seemed to be a tiny wind, as if they were dark weather fans. He smiled, and three of his teeth peeped out and smiled too. "I told Fuzzy a story, Mummy," he said sleepily, "and he liked it."

"You darling," she murmured. She came to him and tucked the covers around his chin. He put up his hand and kept the monster tight against his neck.

"Is Fuzzy sleeping?" asked Mummy, her voice crooning with whimsy.

"No," said Jeremy. "He's hungering himself."

"How does he do that?"

"When I eat, the—the hungry goes away. Fuzzy's different."

21

She looked at him, loving him so much that she did not—could not think. "You're a strange child," she whispered, "and you have the pinkest cheeks in the whole wide world."

"Sure I have," he said.

"What a funny little laugh!" she said, paling.

"That wasn't me. That was Fuzzy. He thinks you're funny."

Mummy stood over the crib, looking down at him. It seemed to be the frown that looked at him, while the eyes looked past. Finally she wet her lips and patted his head. "Good night, baby."

"Good night, Mummy." He closed his eyes. Mummy tiptoed out. The monster kept right on doing it.

It was nap-time the next day, and for the hundredth time Mummy had kissed him and said, "You're so *good* about your nap, Jeremy!" Well, he was. He always went straight up to bed at nap-time, as he did at bedtime. Mummy didn't know why, of course. Perhaps Jeremy did not know. Fuzzy knew.

Jeremy opened the toy-chest and took Fuzzy out. "You're hungry, I bet," he said.

"Yes. Let's hurry."

Jeremy climbed into the crib and hugged the teddy bear close. "I keep thinking about that girl," he said.

"What girl?"

"The one whose hair I changed."

"Maybe because it's the first time you've changed a person."

"It is not! What about the man who fell into the subway hole?"

"You moved the hat. The one that blew off. You moved it under his feet so that he stepped on the brim with one foot and caught his toe in the crown, and tumbled in."

"Well, what about the little girl I threw in front of the truck?"

"You didn't touch her," said the monster equably. "She was on roller skates. You broke something in one wheel so it couldn't turn. So she fell right in front of the truck."

Jeremy thought carefully. "Why didn't I ever touch a person before?"

"I don't know," said Fuzzy. "It has something to do with being born in this house, I think."

"I guess maybe," said Jeremy doubtfully.

"I'm hungry," said the monster, settling itself on Jeremy's stomach as he turned on his back.

22

"Oh, all right," Jeremy said. "The next lecture?"

"Yes," said Fuzzy eagerly. "Dream bright, now. The big things that you say, lecturing. Those are what I want. Never mind the people there. Never mind you, lecturing. The things you say."

The strange blood flowed as Jeremy relaxed. He looked up to the ceiling, found the hairline crack that he always stared at while he dreamed real, and began to talk.

"There I am. There's the—the room, yes, and the—yes, it's all there, again. There's the girl. The one who has the brown, shiny hair. The seat behind her is empty. This must be after that other girl broke her neck."

"Never mind that," said the monster impatiently. "What do you say?"

"I—" Jeremy was quiet. Finally Fuzzy nudged him. "Oh. It's all about yesterday's unfortunate occurrence, but, like the show of legend, our studies must go on."

"Go on with it then," panted the monster.

"All right, all right," said Jeremy impatiently. "Here it is. We come now to the Gymnosophists, whose ascetic school has had no recorded equal in its extremism. Those strange gentry regarded clothing and even food as detrimental to purity of thought. The Greeks also called them *Hylobioi,* a term our more erudite students will notice as analogous to the Sanskrit *Vana-Prasthas.* It is evident that they were a profound influence on Diogenes Laërtius, the Elisian founder of pure skepticism. . . ."

And so he droned on and on. Fuzzy crouched on his body, its soft ears making small masticating motions; and sometimes when stimulated by some particularly choice nugget of esoterica, the ears drooled.

At the end of nearly an hour, Jeremy's soft voice trailed off, and he was quiet. Fuzzy shifted in irritation. "What is it?"

"That girl," said Jeremy. "I keep looking back to that girl while I'm talking."

"Well, stop doing it. I'm not finished."

"There isn't any more, Fuzzy. I keep looking and looking back to that girl until I can't lecture any more. Now I'm saying all that about the pages in the book and the assignment. The lecture is over."

Fuzzy's mouth was almost full of blood. From its ears, it

sighed. "That wasn't any too much. But if that's all, then it's all. You can sleep now if you want to."

"I want to watch for a while."

The monster puffed out its cheeks. The pressure inside was not great. "Go on, then." It scrabbled off Jeremy's body and curled up in a sulky huddle.

The strange blood moved steadily through Jeremy's brain. With his eyes wide and fixed, he watched himself as he would be, a slight, balding professor of philosophy.

He sat in the hall, watching the students tumbling up the steep aisles, wondering at the strange compulsion he had to look at that girl, Miss—Miss—what was it?

Oh. "Miss Patchell!"

He started, astonished at himself. He had certainly not meant to call out her name. He clasped his hands tightly, regaining the dry stiffness which was his closest approach to dignity.

The girl came slowly down the aisle steps, her wideset eyes wondering. There were books tucked under her arm, and her hair shone. "Yes, Professor?"

"I—" He stopped and cleared his throat. "I know it's the last class today, and you are no doubt meeting someone. I shan't keep you very long . . . and if I do," he added, and was again astonished at himself, "you can see Bert tomorrow."

"Bert? Oh!" She colored prettily. "I didn't know you knew about—how *could* you know?"

He shrugged. "Miss Patchell," he said. "You'll forgive an old—ah—middle-aged man's rambling, I hope. There is something about you that—that—"

"Yes?" Caution, and an iota of fright were in her eyes. She glanced up and back at the now empty hall.

Abruptly he pounded the table. "I will *not* let this go on for another instant without finding out about it. Miss Patchell, you are becoming afraid of me, and you are wrong."

"I th-think I'd better . . ." she said timidly, and began backing off.

"Sit down!" he thundered. It was the very first time in his entire life that he had thundered at anyone, and her shock was not one whit greater than his. She shrank back and into a front-row seat, looking a good deal smaller than she actually was, except about the eyes, which were much larger.

24

The professor shook his head in vexation. He rose, stepped down off the dais, and crossed to her, sitting in the next seat.

"Now be quiet and listen to me." The shadow of a smile twitched his lips and he said, "I really don't know what I am going to say. Listen, and be patient. It couldn't be more important."

He sat a while, thinking, chasing vague pictures around in his mind. He heard, or was conscious of, the rapid but slowing beat of her frightened heart.

"Miss Patchell," he said, turning to her, his voice gentle, "I have not at any time looked into your records. Until—ah—yesterday, you were simply another face in the class, another source of quiz papers to be graded. I have not consulted the registrar's files for information about you. And, to my almost certain knowledge, this is the first time I have spoken with you."

"That's right, sir," she said quietly.

"Very good, then." He wet his lips. "You are twenty-three years old. The house in which you were born was a two-story affair, quite old, with a leaded bay window at the turn of the stairs. The small bedroom, or nursery, was directly over the kitchen. You could hear the clatter of dishes below you when the house was quiet. The address was 191 Bucyrus Road."

"How—oh yes! How did you know?"

He shook his head, and then put it between his hands. "I don't know. I don't know. I lived in that house, too, as a child. I don't know how I knew that you did. There are things in here—" He rapped his head, shook it again. "I thought perhaps you could help."

She looked at him. He was a small man, brilliant, tired, getting old swiftly. She put a hand on his arm. "I wish I could," she said warmly. "I do wish I could."

"Thank you, child."

"Maybe if you told me more—"

"Perhaps. Some of it is—ugly. All of it is cloudy, long ago, barely remembered. And yet—"

"Please go on."

"I remember," he half whispered, "things that happened long ago that way, and recent things I remember—twice. One memory is sharp and clear, and one is old and misty. And I remember, in the same misty way, what is happening

25

now and—and what *will* happen!"

"I don't understand."

"That girl. That Miss Symes. She—died here yesterday."

"She was sitting right behind me," said Miss Patchell.

"I know it! I knew what was going to happen to her. I knew it mistily, like an old memory. That's what I mean. I don't know what I could have done to stop it. I don't think I could have done anything. And yet, down deep I have the feeling that it's my fault—that she slipped and fell because of something I did."

"Oh, no!"

He touched her arm in mute gratitude for the sympathy in her tone, and grimaced miserably. "It's happened before," he said. "Time and time and time again. As a boy, as a youth, I was plagued with accidents. I led a quiet life. I was not very strong and books were always more my line than baseball. And yet I witnessed a dozen or more violent, useless deaths—automobile accidents, drownings, falls, and one or two—" his voice shook—"which I won't mention. And there were countless minor ones—broken bones, maimings, stabbings . . . and every time, in some way, it was my fault, like the one yesterday . . . and I—I—"

"Don't," she whispered. "Please don't. You were nowhere near Elaine Symes when she fell."

"I was nowhere near any of them! That never mattered. It never took away the burden of guilt. Miss Patchell—"

"Catherine."

"Catherine. Thank you so much! There are people called by insurance actuaries, 'accident prone.' Most of these are involved in accidents through their own negligence, or through some psychological quirk which causes them to defy the world, or to demand attention, by getting hurt. But some are simply present at accidents, without being involved at all —catalysts of death, if you'll pardon a flamboyant phrase. I am, apparently, one of these."

"Then—how could you feel guilty?"

"It was—" He broke off suddenly, and looked at her. She had a gentle face, and her eyes were filled with compassion. He shrugged. "I've said so much," he said. "More would sound no more fantastic, and do me no more damage."

"There'll be no damage from anything you tell me," she said, with a sparkle of decisiveness.

He smiled his thanks this time, sobered, and said, "These

26

horrors—the maimings, the deaths—they were *funny*, once, long ago. I must have been a child, a baby. Something taught me, then, that the agony and death of others was to be promoted and enjoyed. I remember, I—almost remember when that stopped. There was a—a toy, a—a—"

Jeremy blinked. He had been staring at the fine crack in the ceiling for so long that his eyes hurt.

"What are you doing?" asked the monster.

"Dreaming real," said Jeremy. "I am grown up and sitting in the big empty lecture place, talking to the girl with the brown hair that shines. Her name's Catherine."

"What are you talking about?"

"Oh, all the funny dreams. Only—"

"Well?"

"They're not so funny."

The monster scurried over to him and pounced on his chest. "Time to sleep now. And I want to—"

"No," said Jeremy. He put his hands over his throat. "I have enough now. Wait until I see some more of this real-dream."

"What do you want to see?"

"Oh, I don't know. There's something . . ."

"Let's have some fun," said the monster. "This is the girl you can change, isn't it?"

"Yes."

"Go ahead. Give her an elephant's trunk. Make her grow a beard. Stop her nostrils up. Go on. You can do anything." Jeremy grinned briefly, and then said, "I don't want to."

"Oh, go on. Just see how funny. . . ."

"A toy," said the professor. "But more than a toy. It could talk, I think. If I could only remember more clearly!"

"Don't try so hard. Maybe it will come," she said. She took his hand impulsively. "Go ahead."

"It was—something—" the professor said haltingly, "—something soft and not too large. I don't recall . . ."

"Was it smooth?"

"No. Hairy—fuzzy. *Fuzzy!* I'm beginning to get it. Wait, now. . . . A thing like a teddy bear. It talked. It—why, of course! It was alive!"

"A pet, then. Not a toy."

"Oh, no," said the professor, and shuddered. "It was a toy,

27

all right. My mother thought it was, anyway. It made me—dream real."

"You mean, like Peter Ibbetson?"

"No, no. Not like that." He leaned back, rolled his eyes up. "I used to see myself as I would be later, when I was grown. And before. Oh. Oh—I think it was then— Yes! It must have been then that I began to see all those terrible accidents. It was! It was!"

"Steady," said Catherine. "Tell me quietly."

He relaxed. "Fuzzy. The demon—the monster. I know what it did, the devil. Somehow it made me see myself as I grew. It made me repeat what I had learned. It—it ate knowledge! It did; it ate knowledge. It had some strange affinity for me, for something about me. It could absorb knowledge that I gave out. And it—it changed the knowledge into blood, the way a plant changes sunlight and water into cellulose!"

"I don't understand," she said again.

"You don't? How could you? How can I? I know that that's what it did, though. It made me—why, I was spouting my lectures here to the beast when I was four years old! The words of them, the sense of them, came from me *now* to me *then*. And I gave it to the monster, and it ate the knowledge and spiced it with the things it made me do in my real-dreams. It made me trip a man up on a hat, of all absurd things, and fall into a subway excavation. And when I was in my teens, I was right by the excavation to see it happen. And that's the way with all of them! All the horrible accidents I have witnessed, I have half-remembered before they happened. There's no stopping any of them. What am I going to do?"

There were tears in her eyes. "What about me?" she whispered—more, probably to get his mind away from his despair than for any other reason.

"You. There's something about you, if only I could remember. Something about what happened to that—that toy, that beast. You·were in the same environment as I, as that devil. Somehow, you are vulnerable to it and—Catherine, Catherine, I think that something was done to you that—"

He broke off. His eyes widened in horror. The girl sat beside him, helping him, pitying him, and her expression did not change. But—everything else about her did.

Her face shrank, shrivelled. Her eyes lengthened. Her

28

ears grew long, grew until they were like donkey's ears, like rabbit's ears, like horrible, long hairy spider's legs. Her teeth lengthened into tusks. Her arms shrivelled into jointed straws, and her body thickened.

It smelled like rotten meat.

There were filthy claws scattering out of her polished open-toed shoes. There were bright sores. There were—other things. And all the while she—*it*—held his hand and looked at him with pity and friendliness.

The professor—

Jeremy sat up and flung the monster away. "It isn't funny!" he screamed. "It isn't funny, it isn't, it isn't, it *isn't!*"

The monster sat up and looked at him with its soft, bland, teddy-bear expression. "Be quiet," it said. "Let's make her all squashy now, like soft-soap. And hornets in her stomach. And we can put her—"

Jeremy clapped his hands over his ears and screwed his eyes shut. The monster talked on. Jeremy burst into tears, leapt from the crib and, hurling the monster to the floor, kicked it. It grunted. "That's funny!" screamed the child. "Ha ha!" he cried, as he planted both feet in its yielding stomach. He picked up the twitching mass and hurled it across the room. It struck the nursery clock. Clock and monster struck the floor together in a flurry of glass, metal, and blood. Jeremy stamped it all into a jagged, pulpy mass, blood from his feet mixing with blood from the monster, the same strange blood which the monster had pumped into his neck. . . .

Mummy all but fainted when she ran in and saw him. She screamed, but he laughed, screaming. The doctor gave him sedatives until he slept, and cured his feet. He was never very strong after that. They saved him, to live his life and to see his real-dreams; funny dreams, and to die finally in a lecture room, with his eyes distended in horror while horror froze his heart, and a terrified young woman ran crying, crying for help.

BIANCA'S mother was leading her when Ran saw her first. Bianca was squat and small, with dank hair and rotten teeth. Her mouth was crooked and it drooled. Either she was blind or she just didn't care about bumping into things. It didn't really matter because Bianca was an imbecile. Her hands . .

They were lovely hands, graceful hands, hands as soft and smooth and white as snowflakes, hands whose color was lightly tinged with pink like the glow of Mars on Snow. They lay on the counter side by side, looking at Ran. They lay there half closed and crouching, each pulsing with a movement like the panting of a field creature, and they looked. Not watched. Later, they watched him. Now they looked. They did, because Ran felt their united gaze, and his heart beat strongly.

Bianca's mother demanded cheese stridently. Ran brought it to her in his own time while she berated him. She was a bitter woman, as any woman has a right to be who is wife of no man and mother to a monster. Ran gave her the cheese and took her money and never noticed that it was not enough, because of Bianca's hands. When Bianca's mother tried to take one of the hands, it scuttled away from the unwanted touch. It did not lift from the counter, but ran on its finger-tips to the edge and leaped into a fold of Bianca's dress. The mother took the unresisting elbow and led Bianca out.

Ran stayed there at the counter unmoving, thinking of Bianca's hands. Ran was strong and bronze and not very clever. He had never been taught about beauty and strangeness, but he did not need that teaching. His shoulders were wide and his arms were heavy and thick, but he had great soft eyes and thick lashes. They curtained his eyes now. He was seeing Bianca's hands again dreamily. He found it hard to breathe . . .

Harding came back. Harding owned the store. He was a large man whose features barely kept his cheeks apart. He said, "Sweep up, Ran. We're closing early today." Then he went behind the counter, squeezing past Ran.

Ran got the broom and swept slowly.

"A woman bought cheese," he said suddenly. "A poor woman, with very old clothes. She was leading a girl. I can't remember what the girl looked like, except—who was she?"

"I saw them go out," said Harding. "The woman is Bianca's mother, and the girl is Bianca. I don't know their other name. They don't talk to people much. I wish they wouldn't come in here. Hurry up, Ran."

Ran did what was necessary and put away his broom. Before he left he asked, "Where do they live, Bianca and her mother?"

"On the other side. A house on no road, away from people. Good night, Ran."

Ran went from the shop directly over to the other side, not waiting for his supper. He found the house easily, for it was indeed away from the road, and stood rudely by itself. The townspeople had cauterized the house by wrapping it in empty fields.

Harshly, "What do you want?" Bianca's mother asked as she opened the door.

"May I come in?"

"What do you want?"

"May I come in?" he asked again. She made as if to slam the door, and then stood aside. "Come."

Ran went in and stood still. Bianca's mother crossed the room and sat under an old lamp, in the shadow. Ran sat opposite her, on a three-legged stool. Bianca was not in the room.

The woman tried to speak, but embarrassment clutched at her voice. She withdrew into her bitterness, saying nothing. She kept peeping at Ran, who sat quietly with his arms folded and the uncertain light in his eyes. He knew she would speak soon, and he could wait.

"Ah, well . . ." She was silent after that, for a time, but now she had forgiven him his intrusion. Then, "It's a great while since anyone came to see me; a great while . . . it was different before. I was a pretty girl—"

She bit her words off and her face popped out of the shadows, shrivelled and sagging as she leaned forward. Ran saw that she was beaten and cowed and did not want to be laughed at.

"Yes," he said gently. She sighed and leaned back so that her face disappeared again. She said nothing for a moment, sitting looking at Ran, liking him.

"We were happy, the two of us," she mused, "until Bianca came. He didn't like her, poor thing, he didn't, no more than I do now. He went away. I stayed by her because I was her mother. I'd go away myself, I would, but people know me,

31

and I haven't a penny—not a penny. . . . They'd bring me back to her, they would, to care for her. It doesn't matter much now, though, because people don't want me any more than they want her, they don't . . ."

Ran shifted his feet uneasily, because the woman was crying. "Have you room for me here?" he asked.

Her head crept out into the light. Ran said swiftly, "I'll give you money each week, and I'll bring my own bed and things." He was afraid she would refuse.

She merged with the shadows again. "If you like," she said, trembling at her good fortune. "Though why you'd want to . . . still, I guess if I had a little something to cook up nice, and a good reason for it, I could make someone real cosy here. But—why?" She rose. Ran crossed the room and pushed her back into the chair. He stood over her, tall.

"I never want you to ask me that," he said, speaking very slowly. "Hear?"

She swallowed and nodded. "I'll come back tomorrow with the bed and things," he said.

He left her there under the lamp, blinking out of the dimness, folded round and about with her misery and her wonder.

People talked about it. People said, "Ran has moved to the house of Bianca's mother." "It must be because—" "Ah," said some, "Ran was always a strange boy. It must be because—" "Oh, no!" cried others appalled. "Ran is such a good boy. He wouldn't—"

Harding was told. He frightened the busy little woman who told him. He said, "Ran is very quiet, but he is honest and he does his work. As long as he comes here in the morning and earns his wage, he can do what he wants, where he wants, and it is not my business to stop him." He said this so very sharply that the little woman dared not say anything more.

Ran was very happy, living there. Saying little, he began to learn about Bianca's hands.

He watched Bianca being fed. Her hands would not feed her, the lovely aristocrats. Beautiful parasites they were, taking their animal life from the heavy squat body that carried them, and giving nothing in return. They would lie one on each side of her plate, pulsing, while Bianca's mother put food into the disinterested drooling mouth. They were shy, those hands, of Ran's bewitched gaze. Caught out there naked in the light and open of the table-top, they would creep to the edge and drop out of sight—all but four rosy fingertips clutching the cloth.

They never lifted from a surface. When Bianca walked, her hands did not swing free, but twisted in the fabric of her dress. And when she approached a table or the mantelpiece and stood, her hands would run lightly up and leap, landing together, resting silently, watchfully, with that pulsing peculiar to them.

They cared for each other. They would not touch Bianca herself, but each hand groomed the other. It was the only labor to which they would bend themselves.

Three evenings after he came, Ran tried to take one of the hands in his. Bianca was alone in the room, and Ran went to her and sat beside her. She did not move, nor did her hands. They rested on a small table before her, preening themselves. This, then, was when they really began watching him. He felt it, right down to the depths of his enchanted heart. The hands kept stroking each other, and yet they knew he was there, they knew of his desire. They stretched themselves before him, archly, languorously, and his blood pounded hot. Before he could stay himself he reached and tried to grasp them. He was strong, and his move was sudden and clumsy. One of the hands seemed to disappear, so swiftly did it drop into Bianca's lap. But the other—

Ran's thick fingers closed on it and held it captive. It writhed, all but tore itself free. It took no power from the arm on which it lived, for Bianca's arms were flabby and weak. Its strength, like its beauty, was intrinsic, and it was only by shifting his grip to the puffy forearm that Ran succeeded in capturing it. So intent was he on touching it, holding it, that he did not see the other hand leap from the idiot girl's lap, land crouching at the table's edge. It reared back, fingers curling spiderlike, and sprang at him, fastening on his wrist. It clamped down agonizingly, and Ran felt bones give and crackle. With a cry he released the girl's arm. Her hands fell together and ran over each other, feeling for any small scratch, any tiny damage he might have done them in his passion. And as he sat there clutching his wrist, he saw the hands run to the far side of the little table, hook themselves over the edge and, contracting, draw her out of her place. She had no volition of her own—ah, but her hands had! Creeping over the walls, catching obscure and precarious holds in the wainscoting, they dragged the girl from the room.

And Ran sat there and sobbed, not so much from the pain in his swelling arm, but in shame for what he had done. They might have been won to him in another, gentler way . . .

His head was bowed, yet suddenly he felt the gaze of those hands. He looked up swiftly enough to see one of them whisk round the doorpost. It had come back, then, to see . . . Ran rose heavily and took himself and his shame away. Yet he was compelled to stop in the doorway, even as had Bianca's hands. He watched covertly and saw them come into the room dragging the unprotesting idiot girl. They brought her to the long bench where Ran had sat with her. They pushed her on to it, flung themselves to the table, and began rolling and flattening themselves most curiously about. Ran suddenly realized that there was something of his there, and he was comforted, a little. They were rejoicing, drinking thirstily, revelling in his tears.

Afterwards for nineteen days, the hands made Ran do penance. He knew them as inviolate and unforgiving; they would not show themselves to him, remaining always hidden in Bianca's dress or under the supper table. For those nineteen days Ran's passion and desire grew. More—his love became true love, for only true love knows reverence—and the possession of the hands became his reason for living, his goal in the life which that reason had given him.

Ultimately they forgave him. They kissed him coyly when he was not looking, touched him on the wrist, caught and held him for one sweet moment. It was at table . . . a great power surged through him, and he gazed down at the hands, now returned to Bianca's lap. A strong muscle in his jaw twitched and twitched, swelled and fell. Happiness like a golden light flooded him; passion spurred him, love imprisoned him, reverence was the gold of the golden light. The room wheeled and whirled about him and forces unimaginable flickered through him. Battling with himself, yet lax in the glory of it, Ran sat unmoving, beyond the world, enslaved and yet possessor of all. Bianca's hands flushed pink, and if ever hands smiled to each other, then they did.

He rose abruptly, flinging his chair from him, feeling the strength of his back and shoulders. Bianca's mother, by now beyond surprise, looked at him and away. There was that in his eyes which she did not like, for to fathom it would disturb her, and she wanted no trouble. Ran strode from the room and outdoors, to be by himself that he might learn more of this new thing that had possessed him.

It was evening. The crooked-bending skyline drank the

buoyancy of the sun, dragged it down, sucking greedily. Ran stood on a knoll, his nostrils flaring, feeling the depth of his lungs. He sucked in the crisp air and it smelled new to him, as though the sunset shades were truly in it. He knotted the muscles of his thighs and stared at his smooth, solid fists. He raised his hands high over his head and, stretching, sent out such a great shout that the sun sank. He watched it, knowing how great and tall he was, how strong he was, knowing the meaning of longing and belonging. And then he lay down on the clean earth and he wept.

When the sky grew cold enough for the moon to follow the sun beyond the hills, and still an hour after that, Ran returned to the house. He struck a light in the room of Bianca's mother, where she slept on a pile of old clothes. Ran sat beside her and let the light wake her. She rolled over to him and moaned, opened her eyes and shrank from him. "Ran . . . what do you want?"

"Bianca. I want to marry Bianca."

Her breath hissed between her gums. "No!" It was not a refusal, but astonishment. Ran touched her arm impatiently. Then she laughed.

"To—marry—Bianca. It's late, boy. Go back to bed, and in the morning you'll have forgotten this thing, this dream."

"Will you give me Bianca, or not?"

"I've not been to bed," he said patiently, but growing angry.

She sat up and rested her chin on her withered knees. "You're right to ask me, for I'm her mother. Still and all— Ran, you've been good to us, Bianca and me. You're—you are a good boy but—forgive me, lad, but you're something of a fool. Bianca's a monster. I say it though I am what I am to her. Do what you like, and never a word will I say. You should have known. I'm sorry you asked me, for you have given me the memory of speaking so to you. I don't understand you; but do what you like, boy."

It was to have been a glance, but it became a stare as she saw his face. He put his hands carefully behind his back, and she knew he would have killed her else.

"I'll—marry her, then?" he whispered.

She nodded, terrified. "As you like, boy."

He blew out the light and left her.

Ran worked hard and saved his wages, and made one room

beautiful for Bianca and himself. He built a soft chair, and a table that was like an altar for Bianca's sacred hands. There was a great bed, and heavy cloth to hide and soften the walls, and a rug.

They were married, though marrying took time. Ran had to go far afield before he could find one who would do what was necessary. The man came far and went again afterwards, so that none knew of it, and Ran and his wife were left alone. The mother spoke for Bianca, and Bianca's hand trembled frighteningly at the touch of the ring, writhed and struggled and then lay passive, blushing and beautiful. But it was done. Bianca's mother did not protest, for she didn't dare. Ran was happy, and Bianca—well, nobody cared about Bianca.

After they were married Bianca followed Ran and his two brides into the beautiful room. He washed Bianca and used rich lotions. He washed and combed her hair, and brushed it many times until it shone, to make her more fit to be with the hands he had married. He never touched the hands, though he gave them soaps and creams and tools with which they could groom themselves. They were pleased. Once one of them ran up his coat and touched his cheek and made him exultant.

He left them and returned to the shop with his heart full of music. He worked harder than ever, so that Harding was pleased and let him go home early. He wandered the hours away by the bank of a brook, watching the sun on the face of the chuckling water. A bird came to circle him, flew unafraid through the aura of gladness about him. The delicate tip of a wing brushed his wrist with the touch of the first secret kiss from the hands of Bianca. The singing that filled him was part of the nature of laughing, the running of water, the sound of the wind in the reeds by the edge of the stream. He yearned for the hands, and he knew he could go now and clasp them and own them; instead he stretched out on the bank and lay smiling, all lost in the sweetness and poignance of waiting, denying desire. He laughed for pure joy in a world without hatred, held in the stainless palms of Bianca's hands.

As it grew dark he went home. All during that nuptial meal Bianca's hands twisted about one of his while he ate with the other, and Bianca's mother fed the girl. The fingers twined about each other and about his own, so that three hands seemed to be wrought of one flesh, to become a thing of lovely weight at his arm's end. When it was quite dark they went to the beautiful room and lay where he and the hands could watch, through the window, the clean, bright stars swim up out of the forest. The house and the room were dark and silent. Ran was so happy that he hardly dared to breathe.

A hand fluttered up over his hair, down his cheek, and crawled into the hollow of his throat. Its pulsing matched the beat of his heart. He opened his own hands wide and clenched his fingers, as though to catch and hold this moment.

Soon the other hand crept up and joined the first. For perhaps an hour they lay there passive with their coolness against Ran's warm neck. He felt them with his throat, each smooth convolution, each firm small expanse. He concentrated, with his mind and his heart on his throat, on each part of the hands that touched him, feeling with all his being first one touch and then another, though the contact was there unmoving. And he knew it would be soon now, soon.

As if at a command, he turned on his back and dug his head into the pillow. Staring up at the vague dark hangings on the wall, he began to realize what it was for which he had been working and dreaming so long. He put his head back yet farther and smiled, waiting. This would be possession, completion. He breathed deeply, twice, and the hands began to move.

The thumbs crossed over his throat and the fingertips settled one by one under his ears. For a long moment they lay there, gathering strength. Together, then, in perfect harmony, each co-operating with the other, they became rigid, rockhard. Their touch was still light upon him, still light . . . no, now they were passing their rigidity to him, turning it to a contraction. They settled to it slowly, their pressure measured and equal. Ran lay silent. He could not breathe now, and did not want to. His great arms were crossed on his chest, his knotted fists under his armpits, his mind knowing a great peace. Soon, now . . .

Wave after wave of engulfing, glorious pain spread and receded. He saw color impossible, without light. He arched his back, up, up . . . the hands bore down with all their hidden strength, and Ran's body bent like a bow, resting on feet and shoulders. Up, up . . .

Something burst within him—his lungs, his heart—no matter. It was complete.

There was blood on the hands of Bianca's mother when they found her in the morning in the beautiful room, trying

37

to soothe Ran's neck. They took Bianca away, and they buried Ran, but they hanged Bianca's mother because she tried to make them believe Bianca had done it, Bianca whose hands were quite dead, drooping like brown leaves from her wrists.

IF SHE's dead, I thought, I'll never find her in this white flood of moonlight on the white sea, with the surf seething in and over the pale, pale sand like a great shampoo. Almost always, suicides who stab themselves or shoot themselves in the heart carefully bare their chests; the same strange impulse generally makes the sea-suicide go naked.

A little earlier, I thought, or later, and there would be shadows for the dunes and the breathing toss of the foam. Now the only real shadow was mine, a tiny thing just under me, but black enough to feed the blackness of the shadow of a blimp.

A little earlier, I thought, and I might have seen her plodding up the silver shore, seeking a place lonely enough to die in. A little later and my legs would rebel against this shuffling trot through sand, the maddening sand that could not hold and would not help a hurrying man.

My legs did give way then and I knelt suddenly, sobbing—not for her; not yet—just for air. There was such a rush about me: wind, and tangled spray, and colors upon colors and shades of colors that were not colors at all but shifts of white and silver. If light like that were sound, it would sound like the sea on sand, and if my ears were eyes, they would see such a light.

I crouched there, gasping in the swirl of it, and a flood struck me, shallow and swift, turning up and outward like flower petals where it touched my knees, then soaking me to the waist in its bubble and crash. I pressed my knuckles to my eyes so they would open again. The sea was on my lips with the taste of tears and the whole white night shouted and wept aloud.

And there she was.

Her white shoulders were a taller curve in the sloping foam. She must have sensed me—perhaps I yelled—for she turned and saw me kneeling there. She put her fists to her temples and her face twisted, and she uttered a piercing wail of despair and fury, and then plunged seaward and sank.

I kicked off my shoes and ran into the breakers, shouting, hunting, grasping at flashes of white that turned to sea-salt and coldness in my fingers. I plunged right past her, and her body struck my side as a wave whipped my face and tumbled both of us. I gasped in solid water, opened my eyes beneath the surface and saw a greenish-white distorted moon hurtle as I spun. Then there was sucking sand under my feet again and my left hand was tangled in her hair.

The receding wave towed her away and for a moment she streamed out from my hand like steam from a whistle. In that moment I was sure she was dead, but as she settled to the sand, she fought and scrambled to her feet.

She hit my ear, wet, hard, and a huge, pointed pain lanced into my head. She pulled, she lunged away from me, and all the while my hand was caught in her hair. I couldn't have freed her if I had wanted to. She spun to me with the next wave, battered and clawed at me, and we went into deeper water.

"Don't . . . don't . . . I can't swim!" I shouted, so she clawed me again.

"Leave me alone," she shrieked. "Oh, dear God, why can't you *leave*" (said her fingernails) *"me . . ."* (said her fingernails) *"alone!"* (said her small hard fist).

So by her hair I pulled her head down tight to her white shoulder; and with the edge of my free hand I hit her neck twice. She floated again, and I brought her ashore.

I carried her to where a dune was between us and the sea's broad noisy tongue, and the wind was above us somewhere. But the light was as bright. I rubbed her wrists and stroked her face and said, "It's all right," and, "There!" and some names I used to have for a dream I had long, long before I ever heard of her.

She lay still on her back with the breath hissing between her teeth, with her lips in a smile which her twisted-tight, wrinkled-sealed eyes made not a smile but a torture. She was well and conscious for many moments and still her breath hissed and her closed eyes twisted.

"Why couldn't you leave me alone?" she asked at last. She opened her eyes and looked at me. She had so much misery that there was no room for fear. She shut her eyes again and said, "You know who I am."

"I know," I said.

She began to cry.

I waited, and when she stopped crying, there were shadows among the dunes. A long time.

She said, "You don't know who I am. Nobody knows who I am."

I said, "It was in all the papers."

"That!" She opened her eyes slowly and her gaze traveled over my face, my shoulders, stopped at my mouth, touched my eyes for the briefest second. She curled her lips and turned away her head. "Nobody knows who I am."

I waited for her to move or speak, and finally I said, "Tell *me*."

"Who are you?" she asked, with her head still turned away.

"Someone who . . ."

"Well?"

"Not now," I said. "Later, maybe."

She sat up suddenly and tried to hide herself. "Where are my clothes?"

"I didn't see them."

"Oh," she said. "I remember. I put them down and kicked sand over them, just where a dune would come and smooth them over, hide them as if they never were . . . I hate sand. I wanted to drown in the sand, but it wouldn't let me . . . You mustn't look at me!" she shouted. "I hate to have you looking at me!" She threw her head from side to side, seeking. "I can't stay here like this! What can I do? Where can I go?"

"Here," I said.

She let me help her up and then snatched her hand away, half-turned from me. "Don't touch me. Get away from me."

"Here," I said again, and walked down the dune where it curved in the moonlight, tipped back into the wind and down and became not dune but beach. "Here." I pointed behind the dune.

At last she followed me. She peered over the dune where it was chest-high, and again where it was knee-high. "Back there?"

I nodded.

"So dark . . ." She stepped over the low dune and into the aching black of those moon-shadows. She moved away cautiously, feeling tenderly with her feet, back to where the dune was higher. She sank down into the blackness and disappeared there. I sat on the sand in the light. "Stay away from me," she spat.

I rose and stepped back. Invisible in the shadows, she breathed, "Don't go away," I waited, then saw her hand press out of the clean-cut shadows. "There," she said, "over there. In the dark. Just be a . . . Stay away from me now . . . Be a—voice."

I did as she asked, and sat in the shadows perhaps six feet from her.

She told me about it. Not the way it was in the papers.

She was perhaps seventeen when it happened. She was in Central Park in New York. It was too warm for such an early spring day, and the hammered brown slopes had a dusting of green of precisely the consistency of that morning's hoar frost on the rocks. But the frost was gone and the grass was brave and tempted some hundreds of pairs of feet from the asphalt and concrete to tread on it.

Hers were among them. The sprouting soil was a surprise to her feet, as the air was to her lungs. Her feet ceased to be shoes as she walked, her body was consciously more than clothes. It was the only kind of day which in itself can make a city-bred person raise his eyes. She did.

For a moment she felt separated from the life she lived, in which there was no fragrance, no silence, in which nothing ever quite fit nor was quite filled. In that moment the ordered disapproval of the buildings around the pallid park could not reach her; for two, three clean breaths it no longer mattered that the whole wide world really belonged to images projected on a screen; to gently groomed goddesses in these steel and glass towers; that it belonged, in short, always, always to someone else.

So she raised her eyes, and there above her was the saucer.

It was beautiful. It was golden, with a dusty finish like that of an unripe Concord grape. It made a faint sound, a chord composed of two tones and a blunted hiss like the wind in tall wheat. It was darting about like a swallow, soaring and dropping. It circled and dropped and hovered like a fish, shimmering. It was like all these living things, but with that beauty it had all the loveliness of things turned and burnished, measured, machined, and metrical.

At first she felt no astonishment, for this was so different from anything she had ever seen before that it had to be a trick of the eye, a false evaluation of size and speed and distance that in a moment would resolve itself into a sun-flash on an airplane or the lingering glare of a welding arc.

She looked away from it and abruptly realized that many

other people saw it—saw *something*—too. People all around her had stopped moving and speaking and were craning upward. Around her was a globe of silent astonishment, and outside it she was aware of the life-noise of the city, the hard-breathing giant who never inhales.

She looked up again, and at last began to realize how large and how far away the saucer was. No: rather, how small and how very near it was. It was just the size of the largest circle she might make with her two hands, and it floated not quite eighteen inches over her head.

Fear came then. She drew back and raised a forearm, but the saucer simply hung there. She bent far sideways, twisted away, leaped forward, looked back and upward to see if she had escaped it. At first she couldn't see it; then as she looked up and up, there it was, close and gleaming, quivering and crooning, right over her head.

She bit her tongue.

From the corner of her eye, she saw a man cross himself. *He did that because he saw me standing here with a halo over my head, she thought.* And that was the greatest single thing that had ever happened to her. No one had ever looked at her and made a respectful gesture before, not once, not ever. Through terror, through panic and wonderment, the comfort of that thought nestled into her, to wait to be taken out and looked at again in lonely times.

The terror was uppermost now, however. She backed away, staring upward, stepping a ludicrous cakewalk. She should have collided with people. There were plenty of people there, gasping and craning, but she reached none. She spun around and discovered to her horror that she was the center of a pointing, pressing crowd. Its mosaic of eyes all bulged and its inner circle braced its many legs to press back and away from her.

The saucer's gentle note deepened. It tilted, dropped an inch or so. Someone screamed, and the crowd broke away from her in all directions, milled about, and settled again in a new dynamic balance, a much larger ring, as more and more people raced to thicken it against the efforts of the inner circle to escape.

The saucer hummed and tilted, tilted . . .

She opened her mouth to scream, fell to her knees, and the saucer struck.

43

It dropped against her forehead and clung there. It seemed almost to lift her. She came erect on her knees, made one effort to raise her hands against it, and then her arms stiffened down and back, her hands not reaching the ground. For perhaps a second and a half the saucer held her rigid, and then it passed a single ecstatic quiver to her body and dropped it. She plumped to the ground, the backs of her thighs heavy and painful on her heels and ankles.

The saucer dropped beside her, rolled once in a small circle, once just around its edge, and lay still. It lay still and dull and metallic, different and dead.

Hazily, she lay and gazed at the gray-shrouded blue of the good spring sky, and hazily she heard whistles.

And some tardy screams.

And a great stupid voice bellowing "Give her air!" which made everyone press closer.

Then there wasn't so much sky because of the blueclad bulk with its metal buttons and its leatherette notebook. "Okay, okay, what's happened here stand back figods sake."

And the widening ripples of observation, interpretation and comment: "It knocked her down." "Some guy knocked her down." "He knocked her down." "Some guy knocked her down and—" "Right in broad daylight this guy . . ." "The park's gettin' to be . . ." onward and outward, the adulteration of fact until it was lost altogether because excitement is so much more important.

Somebody with a harder shoulder than the rest bulling close, a notebook here, too, a witnessing eye over it, ready to change ". . . a beautiful brunette . . ." to "an attractive brunette" for the afternoon editions, because "attractive" is as dowdy as any woman is allowed to get if she is a victim in the news.

The glittering shield and the florid face bending close: "You hurt bad, sister?" And the echoes, back and back through the crowd, Hurt bad, hurt bad, badly injured, he beat the hell out of her, broad daylight . . ."

And still another man, slim and purposeful, tan gabardine, cleft chin and beard-shadow: "Flyin' saucer, hm? Okay, Officer, I'll take over here."

"And who the hell might you be, takin' over?"

The flash of a brown leather wallet, a face so close behind that its chin was pressed into the gabardine shoulder. The face said, awed: "F.B.I." and that rippled outward, too. The policeman nodded—the entire policeman nodded in one single bobbing genuflection.

"Get some help and clear this area," said the gabardine.

"Yes, *sir!*" said the policeman.

"F.B.I., F.B.I.," the crowd murmured and there was more sky to look at above her.

She sat up and there was glory in her face. "The saucer talked to me," she sang.

"You shut up," said the gabardine. "You'll have lots of chance to talk later."

"Yeah, sister," said the policeman. "My God, this mob could be full of Communists."

"You shut up, too," said the gabardine.

Someone in the crowd told someone else a Communist beat up this girl, while someone else was saying she got beat up because she was a Communist.

She started to rise, but solicitous hands forced her down again. There were thirty police there by that time.

"I can walk," she said.

"Now you just take it easy," they told her.

They put a stretcher down beside her and lifted her onto it and covered her with a big blanket.

"I can walk," she said as they carried her through the crowd.

A woman went white and turned away moaning, "Oh, my God, how awful!"

A small man with round eyes stared and stared at her and licked and licked his lips.

The ambulance. They slid her in. The gabardine was already there.

A white-coated man with very clean hands: "How did it happen, miss?"

"No questions," said the gabardine. "Security."

The hospital.

She said, "I got to get back to work."

"Take your clothes off," they told her.

She had a bedroom to herself then for the first time in her life. Whenever the door opened, she could see a policeman outside. It opened very often to admit the kind of civilians who were very polite to military people, and the kind of military people who were even more polite to certain civilians.

She did not know what they all did nor what they wanted. Every single day they asked her four million, five hundred thousand questions. Apparently they never talked to each other because each of them asked her the same questions over and over.

"What is your name?"

"How old are you?"

"What year were you born?"

Sometimes they would push her down strange paths with their questions.

"Now your uncle. Married a woman from Middle Europe, did he? Where in Middle Europe?"

"What clubs or fraternal organizations did you belong to? Ah! Now about that Rinkeydinks gang on 63rd Street. Who was *really* behind it?"

But over and over again, "What did you mean when you said the saucer talked to you?"

And she would say, "It talked to me."

And they would say, "And it said—"

And she would shake her head.

There would be a lot of shouting ones, and then a lot of kind ones. No one had ever been so kind to her before, but she soon learned that no one was being kind to *her*. They were just getting her to relax, to think of other things, so they could suddenly shoot that question at her: "What do you mean it talked to you?"

Pretty soon it was just like Mom's or school or any place, and she used to sit with her mouth closed and let them yell. Once they sat her on a hard chair for hours and hours with a light in her eyes and let her get thirsty. Home, there was a transom over the bedroom door and Mom used to leave the kitchen light glaring through it all night, every night, so she wouldn't get the horrors. So the light didn't bother her at all.

They took her out of the hospital and put her in jail. Some ways it was good. The food. The bed was all right, too. Through the window she could see lots of women exercising in the yard. It was explained to her that they all had much harder beds.

"You are a very important young lady, you know."

That was nice at first, but as usual it turned out they didn't mean her at all. They kept working on her. Once they brought the saucer in to her. It was inside a big wooden crate with a

46

padlock, and a steel box inside that with a Yale lock. It only weighed a couple of pounds, the saucer, but by the time they got it packed, it took two men to carry it and four men with guns to watch them.

They made her act out the whole thing just the way it happened with some soldiers holding the saucer over her head. It wasn't the same. They'd cut a lot of chips and pieces out of the saucer and, besides, it was that dead gray color. They asked her if she knew anything about that and for once she told them.

"It's empty now," she said.

The only one she would ever talk to was a little man with a fat belly who said to her the first time he was alone with her, "Listen, I think the way they've been treating you stinks. Now get this: I have a job to do. My job is to find out *why* you won't tell what the saucer said. I don't want to know what it said and I'll never ask you. I don't even want you to tell me. Let's just find out why you're keeping it a secret."

Finding out why turned out to be hours of just talking about having pneumonia and the flower pot she made in second grade that Mom threw down the fire escape and getting left back in school and the dream about holding a wine glass in both hands and peeping over it at some man.

And one day she told him why she wouldn't say about the saucer, just the way it came to her: "Because it was talking to *me,* and it's just nobody else's business."

She even told him about the man crossing himself that day. It was the only other thing she had of her own.

He was nice. He was the one who warned her about the trial. "I have no business saying this, but they're going to give you the full dress treatment. Judge and jury and all. You just say what you want to say, no less and no more, hear? And don't let 'em get your goat. You have a right to own something."

He got up and swore and left.

First a man came and talked to her for a long time about how maybe this Earth would be attacked from outer space by beings much stronger and cleverer than we are, and maybe she had the key to a defense. So she owed it to the whole world. And then even if the Earth wasn't attacked, just think of what an advantage she might give this country over its enemies. Then he shook his finger in her face and said that

47

what she was doing amounted to working *for* the enemies of her country. And he turned out to be the man that was defending her at the trial.

The jury found her guilty of contempt of court and the judge recited a long list of penalties he could give her. He gave her one of them and suspended it. They put her back in jail for a few more days, and one fine day they turned her loose.

That was wonderful at first. She got a job in a restaurant, and a furnished room. She had been in the papers so much that Mom didn't want her back home. Mom was drunk most of the time and sometimes used to tear up the whole neighborhood, but all the same she had very special ideas about being respectable, and being in the papers all the time for spying was not her idea of being decent. So she put her maiden name on the mailbox downstairs and told her daughter not to live there any more.

At the restaurant she met a man who asked her for a date. The first time. She spent every cent she had on a red handbag to go with her red shoes. They weren't the same shade, but anyway they were both red. They went to the movies and afterward he didn't try to kiss her or anything, he just tried to find out what the flying saucer told her. She didn't say anything. She went home and cried all night.

Then some men sat in a booth talking and they shut up and glared at her every time she came past. They spoke to the boss, and he came and told her that they were electronics engineers working for the government and they were afraid to talk shop while she was around—wasn't she some sort of spy or something? So she got fired.

Once she saw her name on a juke box. She put in a nickel and punched that number, and the record was all about "the flyin' saucer came down one day, and taught her a brand new way to play, and what it was I will not say, but she took me out of this world." And while she was listening to it, someone in the juke-joint recognized her and called her by name. Four of them followed her home and she had to block the door shut.

Sometimes she'd be all right for months on end, and then someone would ask for a date. Three times out of five, she and the date were followed. Once the man she was with arrested the man who was tailing them. Twice the man who was tailing them arrested the man she was with. Five times out of five, the date would try to find out about the saucer. Sometimes she would go out with someone and pretend that it was a real date, but she wasn't very good at it.

So she moved to the shore and got a job cleaning at night in offices and stores. There weren't many to clean, but that just meant there weren't many people to remember her face from the papers. Like clockwork, every eighteen months, some feature writer would drag it all out again in a magazine or a Sunday supplement; and every time anyone saw a headlight on a mountain or a light on a weather balloon it had to be a flying saucer, and there had to be some tired quip about the saucer wanting to tell secrets. Then for two or three weeks she'd stay off the streets in the daytime.

Once she thought she had it whipped. People didn't want her, so she began reading. The novels were all right for a while until she found out that most of them were like the movies—all about the pretty ones who really own the world. So she learned things—animals, trees. A lousy little chipmunk caught in a wire fence bit her. The animals didn't want her. The trees didn't care.

Then she hit on the idea of the bottles. She got all the bottles she could and wrote on papers which she corked into the bottles. She'd tramp miles up and down the beaches and throw the bottles out as far as she could. She knew that if the right person found one, it would give that person the only thing in the world that would help. Those bottles kept her going for three solid years. Everyone's got to have a secret little something he does.

And at last the time came when it was no use any more. You can go on trying to help someone who *maybe* exists; but soon you can't pretend there is such a person any more. And that's it. The end.

"Are you cold?" I asked when she was through telling me. The surf was quieter and the shadows longer.

"No," she answered from the shadows. Suddenly she said, "Did you think I was mad at you because you saw me without my clothes?"

"Why shouldn't you be?"

"You know, I don't care? I wouldn't have wanted . . . wanted you to see me even in a ball gown or overalls. You

49

can't cover up my carcass. It shows; it's there whatever. I just didn't want you to *see* me. At all."

"Me, or anyone?"

She hesitated. "You."

I got up and stretched and walked a little, thinking. "Didn't the F.B.I. try to stop you throwing those bottles?"

"Oh, sure. They spent I don't know how much taxpayers' money gathering 'em up. They still make a spot check every once in a while. They're getting tired of it, though. All the writing in the bottles is the same." She laughed. I didn't know she could.

"What's funny?"

"All of 'em—judges, jailers, juke-boxes—people. Do you know it wouldn't have saved me a minute's trouble if I'd told 'em the whole thing at the very beginning?"

"No?"

"No. They wouldn't have believed me. What they wanted was a new weapon. Super-science from a super-race, to slap hell out of the super-race if they ever got a chance, or out of our own if they don't. All those brains," she breathed, with more wonder than scorn, "all that brass. They think 'super-race' and it comes out 'super-science.' Don't they ever imagine a super-race has super-feelings, too—super-laughter, maybe, or super-hunger?" She paused. "Isn't it time you asked me what the saucer said?"

"I'll tell you," I blurted.

> *"There is in certain living souls*
> *A quality of loneliness unspeakable,*
> *So great it must be shared*
> *As company is shared by lesser beings.*
> *Such a loneliness is mine; so know by this*
> *That in immensity*
> *There is one lonelier than you."*

"Dear Jesus," she said devoutly, and began to weep. "And how is it addressed?"

"To the loneliest one . . ."

"How did you know?" she whispered.

"It's what you put in the bottles, isn't it?"

"Yes," she said. "Whenever it gets to be too much, that no one cares, that no one ever did . . . you throw a bottle into the sea, and out goes a part of your own loneliness. You sit and think of someone somewhere finding it . . . learning for the first time that the worst there is can be understood."

The moon was setting and the surf was hushed. We looked up and out to the stars. She said, "We don't know what loneliness is like. People thought the saucer was a saucer, but it wasn't. It was a bottle with a message inside. It had a bigger ocean to cross—all of space—and not much chance of finding anybody. Loneliness? We don't know loneliness."

When I could, I asked her why she had tried to kill herself.

"I've had it good," she said, "with what the saucer told me. I wanted to . . . pay back. I was bad enough to be helped; I had to know I was good enough to help. No one wants me? Fine. But don't tell me no one, anywhere, wants my help. I can't stand that."

I took a deep breath. "I found one of your bottles two years ago. I've been looking for you ever since. Tide charts, current tables, maps and . . . wandering. I heard some talk about you and the bottles hereabouts. Someone told me you'd quit doing it, you'd taken to wandering the dunes at night. I knew why. I ran all the way."

I needed another breath now. "I got a club foot. I think right, but the words don't come out of my mouth the way they're inside my head. I have this nose. I never had a woman. Nobody ever wanted to hire me to work where they'd have to look at me. You're beautiful," I said. "You're beautiful."

She said nothing, but it was as if a light came from her, more light and far less shadow than ever the practiced moon could cast. Among the many things it meant was that even to loneliness there is an end, for those who are lonely enough, long enough.

ALL the world knew them as loverbirds, though they were certainly not birds, but humans. Well, say humanoids. Featherless bipeds. Their stay on earth was brief, a nine-day wonder. Any wonder that lasts nine days on an earth of orgasmic trideo shows; time-freezing pills; synapse-inverter fields which make it possible for a man to turn a sunset to perfumes, a masochist to a fur-feeler; and a thousand other euphorics—why, on such an earth, a nine-day wonder is a wonder indeed.

Like a sudden bloom across the face of the world came the peculiar magic of the loverbirds. There were loverbird songs and loverbird trinkets, loverbird hats and pins, bangles and baubles, coins and quaffs and tidbits. For there was that about the loverbirds which made a deep enchantment. No one can be told about a loverbird and feel this curious delight. Many are immune even to a solidograph. But watch loverbirds, only for a moment, and see what happens. It's the feeling you had when you were twelve, and summer-drenched, and you kissed a girl for the very first time and knew a breathlessness you were sure could never happen again. And indeed it never could—unless you watched loverbirds. Then you are spellbound for four quiet seconds, and suddenly your very heart twists, and incredulous tears sting and stay; and the very first move you make afterward, you make on tiptoe, and your first word is a whisper.

This magic came over very well on trideo, and everyone had trideo; so for a brief while the earth was enchanted.

There were only two loverbirds. They came down out of the sky in a single brassy flash, and stepped out of their ship, hand in hand. Their eyes were full of wonder, each at the other, and together at the world. They seemed frozen in a full-to-bursting moment of discovery; they made way for one another gravely and with courtesy, they looked about them and in the very looking gave each other gifts—the color of the sky, the taste of the air, the pressures of things growing and meeting and changing. They never spoke. They simply *were* together. To watch them was to know of their awestruck mounting of staircases of bird notes, of how each knew the warmth of the other as their flesh supped silently on sunlight.

They stepped from their ship, and the tall one threw a yellow powder back to it. The ship fell in upon itself and became a pile of rubble, which collapsed into a pile of gleaming sand, which slumped compactly down to dust and then to an airblown emulsion so fine that Brownian movement itself hammered it up and out and away. Anyone could see that they intended to stay. Anyone could know by simply watching them that next to their wondrous delight in each other came their delighted wonder at earth itself, everything and everybody about it.

Now, if terrestrial culture were a pyramid, at the apex (where the power is) would sit a blind man, for so constituted are we that only by blinding ourselves, bit by bit, may we rise above our fellows. The man at the apex has an immense preoccupation with the welfare of the whole, because he regards it as the source and structure of his elevation, which it is, and as an extension of himself, which it is not. It was such a man who, in the face of immeasurable evidence, chose to find a defense against loverbirds, and fed the matrices and coordinates of the loverbird image into the most marvelous calculator that had ever been built.

The machine sucked in symbols and raced them about, compared and waited and matched and sat still while its bulging memory, cell by cell, was silent, was silent—and suddenly, in a far corner, resonated. It grasped this resonance in forceps made of mathematics, snatched it out (translating furiously as it snatched) and put out a fevered tongue of paper on which was typed:

DIRBANU

Now this utterly changed the complexion of things. For earth ships had ranged the cosmos far and wide, with few hindrances. Of these hindrances, all could be understood but one, and that one was Dirbanu, a transpalactic planet which shrouded itself in impenetrable fields of force whenever an earth ship approached. There were other worlds which could do this, but in each case the crews knew why it was done. Dirbanu, upon discovery, had prohibited landings from the very first until an ambassador could be sent to Terra. In due time one did arrive (so reported the calculator, which was the only entity that remembered the episode) and it was obvious that Earth and Dirbanu had much in common. The ambassador, however, showed a most uncommon disdain of Earth and all its work, curled his lip and went wordlessly home, and ever since then Dirbanu had locked itself tight away from the questing Terrans.

Dirbanu thereby became of value, and fair game, but we could do nothing to ripple the bland face of her defenses. As this impregnability repeatedly proved itself, Dirbanu evolved in our group mind through the usual stages of being: the Curiosity, the Mystery, the Challenge, the Enemy, the Enemy, the Enemy, the Mystery, the Curiosity, and finally That-which-is-too-far-away-to-bother-with, or the Forgotten.

And suddenly, after all this time, Earth had two genuine natives of Dirbanu aboard, entrancing the populace and giving no information. This intolerable circumstance began to make itself felt throughout the world—but slowly, for this time the blind men's din was cushioned and soaked by the magic of the loverbirds. It might have taken a very long time to convince the people of the menace in their midst had there not been a truly startling development:

A direct message was received from Dirbanu.

The collective impact of loverbird material emanating from transmitters on Earth had attracted the attention of Dirbanu, which promptly informed us that the loverbirds were indeed their nationals, that in addition they were fugitives, that Dirbanu would take it ill if Earth should regard itself as a sanctuary for the criminals of Dirbanu but would, on the other hand, find it in its heart to be very pleased if Earth saw fit to return them.

So from the depths of its enchantment, Terra was able to calculate a course of action. Here at last was an opportunity to consort with Dirbanu on a friendly basis—great Dirbanu which, since it had force fields which Earth could not duplicate, must of necessity have many other things Earth could use; mighty Dirbanu before whom we could kneel in supplication (with purely-for-defense bombs hidden in our pockets) with lowered heads (making invisible the knife in our teeth) and ask for crumbs from their table (in order to extrapolate the location of their kitchens).

Thus the loverbird episode became another item in the weary procession of proofs that Terra's most reasonable intolerance can conquer practically anything, even magic.

Especially magic.

So it was that the loverbirds were arrested, that the *Starmite 439* was fitted out as a prison ship, that a most carefully screened crew was chosen for her, and that she struck starward with the cargo that would gain us a world.

Two men were the crew—a colorful little rooster of a man and a great dun bull of a man. They were, respectively, Rootes, who was Captain and staff, and Grunty, who was midship and inboard corps. Rootes was cocky, springy, white and crisp. His hair was auburn and so were his eyes, and the eyes were hard. Grunty was a shambler with big gentle hands and heavy shoulders half as wide as Rootes was high. He should have worn a cowl and rope-belted habit. He should, perhaps, have worn a burnoose. He did neither, but the effect was there. Known only to him was the fact that words and pictures, concepts and comparisons were an endless swirling blizzard inside him. Known only to him and Rootes was the fact that he had books, and books, and books, and Rootes did not care if he had or not. Grunty he had been called since he first learned to talk, and Grunty was name enough for him. For the words in his head would not leave him except one or two at a time, with long moments between. So he had learned to condense his verbal messages to breathy grunts, and when they wouldn't condense, he said nothing.

They were primitives, both of them, which is to say that they were doers, while Modern Man is a thinker and/or a feeler. The thinkers compose new variations and permutations of euphoria, and the feelers repay the thinkers by responding to their inventions. The ships had no place for Modern Man, and Modern Man had only the most casual use for the ships.

Doers can co-operate like cam and pushrod, like ratchet and pawl, and such linkage creates a powerful bond. But Rootes and Grunty were unique among crews in that these machine parts were not interchangeable. Any good captain can command any good crew, surroundings being equivalent. But Rootes would not and could not ship out with anyone but Grunty, and Grunty was just that dependent. Grunty understood this bond, and the fact that the only way it could conceivably be broken would be to explain it to Rootes. Rootes did not understand it because it never occurred to him to try, and had he tried, he would have failed, since he was inherently

55

non-equipped for the task. Grunty knew that their unique bond was for him, a survival matter. Rootes did not know this, and would have rejected the idea with violence.

So Rootes regarded Grunty with tolerance and a modified amusement. The modification was an inarticulate realization of Grunty's complete dependability. Grunty regarded Rootes with . . . well, with the ceaseless, silent flurry of words in his mind.

There was, besides the harmony of functions and the other link, understood only by Grunty, a third adjunct to their phenomenal efficiency as a crew. It was organic, and it had to do with the stellar drive.

Reaction engines were long forgotten. The so-called "warp" drive was used only experimentally and on certain crash-priority war-craft where operating costs were not a factor. The *Starmite* 439 was, like most interstellar craft, powered by an RS plant. Like the transistor, the Referential Stasis generator is extremely simple to construct and very difficult indeed to explain. Its mathematics approaches mysticism and its theory contains certain impossibilities which are ignored in practice. Its effect is to shift the area of stasis of the ship and everything in it from one point of reference to another. For example, the ship at rest on the Earth's surface is in stasis in reference to the ground on which it rests. Throwing the ship into stasis in reference to the center of the earth gives it instantly an effective speed equal to the surface velocity of the planet around its core—some one thousand miles per hour. Stasis referential to the sun moves the Earth out from under the ship at the Earth's orbital velocity. GH stasis "moves" the ship at the angular velocity of the sun about the Galactic Hub. The galactic drift can be used, as can any simple or complex mass center in this expanding universe. There are resultants and there are multipliers, and effective velocities can be enormous. Yet the ship is constantly in stasis, so that there is never an inertia factor.

The one inconvenience of the RS drive is that shifts from one referent to another invariably black the crew out, for psychoneural reasons. The blackout period varies slightly between individuals from one to two and a half hours. But some anomaly in Grunty's gigantic frame kept his blackout periods down to thirty or forty minutes, while Rootes was always out for two hours or more. There was that about Grunty which made moments of isolation a vital necessity, or a man must occasionally be himself, which in anyone's company Grunty was not. But after stasis shifts Grunty had an hour or so to himself while his commander lay numbly spread-eagled on the blackout couch, and he spent these in communions of his own devising. Sometimes this meant only a good book.

This, then, was the crew picked to man the prison ship. It had been together longer than any other crew in the Space Service. Its record showed a metrical efficiency and a resistance to physical and psychic debilitations previously unheard of in a trade where close confinement on long voyages had come to be regarded as hazards. In space, shift followed shift uneventfully, and planetfall was made on schedule and without incident. In port Rootes would roar off to the fleshpots, in which he would wallow noisily until an hour before takeoff, while Grunty found, first, the business office, and next, a bookstore.

They were pleased to be chosen for the Dirbanu trip. Rootes felt no remorse at taking away Earth's new delight, since he was one of the very few who was immune to it. ("Pretty," he said at his first encounter.) Grunty simply grunted, but then, so did everyone else. Rootes did not notice, and Grunty did not remark upon the obvious fact that though the loverbirds' expression of awestruck wonderment in each other's presence had, if anything, intensified, their extreme pleasure in Earth and the things of Earth had vanished. They were locked, securely but comfortably, in the after cabin behind a new transparent door, so that their every move could be watched from the main cabin and control console. They sat close, with their arms about one another, and though their radiant joy in the contact never lessened, it was a shadowed pleasure, a lachrymose beauty like the wrenching music of the wailing wall.

The RS drive laid its hand on the moon and they vaulted away. Grunty came up from blackout to find it very quiet. The loverbirds lay still in each other's arms, looking very human except for the high joining of their closed eyelids, which nictated upward rather than downward like a Terran's. Rootes sprawled limply on the other couch, and Grunty nodded at the sight. He deeply appreciated the silence, since Rootes had filled the small cabin with earthy chatter about his conquests in port, detail by hairy detail, for two solid hours preceding their departure. It was a routine which Grunty found particularly wearing, partly for its content, which interested him not at all, but mostly for its inevitability. Grunty had long ago noted that these recitations, for all their detail, carried the tones of thirst rather than of satiety. He had his own conclusions about it, and, characteristically, kept them to himself. But inside, his spinning gusts of words could shape themselves well to it, and they did. "And man, she moaned!" Rootes would chant. "And take money? She *gave* me money. And what did I do with it? Why, I bought up some more of the same." *And what you could buy with a shekel's worth of tenderness, my prince!* his silent words sang. ". . . across the floor and around the rug until, by damn, I thought we're about to climb the wall. Loaded, Grunty-boy, I tell you, I was loaded!" *Poor little one* ran the hushed susurrus, *thy poverty is as great as thy joy and a tenth as great as thine empty noise.* One of Grunty's greatest pleasures was taken in the fact that this kind of chuntering was limited to the first day out, with barely another word on the varied theme until the next departure, no matter how many months away that might be. *Squeak to me of love, dear mouse,* his words would chuckle. *Stand up on your cheese and nibble away at your dream.* Then, wearily, *But oh, this treasure I carry is too heavy a burden, in all its fullness, to be so tugged at by your clattering vacuum!*

Grunty left the couch and went to the controls. The preset courses checked against the indicators. He logged them and fixed the finder control to locate a certain mass-nexus in the Crab Nebula. It would chime when it was ready. He set the switch for final closing by the push-button beside his couch, and went aft to wait.

He stood watching the loverbirds because there was nothing else for him to do.

They lay quite still, but love so permeated them that their very poses expressed it. Their lax bodies yearned each to each, and the tall one's hand seemed to stream toward the fingers of his beloved, and then back again, like the riven tatters of a torn fabric straining toward oneness again. And as their mood was a sadness too, so their pose, each and both, together and singly expressed it, and singly each through the other silently spoke of the loss they had suffered, and how it ensured greater losses to come. Slowly the picture suffused Grunty's thinking, and his words picked and pierced and smoothed it down, and murmured finally, *Brush away the dusting of sadness from the future, bright ones. You've sadness enough for now. Grief should live only after it is truly born, and not before.*

His words sang,

> *Come fill the cup and in the fire of spring*
> *Your winter garment of repentance fling.*
> *The bird of time has but a little way*
> *To flutter—and the bird is on the wing.*

and added *Omar Khayyam, born circa 1073*, for this, too, was one of the words' functions.

And then he stiffened in horror; his great hands came up convulsively and clawed the imprisoning glass . . .

They were smiling at him.

They were smiling, and on their faces and on and about their bodies there was no sadness.

They had *heard* him!

He glanced convulsively around at the Captain's unconscious form, then back to the loverbirds.

That they should recover so swiftly from blackout was, to say the least, an intrusion; for his moments of aloneness were precious and more than precious to Grunty, and would be useless to him under the scrutiny of those jewelled eyes. But that was a minor matter compared to this other thing, this terrible fact that they *heard*.

Telepathic races were not common, but they did exist. And what he was now experiencing was what invariably happened when humans encountered one. He could only send; the loverbirds could only receive. And they *must not* receive him! No one must. No one must know what he was, what he thought. If anyone did, it would be a disaster beyond bearing. It would mean no more flights with Rootes. Which, of course, meant no flights with anyone. And how could he live—where could he go?

He turned back to the loverbirds. His lips were white and drawn back in a snarl of panic and fury. For a blood-thick moment he held their eyes. They drew closer to one another, and together sent him a radiant, anxious, friendly look that made him grind his teeth.

Then, at the console, the finder chimed.

Grunty turned slowly from the transparent door and went to his couch. He lay down and poised his thumb over the push-button.

He *hated* the loverbirds, and there was no joy in him. He pressed the button, the ship slid into a new stasis, and he blacked out.

The time passed.

"Grunty!"

"?"

"You feed them this shift?"

"Nuh."

"Last shift?"

"Nuh."

"What the hell's matter with you, y'big dumb bastich? What you expect them to live on?"

Grunty sent a look of roiling hatred aft. "Love," he said.

"Feed 'em," snapped Rootes.

Wordlessly Grunty went about preparing a meal for the prisoners. Rootes stood in the middle of the cabin, his hard small fists on his hips, his gleaming auburn head tilted to one side, and watched every move. "I didn't used to have to tell you anything," he growled, half pugnaciously, half worriedly. "You sick?"

Grunty shook his head. He twisted the tops of two cans and set them aside to heat themselves, and took down the water suckers.

"You got it in for those honeymooners or something?"

Grunty averted his face.

"We get them to Dirbanu alive and healthy, hear me? They get sick, you get sick, by God. I'll see to that. Don't give me trouble, Grunty. I'll take it out on you. I never whipped you yet, but I will."

Grunty carried the tray aft. "You hear me?" Rootes yelled.

Grunty nodded without looking at him. He touched the control and a small communication window slid open in the glass wall. He slid the tray through. The taller loverbird stepped forward and took it eagerly, gracefully, and gave him a dazzling smile of thanks. Grunty growled low in his throat like a carnivore. The loverbird carried the food back to the couch and they began to eat, feeding each other little morsels.

60

A new stasis, and Grunty came fighting up out of blackness. He sat up abruptly, glanced around the ship. The Captain was sprawled out across the cushions, his compact body and outflung arm forming the poured-out, spring-steel laxness usually seen only in sleeping cats. The loverbirds, even in deep unconsciousness, lay like hardly separate parts of something whole, the small one on the couch, the tall one on the deck, prone, reaching, supplicating.

Grunty snorted and hove to his feet. He crossed the cabin and stood looking down on Rootes.

The hummingbird is a yellowjacket, said his words, *Buzz and dart, hiss and flash away. Swift and hurtful, hurtful . . .*

He stood for a moment, his great shoulder muscles working one against the other, and his mouth trembled.

He looked at the loverbirds, who were still motionless. His eyes slowly narrowed.

His words tumbled and climbed, and ordered themselves:

> *I through love have learned three things,*
> *Sorrow, sin and death it brings.*
> *Yet day by day my heart within*
> *Dares shame and sorrow, death and sin. . . .*

And dutifully he added *Samuel Ferguson, born 1810.* He glared at the loverbirds and brought his fist into his palm with a sound like a club on an anthill. They had heard him again, and this time they did not smile, but looked into each other's eyes and then turned together to regard him, nodding gravely.

Rootes went through Grunty's books, leafing and casting aside. He had never touched them before. "Buncha crap," he jeered. "Garden of the Plynck. Wind in the Willows. Worm Ouroborous. Kid stuff."

Grunty lumbered across and patiently gathered up the books the Captain had flung aside, putting them one by one back into their places, stroking them as if they had been bruised.

"Isn't there nothing in here with pictures?"

Grunty regarded him silently for a moment and then took down a tall volume. The Captain snatched it, leafed through it. "Mountains," he growled. "Old houses." He leafed. "Damn boats." He smashed the book to the deck. "Haven't you got *any* of what I want?"

Grunty waited attentively.

"Do I have to draw a diagram?" the Captain roared. "Got that ol' itch, Grunty. You wouldn't know. I feel like looking at pictures, get what I mean?"

Grunty stared at him, utterly without expression, but deep within him a panic squirmed. The Captain never, *never* behaved like this in mid-voyage. It was going to get worse, he realized. Much worse. And quickly.

He shot the loverbirds a vicious, hate-filled glance. If they weren't aboard . . .

There could be no waiting. Not now. Something had to be done. Something . . .

"Come on, come on," said Rootes. "Goddlemighty Godfrey, even a deadbutt like you must have *something* for kicks."

Grunty turned away from him, squeezed his eyes closed for a tortured second, then pulled himself together. He ran his hand over the books, hesitated, and finally brought out a large, heavy one. He handed it to the Captain and went forward to the console. He slumped down there over the file of computer tapes, pretending to be busy.

The Captain sprawled onto Grunty's couch and opened the book. "Michelangelo, what the hell," he growled. He grunted, almost like his shipmate. "Statues," he half-whispered, in withering scorn. But he ogled and leafed at last, and was quiet.

The loverbirds looked at him with a sad tenderness, and then together sent beseeching glances at Grunty's angry back.

The matrix-pattern for Terra slipped through Grunty's fingers, and he suddenly tore the tape across, and across again. A filthy place, Terra. *There is nothing,* he thought, *like the conservatism of license.* Given a culture of sybaritics, with an endless choice of mechanical titillations, and you have a people of unbreakable and hidebound formality, a people with few but massive taboos, a shockable, narrow, prissy people obeying the rules—even the rules of their calculated depravities—and protecting their treasured, specialized pruderies. In such a group there are words one may not use for fear of their fanged laughter, colors one may not wear, gestures and intonations one must forego, on pain of being torn to pieces. The rules are complex and absolute, and in such a place one's heart may not sing lest, through its warm free joyousness, it betray one.

And if you must have joy of such a nature, if you must be free to be your pressured self, then off to space . . . off to the

62

glittering black loneliness. And let the days go by, and let the time pass, and huddle beneath your impenetrable integument, and wait, and wait, and every once in a long while you will have that moment of lonely consciousness when there is no one around to see; and then it may burst from you and you may dance, or cry, or twist the hair on your head till your eyeballs blaze, or do any of the other things your so unfashionable nature thirstily demands.

It took Grunty half a lifetime to find this freedom: No price would be too great to keep it. Not lives, nor interplanetary diplomacy, nor Earth itself were worth such a frightful loss.

He would lose it if anyone knew, and the loverbirds knew.

He pressed his heavy hands together until the knuckles crackled. Dirbanu, reading it all from the ardent minds of the loverbirds; Dirbanu flashing the news across the stars; the roar of reaction, and then Rootes, Rootes, when the huge and ugly impact washed over him . . .

So let Dirbanu be offended. Let Terra accuse this ship of fumbling, even of treachery—anything but the withering news the loverbirds had stolen.

Another new stasis, and Grunty's first thought as he came alive in the silent ship was *It has to be soon.*

He rolled off the couch and glared at the unconscious loverbirds. The helpless loverbirds.

Smash their heads in.

Then Rootes . . . what to tell Rootes?

The loverbirds attacked him, tried to seize the ship?

He shook his head like a bear in a beehive. Rootes would never believe that. Even if the loverbirds could open the door, which they could not, it was more than ridiculous to imagine those two bright and slender things attacking anyone —especially so rugged and massive an opponent.

Poison? No—there was nothing in the efficient, unfailingly beneficial food stores that might help.

His glance strayed to the Captain, and he stopped breathing.

Of *course!*

He ran to the Captain's personal lockers. He should have known that such a cocky little hound as Rootes could not live, could not strut and prance as he did unless he had a weapon. And if it was the kind of weapon that such a man would characteristically choose—

A movement caught his eye as he searched.

The loverbirds were awake.

That wouldn't matter.

He laughed at them, a flashing, ugly laugh. They cowered close together and their eyes grew very bright.

They knew.

He was aware that they were suddenly very busy, as busy as he. And then he found the gun.

It was a snug little thing, smooth and intimate in his hand. It was exactly what he had guessed, what he had hoped for— just what he needed. It was silent. It would leave no mark. It need not even be aimed carefully. Just a touch of its feral radiation and throughout the body the axones suddenly refuse to propagate nerve impulses. No thought leaves the brain, no slightest contraction of heart or lung occurs again, ever. And afterward, no sign remains that a weapon has been used.

He went to the serving window with the gun in his hand. *When he wakes, you will be dead,* he thought. *Couldn't recover from stasis blackout. Too bad. But no one's to blame, hm? We never had Dirbanu passengers before. So how could we know?*

The loverbirds, instead of flinching, were crowding close to the window, their faces beseeching, their delicate hands signing and signalling, frantically trying to convey something.

He touched the control, and the panel slid back.

The taller loverbird held up something as if it would shield him. The other pointed at it, nodded urgently, and gave him one of those accursed, hauntingly sweet smiles.

Grunty put up his hand to sweep the thing aside, and then checked himself.

It was only a piece of paper.

All of the cruelty of humanity rose up in Grunty. *A species that can't protect itself doesn't deserve to live.* He raised the gun.

And then he saw the pictures.

Economical and accurate, and for all their subject, done with the ineffable grace of the loverbirds themselves, the pictures showed three figures:

Grunty himself, hulking, impassive, the eyes glowing, the tree-trunk legs and hunched shoulders.

Rootes, in a pose so characteristic and so cleverly done that Grunty gasped. Crisp and clean, Rootes' image had one foot up on a chair, both elbows on the high knee, the head half turned. The eyes fairly sparkled from the paper.

And a girl.

She was beautiful. She stood with her arms behind her, her feet slightly apart, her face down a little. She was deep-eyed, pensive, and to see her was to be silent, to wait for those downcast lids to lift and break the spell.

Grunty frowned and faltered. He lifted a puzzled gaze from these exquisite renderings to the loverbirds, and met the appeal, the earnest, eager, hopeful faces.

The loverbird put a second paper against the glass.

There were the same three figures, identical in every respect to the previous ones, except for one detail: they were all naked.

He wondered how they knew human anatomy so meticulously.

Before he could react, still another sheet went up.

The loverbirds, this time—the tall one, the shorter one, hand in hand. And next to them a third figure, somewhat similar, but tiny, very round, and with grotesquely short arms.

Grunty stared at the three sheets, one after the other. There was something . . . something . . .

And then the loverbird put up the fourth sketch, and slowly, slowly, Grunty began to understand. In the last picture, the loverbirds were shown exactly as before, except that they were naked, and so was the small creature beside them. He had never seen loverbirds naked before. Possibly no one had.

Slowly he lowered the gun. He began to laugh. He reached through the window and took both the loverbirds' hands in one of his, and they laughed with him.

Rootes stretched easily with his eyes closed, pressed his face down into the couch, and rolled over. He dropped his feet to the deck, held his head in his hands and yawned. Only then did he realize Grunty was standing just before him.

"What's the matter with you?"

He followed Grunty's grim gaze.

The glass door stood open.

Rootes bounced to his feet as if the couch had turned white-hot. "Where—what—"

Grunty's crag of a face was turned to the starboard bulkhead. Rootes spun to it, balanced on the balls of his feet as if he were boxing. His smooth face gleamed in the red glow of the light over the airlock.

"The lifeboat . . . you mean they took the lifeboat? They got away?"

Grunty nodded.

Rootes held his head. "Oh, fine," he moaned. He whipped around to Grunty. "And where the hell were you when this happened?"

"Here."

"Well, what in God's name happened?" Rootes was on the trembling edge of foaming hysteria.

Grunty thumped his chest.

"You're not trying to tell me you let them go?"

Grunty nodded, and waited—not for very long.

"I'm going to burn you down," Rootes raged. "I'm going to break you so low you'll have to climb for twelve years before you get a barracks to sweep. And after I get done with you I'll turn you over to the Service. What do you think they'll do to you? What do you think they're going to do to *me?*"

He leapt at Grunty and struck him a hard, cutting blow to the cheek. Grunty kept his hands down and made no attempt to avoid the fist. He stood immovable, and waited.

"Maybe those were criminals, but they were Dirbanu nationals," Rootes roared when he could get his breath. "How are we going to explain this to Dirbanu? Do you realize this could mean war?"

Grunty shook his head.

"What do you mean? You know something. You better talk while you can. Come on, bright boy—what are we going to tell Dirbanu?"

Grunty pointed at the empty cell. "Dead," he said.

"What good will it do us to say they're dead? They're not. They'll show up again some day, and—"

Grunty shook his head. He pointed to the star chart. Dirbanu showed as the nearest body. There was no livable planet within thousands of parsecs.

"They didn't go to Dirbanu!"

"Nuh."

"Damn it, it's like pulling rivets to get anything out of you. In that lifeboat they go to Dirbanu—which they won't—or they head out, maybe for years, to the Rim stars. That's all they can do!"

Grunty nodded.

66

"And you think Dirbanu won't track them, won't bring 'em down?"

"No ships."

"They have ships!"

"Nuh."

"The loverbirds told you?"

Grunty agreed.

"You mean their own ship that they destroyed, and the one the ambassador used were all they had?"

"Yuh."

Rootes strode up and back. "I don't get it. I don't begin to get it. What did you do it for, Grunty?"

Grunty stood for a moment, watching Rootes' face. Then he went to the computing desk. Rootes had no choice but to follow. Grunty spread out the four drawings.

"What's this? Who drew these? *Them?* What do you know. *Damn!* Who is the chick?"

Grunty patiently indicated all of the pictures in one sweep. Rootes looked at him, puzzled, looked at one of Grunty's eyes, then the other, shook his head, and applied himself to the pictures again. "This is more like it," he murmured. "Wish I'd 'a known they could draw like this." Again Grunty drew his attention to all the pictures and away from the single drawing that fascinated him.

"There's you, there's me. Right? Then this chick. Now, here we are again, all buff naked. Damn, what a carcass. All right, all right, I'm going on. Now, this is the prisoners, right? And who's the little fat one?"

Grunty pushed the fourth sheet over. "Oh," said Rootes. "Here everybody's naked too. Hm."

He yelped suddenly and bent close. Then he rapidly eyed all four sheets in sequence. His face began to get red. He gave the fourth picture a long, close scrutiny. Finally he put his finger on the sketch of the round little alien. "This is . . . a . . . a Dirbanu—"

Grunty nodded. "Female."

"Then those two—they were—"

Grunty nodded.

"So that's it!" Rootes fairly shrieked in fury. "You mean we been shipped out all this time with a coupla God damned *fairies?* Why, if I'd a' known that I'd a' killed 'em!"

"Yuh."

Rootes looked up at him with a growing respect and considerable amusement. "So you got rid of 'em so's I wouldn't kill 'em and mess everything up?" He scratched his head. "Well, I'll be billy-be-damned. You got a think-tank on you after all. Anything I can't stand, it's a fruit."

Grunty nodded.

"God," said Rootes, "it figures. It really figures. Their females don't look anything like the males. Compared with them, our females are practically identical to us. So the ambassador comes, and sees what looks like a planet full of queers. He knows better but he can't stand the sight. So back he goes to Dirbanu, and Earth gets brushed off."

Grunty nodded.

"Then these pansies here run off to Earth, figuring they'll be at home. They damn near made it, too. But Dirbanu calls 'em back, not wanting the likes of them representing their planet. I don't blame 'em a bit. How would you feel if the only Terran on Dirbanu was a fluff? Wouldn't you want him out of there, but quick?"

Grunty said nothing.

"And now," said Rootes, "we better give Dirbanu the good news."

He went forward to the communicator.

It took a surprisingly short time to contact the shrouded planet. Dirbanu acknowledged and coded out a greeting. The decoder over the console printed the message for them:

GREETINGS STARMITE 439. ESTABLISH ORBIT. CAN YOU DROP PRISONERS TO DIRBANU? NEVER MIND PARACHUTE.

"Whew," said Rootes. "Nice people. Hey, you notice they don't say come on in. They never expected to let us land. Well, what'll we tell 'em about their lavender lads?"

"Dead," said Grunty.

"Yeah," said Rootes. "That's what they want anyway." He sent rapidly.

In a few minutes the response clattered out of the decoder.

STAND BY FOR TELEPATH SWEEP. WE MUST CHECK. PRISONERS MAY BE PRETENDING DEATH.

"Oh-oh," said the Captain. "This is where the bottom drops out."

"Nuh," said Grunty, calmly.

"But their detector will locate—oh—I see what you're driving at. No life, no signal. Same as if they weren't here at all."

"Yuh."

68

The decoder clattered.

DIRBANU GRATEFUL. CONSIDER MISSION COMPLETE. DO NOT WANT BODIES. YOU MAY EAT THEM.

Rootes retched. Grunty said, "Custom."

The decoder kept clattering.

NOW READY FOR RECIPROCAL AGREEMENT WITH TERRA.

"We go home in a blaze of glory," Rootes exulted. He sent, TERRA ALSO READY. WHAT DO YOU SUGGEST?

The decoder paused, then:

TERRA STAY AWAY FROM DIRBANU AND DIRBANU WILL STAY AWAY FROM TERRA. THIS IS NOT A SUGGESTION. TAKES EFFECT IMMEDIATELY.

"Why that bunch of bastards!"

Rootes pounded his codewriter, and although they circled the planet at a respectful distance for nearly four days, they received no further response.

The last thing Rootes had said before they established the first stasis on the way home was: "Well, anyway—it does me good to think of those two queens crawling away in that lifeboat. Why, they can't even starve to death. They'll be cooped up there for *years* before they get anywhere they can sit down."

It still rang in Grunty's mind as he shook off the blackout. He glanced aft to the glass partition and smiled reminiscently. "For years," he murmured. His words curled up and spun, and said,

> ... *Yes; love requires the focal space*
> *Of recollection or of hope,*
> *Ere it can measure its own scope.*
> *Too soon, too soon comes death to show*
> *We love more deeply than we know!*

Dutifully, then, came the words: *Coventry Patmore, born 1823.*

He rose slowly and stretched, revelling in his precious privacy. He crossed to the other couch and sat down on the edge of it.

For a time he watched the Captain's unconscious face,

reading it with great tenderness and utmost attention, like a mother with an infant.

His words said, *Why must we love where the lightning strikes, and not where we choose?*

And they said, *But I'm glad it's you, little prince. I'm glad it's you.*

He put out his huge hand, and with a feather touch, stroked the sleeping lips.

BETTER not read it. I mean it. No—this isn't one of those "perhaps it will happen to you" things. It's a lot worse than that. It might very possibly be happening to you right now. And you won't know until it's over. You can't, by the very nature of things.

(I wonder what the population really is?)

On the other hand, maybe it won't make any difference if I do tell you about it. Once you get used to the idea, you might even be able to relax and enjoy it. Heaven knows there's plenty to enjoy—and again I say it—by the very nature of things.

All right, then, if you think you can take it. . . .

I met her in a restaurant. You may know the place— Murphy's. It has a big oval bar and then a partition. On the other side of the partition are small tables, then an aisle, then booths.

Gloria was sitting at one of the small tables. All of the booths but two were empty; all the other small tables but one were unoccupied, so there was plenty of room in the place for me.

But there was only one place I could sit—at her table. That was because, when I saw Gloria, there wasn't anything else in the world. I have never been through anything like that. I just stopped dead. I dropped my briefcase and stared at her. She had gleaming auburn hair and olive skin. She had delicate high-arched nostrils and a carved mouth, lips that were curved above like gull's wings on the down-beat, and full below. Her eyes were as sealed and spice-toned as a hot buttered rum, and as deep as a mountain night.

Without taking my eyes from her face, I groped for a chair and sat opposite her. I'd forgotten everything. Even about being hungry. Helen hadn't, though. Helen was the head waitress and a swell person. She was fortyish and happy. She didn't know my name but used to call me "The Hungry Fella." I never had to order. When I came in she'd fill me a bar-glass full of beer and pile up two orders of that day's Chef's Special on a steak platter. She arrived with the beer, picked up my briefcase, and went for the fodder. I just kept on looking at Gloria, who, by this time, was registering considerable amazement, and a little awe. The awe, she told me later, was conceived only at the size of the beer-glass, but I have my doubts about that.

She spoke first. "Taking an inventory?"

She had one of those rare voices which makes noises out of all other sounds. I nodded. Her chin was rounded, with the barest suggestion of a cleft, but the hinges of her jaw were square.

I think she was a little flustered. She dropped her eyes— I was glad, because I could see then how very long and thick her lashes were—and poked at her salad. She looked up again, half-smiling. Her teeth met, tip to tip. I'd read about that but had never actually seen it before. "What is it?" she asked. "Have I made a conquest?"

I nodded again. "You certainly have."

"Well!" she breathed.

"Your name's Gloria," I said positively.

"How did you know?"

"It had to be, that's all."

She looked at me carefully, at my eyes, my forehead, my shoulders. "If your name is Leo, I'll scream."

"Scream then. But why?"

"I—I've always thought I'd meet a man named Leo, and—"

Helen canceled the effects of months of good relations between herself and me, by bringing my lunch just then. Gloria's eyes widened when she saw it. "You must be very fond of lobster hollandaise."

"I'm very fond of all subtle things," I said, "and I like them in great masses."

"I've never met anyone like you," she said candidly.

"No one like you ever has."

"Oh?"

I picked up my fork. "Obviously not, or there'd be a race of us." I scooped up some lobster. "Would you be good enough to watch carefully while I eat? I can't seem to stop looking at you, and I'm afraid I might stab my face with the fork."

She chortled. It wasn't a chuckle, or a gargle. It was a true Lewis Carroll chortle. They're very rare. "I'll watch."

"Thank you. And while you watch, tell me what you don't like."

"What I *don't* like? Why?"

"I'll probably spend the rest of my life finding out the things you do like, and doing them with you. So let's get rid of the nonessentials."

She laughed. "All right. I don't like tapioca because it makes me feel conspicuous, staring that way. I don't like furniture with buttons on the upholstery; lace curtains that cross each other; small flower-prints, hooks-and-eyes and snap fasteners where zippers ought to be; that orchestra leader with the candy saxophones and the yodeling brother; tweedy men who smoke pipes; people who can't look me in the eye when they're lying; night clothes; people who make mixed drinks with Scotch—my, you eat fast."

"I just do it to get rid of my appetite so I can begin eating for esthetic reasons. I like that list."

"What don't *you* like?"

"I don't like literary intellectuals with their conversations all dressed up in overquotes. I don't like bathing-suits that don't let the sun in and I don't like weather that keeps bathing-suits in. I don't like salty food; clinging-vine girls; music that doesn't go anywhere or build anything; people who have forgotten how to wonder like children; automobiles designed to be better streamlined going backwards than going forward; people who will try anything once but are afraid to try it twice and acquire a taste; and professional sceptics." I went back to my lunch.

"You bat a thousand," she said. "Something remarkable is happening here."

"Let it happen," I cautioned. "Never mind what it is or why. Don't be like the guy who threw a light-bulb on the floor to find out if it was brittle." Helen passed and I ordered a Slivovitz.

"Prune brandy!" cried Gloria. "I love it!"

"I know. It's for you."

"Some day you're going to be wrong," she said, suddenly somber, "and that will be bad."

"That will be good. It'll be the difference between harmony and contrast, that's all."

"Leo—"

"Mm?"

She brought her gaze squarely to me, and it was so warm I could feel it on my face. "Nothing. I was just saying it, Leo. *Leo!*"

Something choked me—not the lobster. It was all gone.

"I have no gag for that. I can't top it. I can match it, Gloria."

Another thing was said, but without words.

There are still no words for it. Afterward she reached across and touched my hand with her fingertips. I saw colors.

I got up to go, after scribbling on a piece of the menu. "Here's my phone number. Call me up when there's no other way out."

She raised her eyebrows. "Don't you want my phone, or my address, or anything?"

"No," I said.

"But—"

"This means too much," I said. "I'm sorry if I seem to be dropping it in your lap like this. But any time you are with me, I want it to be because you want to be with me, not because you think it's what I might want. We've got to be together because we are traveling in the same direction at approximately the same speed, each under his own power. If I call you up and make all the arrangements, it could be that I was acting on a conditioned reflex, like any other wolf. If you call, we can both be sure."

"It makes sense." She raised those deep eyes to me. Leaving her was coming up out of those eyes hand over hand. A long haul. I only just made it.

Out on the street I tried valiantly to get some sense of proportion. The most remarkable thing about the whole remarkable business was simply this: that in all my life before, I had never been able to talk to anyone like that. I had always been diffident, easy-going, unaggressive to a fault, and rather slow on the uptake.

I felt like the daydreams of the much advertised 97-pound weakling as he clipped that coupon.

"Hey—you!"

I generally answered to that as well as anything else. I looked up and recoiled violently. There was a human head floating in midair next to me. I was so startled I couldn't even stop walking. The head drifted along beside me, bobbing slightly as if invisible legs carried an invisible body to which the visible head was attached. The face was middle-aged, bookish, dryly humorous.

"You're quite a hell of a fellow, aren't you?"

Oddly, my tongue loosened from the roof of my mouth.

"Some pretty nice people think so," I faltered. I looked around nervously, expecting a stampede when other people saw this congenial horror.

"No one can see me but you," said the head. "No one that's likely to make a fuss, at any rate."

"Wh-what do you want?"

"Just wanted to tell you something," said the head. It must have had a throat somewhere because it cleared it. "Parthenogenesis," it said didactically, "has little survival value, even with syzygy. Without it—" The head disappeared. A little lower down, two bony, bare shoulders appeared, shrugged expressively, and vanished. The head reappeared. "—there isn't a chance."

"You don't say," I quavered.

It didn't say. Not any more, just then, It was gone.

I stopped, spun around, looking for it. What it had told me made as little sense to me, then, as its very appearance. It took quite a while for me to discover that it had told me the heart of the thing I'm telling you. I do hope I'm being a little more lucid than the head was.

Anyway, that was the first manifestation of all. By itself, it wasn't enough to make me doubt my sanity. As I said, it was only the first.

I might as well tell you something about Gloria. Her folks had been poor enough to evaluate good things, well enough off to be able to have a sample or two of these good things. So Gloria could appreciate what was good as well as the effort that was necessary to get it. At twenty-two she was the assistant buyer of a men's department store. (This was toward the end of the war.) She needed some extra money for a pet project, so she sang at a club every night. In her "spare" time she practiced and studied and at the end of a year she had her commercial pilot's license. She spent the rest of the war ferrying airplanes.

Do you begin to get the idea of what kind of people she was?

She was one of the most dynamic women who ever lived. She was thoughtful and articulate and completely un-phony.

She was strong. You can have no idea—no; some of you do know how strong. I had forgotten. . . . She radiated her strength. Her strength surrounded her like a cloud rather than like armor, for she was tangible through it. She influenced everything and everyone she came near. I felt, sometimes, that the pieces of ground which bore her footprints, the chairs she used, the doors she touched and the books she held, continued to radiate for weeks afterward, like the Bikini ships.

She was completely self-sufficient. I had hit the matter squarely when I insisted that she call me before we saw each other again. Her very presence was a compliment. When she was with me, it was, by definition, because that was where she would rather be than any other place on earth. When she was away from me, it was because to be with me at that time would not have been a perfect thing, and in her way she was a perfectionist.

Oh, yes—a perfectionist. I should know!

You ought to know something about me, too, so that you can realize how completely a thing like this is done, and how it is being done to so many of you.

I'm in my twenties and I play guitar for a living. I've done a lot of things and I carry around a lot of memories from each of them—things that only I could possibly know. The color of the walls in the rooming house where I stayed when I was "on the beach" in Port Arthur, Texas, when the crew of my ship went out on strike. What kind of flowers that girl was wearing the night she jumped off the cruise ship in Montego Bay, down in Jamaica.

I can remember, hazily, things like my brother's crying because he was afraid of the vacuum cleaner, when he was four. So I couldn't have been quite three then. I can remember fighting with a kid called Boaz, when I was seven. I remember Harriet, whom I kissed under a fragrant tulip poplar one summer dusk when I was twelve. I remember the odd little lick that drummer used to tear off when, and only when he was really riding, while I was playing at the hotel, and the way the trumpet man's eyes used to close when he heard it. I remember the exact smell of the tiger's wagon when I was pulling ropes on the Barnes Circus, and the one-armed roustabout who used to chantey us along when we drove the stakes, he swinging a twelve-pound maul with the rest of us—

> "*Hit* down, *slap it* down, *haul* back, *snub*, bub,
> "*Half* back, *quarter* back, *all* back, *whoa!*"

—he used to cry, with the mauls rat-tatting on the steelbound peg and the peg melting into the ground, and the snubber grunting over his taut half-hitch while the six of us stood in a circle around the peg. And those other hammers, in the blacksmith's shop in Puerto Rico, with the youngster swinging a sledge in great full circles, clanging on the anvil, while the old smith touched the work almost delicately with his shaping hammer and then tinkled out every syncopation known to man by bouncing it on the anvil's horn and face between his own strokes and those of the great metronomic sledge. I remember the laboring and servile response of a power shovel under my hands as they shifted from hoist to crowd to swing to rehaul controls, and the tang of burning drum-frictions and hot crater compound. That was at the same quarry where the big Finnish blast foreman was killed by a premature shot. He was out in the open and knew he couldn't get clear. He stood straight and still and let it come, since it was bound to come, and he raised his right hand to his head. My mechanic said he was trying to protect his face but I thought at the time he was saluting something.

Details; that's what I'm trying to get over to you. My head was full of details that were intimately my own.

It was a little over two weeks—sixteen days, three hours, and twenty-three minutes, to be exact—before Gloria called. During that time I nearly lost my mind. I was jealous, I was worried, I was frantic. I cursed myself for not having gotten her number—why, I didn't even know her last name! There were times when I determined to hang up on her if I heard her voice, I was so sore. There were times when I stopped work—I did a lot of arranging for small orchestras—and sat before the silent phone, begging it to ring. I had a routine worked out: I'd demand a statement as to how she felt about me before I let her say another thing. I'd demand an explanation of her silence. I'd act casual and disinterested. I'd—

The phone did ring, though, and it was Gloria, and the dialogue went like so:

"Hello?"

"Leo."

"Yes, Gloria!"

"I'm coming up."

"I'm waiting."

And that was it. I met her at the door. I had never touched her before, except for that one brief contact of her hands; and yet, with perfect confidence, with no idea of doing anything different, I took her in my arms and kissed her. This whole thing has its terrible aspects, and yet, sometimes I wonder if moments like that don't justify the horror of it.

I took her hand and led her into the living room. The room wavered like an underwater scene because she was in it. The air tasted different. We sat close together with our hands locked, saying that wordless thing with our eyes. I kissed her again. I didn't ask her anything at all.

She had the smoothest skin that ever was. She had a skin smoother than a bird's throat. It was like satin-finished aluminum, but warm and yielding. It was smooth like Gran' Marnier between your tongue and the roof of your mouth.

We played records—Django Reinhardt and The New Friends of Rhythm, and Bach's *Passacaglia and Fugue* and *Tubby the Tuba*. I showed her the Smith illustrations from *Fantazius Mallare* and my folio of Ed Weston prints. I saw things and heard things in them all that I had never known before, though they were things I loved.

Not one of them—not a book, nor a record, nor a picture, was new to her. By some alchemy, she had culled the random flood of esthetic expression that had come her way, and had her choices; and her choices were these things that I loved, but loved in a way exclusively hers, a way in which I could share.

We talked about books and places, ideas and people. In her way, she was something of a mystic. "I believe that there is something behind the old superstitions about calling up demons and materializations of departed spirits," she said thoughtfully. "But I don't think it was ever done with mumbo-jumbo—witches' brew and pentagrams and toads' skins stuffed with human hair buried at the crossroads on a May midnight, unless these rituals were part of a much larger thing —a purely psychic and un-ghostly force coming from the 'wizard' himself."

"I never thought much about it," I said, stroking her hair. It is the only hair that was not fine that I have ever touched with pleasure. Like everything else about her, it was strong and controlled and glowing. "Have you ever tried anything like that?

78

You're some sort of a sorceress. I know when I'm enchanted at any rate."

"You're not enchanted," she said gravely. "You're not a thing with magic on it. You're a real magic all by yourself."

"You're a darling," I said. "Mine."

"I'm not!" she answered, in that odd way she had of turning aside fantasy for fact. "I don't belong to you. I belong to *me!*"

I must have looked rather stricken, for she laughed suddenly and kissed my hand. "What belongs to you is only a large part of 'us,' " she explained carefully. "Otherwise you belong to you and I belong to me. Do you see?"

"I think I do," I said slowly. "I said I wanted us to be together because we were both travelling together under our own power. I—didn't know it was going to be so true, that's all."

"Don't try to make it any different, Leo. Don't *ever*. If I started to really belong to you, I wouldn't be *me* any more, and then you wouldn't have anything at all."

"You seem so sure of these hazy things."

"They aren't hazy things! They're important. If it weren't for these things, I'd have to stop seeing you. I—*would* stop seeing you."

I put my arms tight around her. "Don't talk about that," I whispered, more frightened than I have ever been in my life before. "Talk about something else. Finish what you were saying about pentagrams and spirits."

She was still a moment. I think her heart was pounding the way mine was, and I think she was frightened too.

"I spend a lot of time reading and mulling over those things," she said after a quiet time. "I don't know why. I find them fascinating. You know what, Leo? I think too much has been written about manifestations of evil. I think it's true that good is more powerful than evil. And I think that far too much has been written and said about ghosties an' ghoulies an' things that go 'boomp' i' th' nicht, as the old Scottish prayer has it. I think those things have been too underlined. They're remarkable enough, but have you ever realized that things that are remarkable are by definition, rare?"

"If the cloven-hoofed horrors and the wailing banshees are remarkable—which they are—then what's commonplace?"

She spread her hands—square, quite large hands, capable and beautifully kept. "The manifestations of good, of course. I believe that they're much easier to call up. I believe they happen all the time. An evil mind has to be very evil before

79

it can project itself into a new thing with a life of its own. From all accounts I have read, it takes a tremendously powerful mind to call up even a little demon. Good things must be much easier to materialize, because they fall in the pattern of good living. More people live good lives than such thoroughly bad ones that they can materialize evil things."

"Well then, why don't more people bring more good things from behind this mystic curtain?"

"But they do!" she cried. "They must! The world is so full of good things! Why do you suppose they're so good? What put the innate goodness into Bach and the Victoria Falls and the color of your hair and Negro laughter and the way ginger ale tickles your nostrils?"

I shook my head slowly. "I think that's lovely, and I don't like it."

"Why not?"

I looked at her. She was wearing a wine-colored suit and a marigold silken kerchief tucked into the throat. It reflected on the warm olive of her chin. It reminded me of my grandmother's saying when I was very small. "Let's see if you like butter," as she held a buttercup under my chin to see how much yellow it reflected. "You are good," I said slowly, searching hard for the words. "You are about the—the goodest thing that ever happened. If what you say is really true, then you might be just a shadow, a dream, a glorious thought that someone had."

"Oh, you idiot," she said, with sudden tears in her eyes. "You big, beautiful hunk of idiot!" She pressed me close and bit my cheek so hard that I yelped. "Is that real?"

"If it isn't," I said, shaken, "I'll be happy to go on dreaming.

She stayed another hour—as if there were such a thing as time when we were together—and then she left. I had her phone number by then. A hotel. And after she was gone, I wandered around my apartment, looking at the small wrinkles in the couch-cover where she had sat, touching the cup she had held, staring at the bland black surface of a record, marvelling at the way its grooves had unwound the *Passacaglia* for her. Most wonderful of all was a special way I discovered to turn my head as I moved. Her fragrance clung to my cheek, and if I turned my face just so, I could sense it. I thought about every one of those many minutes with her, each by itself, and the things we had done. I thought, too,

about the things we had not done—I know you wondered—
and I gloried in them. For, without a word spoken, we had
agreed that a thing worth having was a thing worth awaiting
and that where faith is complete, exploration is uncalled for.

She came back next day, and the day after. The first of
these two visits was wonderful. We sang, mostly. I seemed
to know all her very favorite songs. And by a happy accident,
my pet key on the guitar—B flat—was exactly within her
lovely contralto range. Though I say it as shouldn't, I played
some marvellous guitar behind and around what she sang.
We laughed a lot, largely at things that were secret between
us—is there a love anywhere without its own new language?
—and we talked for a long time about a book called "The
Fountainhead" which seemed to have had the same extraordinary effect on her that it had on me; but then, it's an
extraordinary book.

It was after she left that day that the strangeness began—
the strangeness that turned into such utter horror. She hadn't
been gone more than an hour when I heard the frightened
scramble of tiny claws in the front room. I was poring over
the string-bass part of a trio arrangement I was doing (and
not seeing it for my Gloria-flavored thoughts) and I raised
my head and listened. It was the most panic-struck scurrying
imaginable, as if a regiment of newts and salamanders had
broken ranks in a wild retreat. I remember clearly that the little claw susurrus did not disturb me at all, but the terror behind the movement startled me in ways that were not pleasant.

What were they running from? was infinitely more important than *What were they?*

Slowly I put down the manuscript and stood up. I went to
the wall and along it to the archway, not so much to keep out
of sight as to surprise the *thing* that had so terrorized the
possessors of those small frightened feet.

And that was the first time I have ever been able to smile
while the hackles on the back of my neck were one great
crawling prickle. For there was nothing there at all; nothing
to glow in the dark before I switched on the overhead light,
nothing to show afterward. But the little feet scurried away
faster—there must have been hundreds of them—tapping and
scrabbling out a perfect crescendo of horrified escape. That
was what made my hackles rise. What made me smile—

The sounds radiated from *my* feet!

I stood there in the archway, my eyeballs throbbing with the effort to see this invisible rout; and from the threshold, to right and left and away into the far corners of the front room, ran the sounds of the little paws and tiny scratching claws. It was as if they were being generated under my soles, and then fleeing madly. None ran behind me. There seemed to be something keeping them from the living room. I took a cautious step further into the front room, and now they did run behind me, but only as far as the archway. I could hear them reach it and scuttle off to the side walls. You see what made me smile?

I was the horror that frightened them so!

The sound gradually lessened. It was not that it lessened in over-all intensity. It was just there were fewer and fewer creatures running away. It diminished rapidly, and in about ninety seconds it had reduced to an occasional single scampering. One invisible creature ran around and around me, as if all the unseen holes in the walls had been stopped up and it was frantically looking for one. It found one, too, and was gone.

I laughed then and went back to my work. I remember that I thought quite clearly after that, for a while. I remember writing in a *glissando* passage that was a stroke of genius—something to drive the dog-house slapper crazy but guaranteed to drive the customers even crazier if it could be done at all. I remember zoom-zooming it off under my breath, and feeling mightily pleased with myself over it.

And then the reaction struck me.

Those little claws—

What was happening to me?

I thought instantly of Gloria. *There's some deadly law of compensation working here,* I thought. For every yellow light, a purple shadow. For every peal of laughter, a cry of anguish somewhere. For the bliss of Gloria, a touch of horror to even things up.

I licked my lips, for they were wet and my tongue was dry. *What was happening to me?*

I thought again of Gloria, and the colors and sounds of Gloria, and most of all, the reality, the solid normalcy of Gloria, for all her exquisite sense of fantasy.

I couldn't go crazy. I *couldn't!* Not *now!* I'd be—unfit.

Unfit! As terrifying to me, then, as the old cry of *"Unclean"* was in the Middle Ages.

"Gloria, darling," I'd have to say, *"Honey, we'll just have*

to call it quits. You see, I'm off my trolley. Oh, I'm quite serious. Yes indeedy. The men in the white coats will come around and back up their little wagon to the door and take me away to the laughing academy. And we won't see each other any more. A pity. A great pity. Just give me a hearty little old handshake, now, and go find yourself another fellow."

"Gloria!" I yelled. Gloria was all those colors, and the lovely sounds, and the fragrance that clung to my cheek and came to me when I moved and held my head just so.

"Oh, I dunno," I moaned. "I just don't know what to do! What is it? What is it?"

"Syzygy."

"Huh?" I came bolt upright, staring around wildly. Twenty inches over the couch hovered the seamed face of my jovial phantom of the street outside Murphy's. "You! Now I know I'm off my—hey! What is syzygy?"

"What's happening to you."

"Well, what is happening to me?"

"Syzygy." The head grinned engagingly. I put my head in my hands. There is an emotional pitch—an *un*emotional pitch, really—at which nothing is surprising, and I'd reached it. "Please explain," I said dully. "Tell me who you are, and what you mean by this sizz-sizz whatever-it-is."

"I'm not anybody," said the head, "and syzygy is a concomitant of parthenogenetic and certain other low types. I think what's happening *is* syzygy. If it isn't—" The head disappeared, a hand with spatulate fingers appeared and snapped its fingers explosively; the hand disappeared, the head reappeared and smiled, "—you're a gone goose."

"Don't *do* that," I said miserably.

"Don't do what?"

"That—that piecemeal business. Why do you do it?"

"Oh—that. Conservation of energy. It works here too, you know."

"Where is 'here'?"

"That's a little difficult to explain until you get the knack of it. It's the place where reverse ratios exist. I mean, if something stacks up in a three to five ratio there, it's a five to three ratio here. Forces must balance."

I almost had it. What he said almost made sense. I opened my mouth to question him but he was gone.

After that I just sat there. Perhaps I wept.

And Gloria came the next day, too. That was bad. I did two wrong things. First, I kept information from her, which was inexcusable. If you are going to share at all, you must share the bad things too. The other thing I did was to question her like a jealous adolescent.

But what else could be expected? Everything was changed. Everything was different. I opened the door to her and she brushed past me with a smile, and not a very warm one at that, leaving me at the door all outstretched arms and large clumsy feet.

She shrugged out of her coat and curled up on the couch. "Leo, play some music."

I felt like hell and I know I looked it. Did she notice? Did she even care? Didn't it make any difference at all how I felt, what I was going through?

I went and stood in front of her. "Gloria," I said sternly, "where have you been?"

She looked up at me and released a small, retrospective sigh that turned me bright green and sent horns sprouting out of my scalp. It was such a happy, satisfied little sound. I stood there glowering at her. She waited a moment more and then got up, switched on the amplifier and turntable, dug out the "Dance of the Hours," turned the volume up, added too much bass, and switched in the volume expander, which is quite the wrong thing to use on that record. I strode across the room and turned the volume down.

"Please, Leo," she said in a hurt tone. "I like it that way."

Viciously I turned it back up and sat down with my elbows on my knees and my lower lip stuck out. I was wild. This was all wrong.

I know what I should do, I thought sullenly. *I ought to yank the plug on the rig and stand up and tell her off.*

How right I was! But I didn't do it. How could I do it? This was *Gloria!* Even when I looked up at her and saw her staring at me, saw the slight curl to her lip, I didn't do it. Well, it was too late then. She was watching me, comparing me with—

Yes, that was it. She was comparing me with somebody. Somebody who was different from her, someone who rode roughshod over everything delicate and subtle about her, everything about her that I liked and shared with her. And she, of course, ate it up.

84

I took refuge in the tactic of letting her make the first move. think, then, that she despised me. And rightly.

A bit of cockney dialogue I had once heard danced through my mind:

"D'ye love us, Alf?"

"Yus."

"Well, knock us abaht a bit."

You see? I knew the right things to do, but—

But this was Gloria. I *couldn't.*

The record finished, and she let the automatic shut off the turntable. I think she expected me to turn it over. I didn't. She said, "All right, Leo. What is it?" tiredly.

I said to myself, "I'll start with the worst possible thing that could happen. She'll deny that, and then at least I'll feel better." So I said to her, "You've changed. There's somebody else."

She looked up at the picture molding and smiled sleepily. "Yes," she said. "There certainly is."

"Uff!" I said, because that caught me right in the solar plexus. I sat down abruptly.

"His name's Arthur," she said dreamily. "He's a real man, Leo."

"Oh," I said bitterly. "I can see it. Five o'clock shadow and a head full of white matter. A toupée on his chest and a vernacular like a boatswain. Too much shoulders, too little hips, and, to quote Thorne Smith, a voice as low as his intentions. A man who never learned the distinction between eating and dining, whose idea of a hot time consists of—"

"Stop it," she said. She said it quite casually and very quietly. Because my voice was raised, it contrasted enough to have a positively deafening effect. I stood there with my jaw swinging like the lower gate of a steam-shovel as she went on, "Don't be catty, Leo."

It was a studied insult for her to use such a woman-to-woman phrase, and we both knew it. I was suddenly filled with what the French call *ésprit d'éscalier*—the wit of the staircase; in other words, the belated knowledge of the thing you should have said if you'd only thought of it in time, which you mumble frustratedly to yourself as you go down the stairs on your way out. I should have caught her to me as she tried to brush past me when she arrived, smothered her with—

what was that corny line? "kisses—naru tooth-raking kisses, that broke his lips and hers in exquisite, salty pain." Then I should have threatened her with pinking scissors—

And then I thought of the glittering, balanced structure of self-denial I had built with her, and I could have cried. . . .

"Why come here and parade it in front of me?" I shouted. "Why don't you take your human bulldozer and cross a couple of horizons with him? Why come here and rub my nose in it?"

She stood up, pale, and lovelier than I had thought a human being could be—so beautiful that I had to close my eyes. "I came because I had to have something to compare him with," she said steadily. "You are everything I have ever dreamed about, Leo, and my dreams are . . . very detailed. . . ." At last she faltered, and her eyes were bright. "Arthur is—is—" She shook her head. Her voice left her; she had to whisper. "I know everything about you, Leo. I know how you think, and what you will say, and what you like, and it's wonderful, wonderful . . . but Leo, Arthur is something outside of me. Don't you see? Can't you see? I don't always like what Arthur does. *But I can't tell what he's going to do!* You—you share everything, Leo, Leo darling, but you don't—*take* anything!"

"Oh," I said hoarsely. My scalp was tight. I got up and started across the room toward her. My jaws hurt.

"Stop, Leo," she gasped. "Stop it, now. You can do it, but you'll be acting. You've never acted before. It would be wrong. Don't spoil what's left. No, Leo—no . . . no . . ."

She was right. She was so right. She was always right about me; she knew me so well. This kind of melodrama was away out of character for me. I reached her. I took her arm and she closed her eyes. It hurt when my fingers closed on her arm. She trembled but she did not try to pull away. I got her wrist and lifted it. I turned her hand over and put a kiss on the palm, closing her fingers on it. "Keep that," I said. "You might like to have it some time." Then I let her go.

"Oh Leo, darling," she said. "Darling," she said, with a curl to her lip. . . .

She turned to go. And then—

"*Arhgh!*" She uttered a piercing scream and turned back to me, all but bowling me over in her haste to get away from Abernathy. I stood there holding her tight while she pressed, crouched, squeezed against me, and I burst into laughter. Maybe it was reaction—I don't know. But I roared.

Abernathy is my mouse.

Our acquaintance began shortly after I took the apartment. I knew the little son-of-a-gun was there because I found evidences of his depredations under the sink where I stored my potatoes and vegetables. So I went out and got a trap. In those days the kind of trap I wanted was hard to find; it took me four days and a young fortune in carfare to run one of them down. You see, I can't abide the kind of trap that hurls a wire bar down on whatever part of the mouse happens to be available, so that the poor shrieking thing dies in agony. I wanted—and by heaven, I got—one of those wirebasket effects made so that a touch on the bait trips a spring which slams a door on the occupant.

I caught Abernathy in the contraption the very first night. He was a small gray mouse with very round ears. They were like the finest tissue, and covered with the softest fuzz in the world. They were translucent, and if you looked very closely you could see the most meticulous arrangement of hairline blood-vessels in them. I shall always maintain that Abernathy owed his success in life to the beauty of his ears. No one with pretensions to a soul could destroy such divine tracery.

Well, I let him alone until he got over being frightened and frantic, until he got hungry and ate all the bait, and a few hours over. When I thought he was good and ready to listen to reason, I put the trap on my desk and gave him a really good talking-to.

I explained very carefully (in simple language, of course) that for him to gnaw and befoul in his haphazard fashion was downright antisocial. I explained to him that when I was a child I was trained to finish whatever I started to eat, and that I did it to this day, and I was a human being and much bigger and stronger and smarter than he was. And whatever was good enough for me was at least good enough for him to take a crack at. I really laid down the law to that mouse. I let him mull over it for a while and then I pushed cheese through the bars until his tummy was round like a ping-pong ball. Then I let him go.

There was no sign of Abernathy for a couple of days after that. Then I caught him again; but since he had stolen nothing I let him off with a word of warning—very friendly this time; I had been quite stern at first, of course—and some more cheese. Inside of a week I was catching him every other night, and the only trouble I ever had with him was one time when I baited the trap and left it closed. He couldn't get in to the cheese and he just raised Cain until I woke up and let him in. After that I knew good relations had been established and I did without the trap and just left cheese out for him. At first he wouldn't take the cheese unless it was in the trap, but he got so he trusted me and would take it lying out on the floor. I had long since warned him about the poisoned food that the neighbors might leave out for him, and I think he was properly scared. Anyhow, we got along famously.

So here was Gloria, absolutely petrified, and in the middle of the floor in the front room was Abernathy, twinkling his nose and rubbing his hands together. In the middle of my bellow of laughter, I had a severe qualm of conscience. Abernathy had had no cheese since the day before yesterday! *Sic semper amoris.* I had been fretting so much over Gloria that I had overlooked my responsibilities.

"Darling, I'll take care of him," I said reassuringly to Gloria. I led her to an easy-chair and went after Abernathy. I have a noise I make by pressing my tongue against my front teeth—a sort of a squishy-squeaky noise, which I always made when I gave cheese to Abernathy. He ran right over toward me, saw Gloria, hesitated, gave a "the hell with it" flirt with his tail, turned to me and ran up my pants-leg.

The outside, fortunately.

Then he hugged himself tight into my palm while I rummaged in the icebox with my other hand for his cheese. He didn't snatch at it, either, until he let me look at his ears again. You never saw such beautiful ears in your life. I gave him the cheese, and broke off another piece for his dessert, and set him in the corner by the sink. Then I went back to Gloria, who had been watching me, big-eyed and trembling.

"Leo—how can you *touch* it?"

"Makes nice touching. Didn't you ever touch a mouse?"

She shuddered, looking at me as if I were Horatio just back from the bridge. "I can't stand them."

"Mice? Don't tell me that you, of all people, really and truly have the traditional Victorian mouse phobia!"

"Don't laugh at me," she said weakly. "It isn't only mice. It's any little animal—frogs and lizards and even kittens and puppies. I like big dogs and cats and horses. But somehow—" She trembled again. "If I hear anything like little claws run-

88

ing across the floor, or see small things scuttling around the walls, it drives me crazy."

I goggled. "If you hear—hey; it's a good thing you didn't stay another hour last night, then."

"Last night?" Then, "Last night. . . ." she said, in a totally different voice, with her eyes looking inward and happy. She chuckled. "I was telling—Arthur about that little phobia of mine last night."

If I had thought my masterful handling of the mouse was going to do any good, apparently I was mistaken. "You better shove off," I said bitterly. "Arthur might be waiting."

"Yes," she said, without any particular annoyance, "he might. Goodbye, Leo."

"Goodbye."

Nobody said anything for a time.

"Well," she said, "goodbye."

"Yes," I said, "I'll call you."

"Do that," she said, and went out.

I sat still on the couch for a long time, trying to get used to it. Wishful thinking was no good; I knew that. Something had happened between us. Mostly, its name was Arthur. The thing I couldn't understand was how he ever got a show, the way things were between Gloria and me. In all my life, in all my reading, I had never heard of such a complete fusion of individuals. We both felt it when we met; it had had no chance to get old. Arthur was up against some phenomenal competition; for one thing that was certain was that Gloria reciprocated my feelings perfectly, and one of my feelings was faith. I could understand—if I tried hard—how another man might overcome this hold, or that hold, which I had on her. There are smarter men than I, better looking ones, stronger ones. Any of several of those items could go by the board, and leave us untouched.

But not faith! Not that! It was too big; nothing else we had was important enough to compensate for a loss of faith.

I got up to turn on the light, and slipped. The floor was wet. Not only was it wet; it was soft. I floundered to the seven-way lamp and cranked both switches all the way around.

The room was covered with tapioca. Ankle-deep on the floor, inches deep on the chairs and the couch.

"She's thinking about it now," said the head. Only it wasn't a head this time. It was a flaccid mass of folded tissue. In it I could see pulsing blood vessels. My stomach squirmed.

"Sorry. I'm out of focus." The disgusting thing—a sectioned brain, apparently—moved closer to me and became a face.

I lifted a foot out of the gummy mass, shook it, and put it back in again. "I'm glad she's gone," I said hoarsely.

"Are you afraid of the stuff?"

"No!" I said. "Of course not!"

"It will go away," said the head. "Listen; I'm sorry to tell you; it isn't syzygy. You're done, son."

"What isn't syzygy?" I demanded. "And what is syzygy?"

"Arthur. The whole business with Arthur."

"Go away," I gritted. "Talk sense, or go away. Preferably— go away."

The head shook from side to side, and its expression was gentle. "Give up," it said. "Call it quits. Remember what was good, and fade out."

"You're no good to me," I muttered, and waded over to the book case. I got out a dictionary, glowering at the head, which now was registering a mixture of pity and amusement.

Abruptly, the tapioca disappeared.

I leafed through the book. Sizable, sizar, size, sizzle—"Try S-Y," prompted the head.

I glared at it and went over to the S-Y's. Systemize, systole—

"Here it is," I said, triumphantly. "The last word in the S section." I read from the book. " 'Syzygy—either of the points at which the moon is most nearly in line with the earth and the sun, as when it is new or full.' What are you trying to tell me—that I'm caught in the middle of some astrological mumbo-jumbo?"

"Certainly not," it snapped. "I will tell you, however, that if that's all your dictionary says, it's not a very good one." It vanished.

"But—" I said vaguely. I went back to the dictionary. That's all it had to say about syzygy. Shaking, I replaced it.

Something cat-sized and furry hurtled through the air, clawed at my shoulder. I startled, backed into my record cabinet and landed with a crash on the middle of my back in the doorway. The thing leaped from me to the couch and sat up, curling a long wide tail against its back and regarding me with its jewelled eyes. A squirrel.

"Well, hello!" I said, getting to my knees and then to my feet. "Where on earth did you come from?"

The squirrel, with the instantaneous motion of its kind, dived to the edge of the couch and froze with its four legs wide apart, head up, tail describing exactly its recent trajectory, and ready to take off instantly in any direction including up. I looked at it with some puzzlement. "I'll go see if I have any walnuts," I told it. I moved toward the archway, and as I did so the squirrel leaped at me. I threw up a hand to protect my face. The squirrel struck my shoulder again and leaped from it—

And as far as I know it leaped into the fourth dimension or somewhere. For I searched under and into every bed, chair, closet, cupboard and shelf in the house, and could find no sign of anything that even looked like a squirrel. It was gone as completely as the masses of tapioca. . . .

Tapioca! What had the head said about the tapioca? "She's thinking about it now." *She*—Gloria, of course. This whole insane business was tied up with Gloria in some way.

Gloria not only disliked tapioca—she was afraid of it.

I chewed on that for a while, and then looked at the clock. Gloria had had time enough to get to the hotel. I ran to the phone, dialled.

"Hotel San Dragon," said a chewing-gum voice.

"748, please," I said urgently.

A couple of clicks. Then, "Hello?"

"Gloria," I said. "Listen; I—"

"Oh, you. Listen—can you call me back later? I'm very busy."

"I can and I will, but tell me something quickly: Are you afraid of squirrels?"

Don't tell me a shudder can't be transmitted over a telephone wire. One was that time, "I hate them. Call me back in about—"

"Why do you hate them?"

With exaggerated patience, she said carefully, "When I was a little girl, I was feeding some pigeons and a squirrel jumped right up on my shoulder and scared me half to death. Now, *please*—"

"Okay, okay," I said. "I'll speak to you later." I hung up. She shouldn't talk to me that way. She had no right—

What was she doing in that hotel room, anyway?

I pushed the ugly thought down out of sight, and went and poured myself a beer. Gloria is afraid of tapioca, I thought, and tapioca shows up here. She is afraid of the sound of small animals' feet, and I hear them here. She is afraid of squirrels that jump on people, and I get a squirrel that jumps on people.

That must all make some sense. Of course, I could take the easy way out, and admit that I was crazy. But somehow, I was no longer so ready to admit anything like that. Down deep inside, I made an agreement with myself not to admit that until I had exhausted every other possibility.

A very foolish piece of business. See to it that you don't do likewise. It's probably much smarter not to try to figure things out.

There was only one person who could straighten this whole crazy mess out—since the head wouldn't—and that was Gloria, I thought suddenly. I realized, then, why I had not called all bets before now. I had been afraid to jeopardize the thing that Gloria and I shared. Well, let's face it. We didn't share it any longer. That admission helped.

I strode to the telephone, and dialled the hotel.

"Hotel San Dragon."

"748, please."

A moment's silence. Then, "I'm sorry, sir. The party does not wish to be disturbed."

I stood there looking blankly at the phone, while pain swirled and spiralled up inside me. I think that up to this moment I had treated the whole thing as part sickness, part dream; this, somehow, brought it to a sharp and agonizing focus. Nothing that she could have done could have been so calculated and so cruel.

I cradled the receiver and headed for the door. Before I could reach it, gray mists closed about me. For a moment I seemed to be on some sort of a treadmill; I was walking, but I could not reach anything. Swiftly, then, everything was normal.

"I must be in a pretty bad way," I muttered. I shook my head. It was incredible. I felt all right, though a little dizzy. I went to the door and out.

The trip to the hotel was the worst kind of a nightmare. I could only conclude that there was something strange and serious wrong with me, completely aside from my fury and

92

my hurt at Gloria. I kept running into these blind spells, when everything about me took on an unreal aspect. The light didn't seem right. I passed people on the street who weren't there when I turned to look at them. I heard voices where there were no people, and I saw people talking but couldn't hear them. I overcame a powerful impulse to go back home. I couldn't go back; I knew it; I knew I had to face whatever crazy thing was happening, and that Gloria had something to do with it.

I caught a cab at last, though I'll swear one of them disappeared just as I was about to step into it. Must have been another of those blind spells. After that it was easier. I slouched quivering in a corner of the seat with my eyes closed.

I paid off the driver at the hotel and stumbled in through the revolving doors. The hotel seemed much more solid than anything else since this horrible business had started to happen to me. I started over to the desk, determined to give some mad life-and-death message to the clerk to break that torturing "do not disturb" order. I glanced into the coffee room as I passed it and stopped dead.

She was in there, in a booth, with—with someone else. I couldn't see anything of the man but a glossy black head of hair and a thick, ruddy neck. She was smiling at him, the smile that I thought had been born and raised for me.

I stalked over to them, trembling. As I reached them, he half-rose, leaned across the table, and kissed her.

"Arthur . . ." she breathed.

"That," I said firmly, "will do."

They did not move.

"Stop it!" I screamed. They did not move. Nothing moved, anywhere. It was a tableau, a picture, a hellish frozen thing put there to tear me apart.

"That's all," said a now familiar voice, gently. "That kiss did it, son. You're through." It was the head, but now he was a whole man. An ordinary-looking, middle-sized creature he was, with a scrawny frame to match his unimpressive middle-aged face. He perched on the edge of the table, mercifully between me and that torturing kiss.

I ran to him, grasped his thin shoulders. "Tell me what it is," I begged him. "Tell me, if you know—and I think you know. Tell me!" I roared, sinking my fingers into his flesh.

He put his hands up and laid them gently on my wrists, holding them there until I quieted down a little. I let him go. "I *am* sorry, son," he said. "I hoped you would figure it all out by yourself."

"I tried," I said. I looked around me. The grayness was closing in again, and through it I could see the still figures of the people in the coffee-shop, all stopped in mid-action. It was one three-dimensional frame of some unthinkable movie-film. I felt cold sweat all but squirt from the pores of my face. "Where am I?" I shrieked.

"Please," he soothed. "Take it easy, and I'll tell you. Come over here and sit down and relax. Close your eyes and don't try to think. Just listen."

I did as he asked, and gradually I stopped shaking. He waited until he felt that I was calm, and then began talking.

"There is a world of psychic things—call them living thought, call them dreams if you like. Now, you know that of all animals, only human beings can reach these psychic things. It was a biological accident. There is something about humans which is tangent to this psychic world. Humans have the power to open a gate between the two worlds. They can seldom control the power; often they're not aware of it. But when that gate is opened, something materializes in the world of the humans. Imagination itself is enough to do it. If you are hungry, down deep inside, for a certain kind of woman, and if you picture her to yourself vividly enough, such a gate might open, and there she'll be. You can see her and touch her; she'll be little different from a real one."

"But—there is a difference?"

"Yes, there is. She is not a separate thing from you. She is a part of you. She is your product. That's what I was driving at when I mentioned parthenogenesis. It works like that."

"Parthenogenesis—let's see. That's the process of reproducing without fertilization, isn't it?"

"That's right. This 'materialization' of yours is a perfect parallel to that. As I told you before, however, it is not a process with high survival value. For one thing, it affords no chance to cross strains. Unless a living creature can bring into itself other characteristics, it must die out."

"Then why don't all parthenogenetic creatures die out?"

"There is a process used by which the very simple, one-celled forms of life take care of that. Mind you," he broke off

94

suddenly, "I'm just using all of this biological talk as symbolism. There are basic laws that work in both worlds, that work equally on the high forms of life and the low. Do you see?"

"I see. These are just examples. But go on about this process that the parthenogenetic creatures use to mix their strains."

"It's very simple. Two of these organisms let their nuclei flow together for a time. Then they separate and go their ways again. It isn't a reproductive process at all. It's merely a way in which each may gain a part of the other. It's called —syzygy."

"Oh," I said. "That. But I still don't—let me see. You mentioned it first when that—that—"

"When Gloria met Arthur," the man finished smoothly. "I said that if it were syzygy, you'd be all right. Well, it wasn't, as you saw for yourself. The outside strain, even though it didn't suit her as well as you did, was too strong. You got hurt. Well, in the workings of really basic laws, something always gets hurt."

"What about you? Who are you?"

"I am somebody who has been through it, that's all. You must understand that my world is different from the one you remember. Time itself is different. Though I started from a time perhaps thirty years away, I was able to open a gate near you. Just a little one, of course. I did it so that I could try to make you think this thing out in time. I believe that if you could, you would have been spared all this. You might even have been able to keep Gloria."

"What's it to you?"

"You don't know, do you? You really don't know?"

I opened my eyes and looked at him, and shook my head. "No, I don't. I—like you, old man."

He chuckled. "That's odd, you know. I don't like me."

I craned around and looked over at Gloria and her man, still frozen in that strange kiss. "Will those dream-people stay like that forever?"

"Dream people?"

"I suppose that's what they are. You know, I'm a little proud of Gloria. How I managed to dream up anything so—so lovely, I'll never know. I—hey—what's the matter?"

"Didn't you understand what I was telling you? Gloria is real. Gloria goes on living. What you see over there is the

95

thing that happened when you were no longer a part of her. Leo: she dreamed *you!*"

I rose to my feet and put my fists on the table between us. "That's a lie," I choked. "I'm—I'm me, damn you!"

"You're a detailed dream, Leo, and a splendid job. You're a piece of sentient psyche from another world injection-molded into an ideal that Gloria dreamed. Don't try to be anything else. There aren't many real humans, Leo. Most of the world is populated by the dreams of a few of them; didn't you know, Leo? Why do you suppose that so few people you met knew anything about the world as a whole? Why do you suppose that humans keep their interests confined and their environments small? Most of them aren't humans at all, Leo!"

"I'm *me,*" I said stubbornly. "Gloria *couldn't* have thought of all of me! Gloria can't run a power shovel! Gloria can't play a guitar! Gloria doesn't know enything about the circus foreman who sang, or the Finn dynamite boss who was killed!"

"Of course not. Gloria only dreamed a kind of man who was the product of those things, or things like them. Have you run a shovel since you met her? You'd find that you couldn't, if you really tried. You've played guitar for no one but her since you met her. You've spent all your time arranging music that no one will ever see or play!"

"I'm *not* anybody's dream!" I shouted. "I'm not. If I was an ideal of hers, we would have stayed together. I failed with her, old man; don't you know that? She wanted me to be aggressive, and I wasn't."

He looked at me so sadly that I thought he was going to cry. "She wanted you to *take*. You were a part of her, no human can take from himself."

"She was deathly afraid of some things that didn't bother me at all. What about that?"

"The squirrels, and the sound of all the little feet? No, Leo; they were baseless phobias, and she had the power to overcome any of them. She never tried, but it was not difficult to create you without them."

I stared at him. "Do you mean to—Old man, are there more like me, really?"

"Many, many," he sighed. "But few who cling to their nonexistent, ghostly egos as you are doing."

"Do the real people know what they are doing?"

"Very few of them. Very few. The world is full of people who feel incomplete, people who have everything they can possibly want and yet are unhappy, people who feel alone in a crowd. The world is mostly peopled by ghosts."

"But—the war! Roman history! The new car models! What about them?"

He shook his head again. "Some of it's real, some not. It depends on what the real humans want from moment to moment."

I thought a minute, bitterly. Then I asked him, "What was that you said about coming back in world-time, and looking through a little gateway at things that had happened?"

He sighed. "If you *must* hang on to the ego she gave you," he said wearily, "you'll stay the way you are now. But you'll age. It will take you the equivalent of thirty or so years to find your way around in that strange psychic world, for you will have to move and think like a human. Why do you want to do that?"

I said, with determination, "I am going back, then, if it takes me a century. I'm going to find me right after I met Gloria, and I'm going to warn me in such a way that I'll figure out a way to be with Gloria for the rest of her life."

He put his hands on my shoulders, and now there really were tears in his eyes. "Oh, you poor kid," he said.

I stared at him. Then, "What's—your name, old man?"

"My name is Leo."

"Oh," I said. "Oh."

Hospital . . .

They wouldn't let me go, even when the clatter of dishes and the meaningless talk and complaining annoyed me. They knew it annoyed me; they must have. Starch and boredom and the flat-white dead smell. They knew it. They knew I hated it, so every night was the same.

I could go out. Not really; not all the way out, to the places where people were not dressed in gray robes and long itchy flannel. But I could go outside where I could see the sky and smell the river smell and smoke a cigarette. If I closed the door tight and moved all the way over to the rail, and watched and smelled very carefully, sometimes I could forget the things inside the building and those inside me, too.

I liked the night. I lit my cigarette and I looked at the sky. Clotted, it was, and clean between clouds. The air was cold and warmed me, and down on the river a long golden ribbon was tied to a light on the other side, and lay across the water. My music came to me again, faintly, tuning up. I was very proud of my music because it was mine. It was a thing that belonged to me, and not to the hospital like the itchy flannel and the gray robe. The hospital had old red buildings and fences and a great many nurses who knew briskly of bedpans, but it had no music about it, anywhere, anywhere.

A light mist lay just above the ground because there were garbage cans in a battered row, and the mist was very clean and would not go among them. Entrance music played gently for the cat.

It was a black and white mangy cat. It padded out of the shadow into the clearing before the cans and stood with its head on one side, waving its tail. It was lean and moved like a beautiful thing.

Then there was the rat, the fat little brown bundle with its long worm of a tail. The rat glided out from between the cans, froze, and dropped on its belly. The music fell in pitch to meet the rise in volume, and the cat tensed. There was a pain about me somewhere and I realized distantly that my fingernails were biting into my tongue. *My* rat, *my* cat, *my* music. The cat sprang, and the rat drew first blood and squealed and died out there in the open where it could see its own blood. The cat licked its wound and yowled and tore at the quivering thing. There was blood on the rat and on the cat and on my tongue.

I turned away, shaken and exultant, as the music repeated its death-motif in echo. She was coming out of the building. Inside she was Miss Starchy but now she was a brown bundle —a little fat brown bundle. I was lean and moved like a beautiful thing . . . she smiled at me and turned to the steps. I was very happy and I moved along beside her, looking down at her soft throat. We went out into the mist together. In front of the cans she stopped and looked at me with her eyes very wide.

The cat watched curiously and then went on eating. We went on eating and listening to the music.

THERE is a time when a thing in the mind is a heavy thing to carry, and then it must be put down. But such is its nature that it cannot be set on a rock or shouldered off on to the fork of a tree, like a heavy pack. There is only one thing shaped to receive it, and that is another human mind. There is only one time when it can be done, and that is in a shared solitude. It cannot be done when a man is alone, and no man aloof in a crowd ever does it.

Riding fence gives a man this special solitude until his throat is full of it. It will come maybe two or three weeks out, with the days full of heat and gnats and the thrum of wire under the stretcher, and the nights full of stars and silence. Sometimes in those nights a chunk will fall in the fire, or a wolf will howl, and just then a man might realize that his partner is awake too, and that a thing in his mind is growing and swelling and becoming heavy. If it gets to be heavy enough, it is put down softly, like fine china, cushioned apart with thick strips of quiet.

That is why a wise foreman pairs his fence riders carefully. A man will tell things, sometimes, things grown into him like the calluses from his wire cutters, things as much a part of him, say, as a notched ear or bullet scars in his belly; and his hearer should be a man who will not mention them after sun-up—perhaps not until his partner is dead—perhaps never.

Kellet was a man who had calluses from wire cutters, and a notched ear, and old bullet scars low down on his belly. He's dead now. Powers never asked to hear about the scars. Powers was a good fence man and a good partner. They worked in silence, mostly, except for a grunt when a post-hole was deep enough, or "Here," when one of them handed over a tool. When they pitched for the night, there was no saying "You get the wood," or "Make the coffee." One or the other would just do it. Afterward they sat and smoked, and sometimes they talked, and sometimes they did not, and sometimes what they said was important to them, and sometimes it was not.

Kellet told about the ear while he was cooking one evening. Squatting to windward of the fire, he rolled the long-handled skillet deftly, found himself looking at it like a man suddenly scanning the design of a ring he has worn for years.

100

"Was in a fight one time," he said.

Powers said, "Woman."

"Yup," said Kellet. "Got real sweet on a dressmaker in Kelso when I was a bucko like you. Used to eat there. Made good mulligan."

They were eating, some ten minutes later, when he continued. " 'Long comes this other feller, had grease on his hair. He shore smelt purty."

"Mexican?"

"Easterner."

Powers' silence was contributory rather than receptive at this point.

"She said to come right in. Spoons him out what should be my seconds o' stew. Gets to gigglin' an' fussin' over him." He paused and chewed, and when the nutritious obstacle was out of the way, spat vehemently. "Reckon I cussed a little. Couldn't he'p m'self. Next thing you know, he's a-tellin' me what language not to use in front of a lady. We went round and round together and that ended quick. See this ear?"

"Pulled a knife on you."

Kellet shook his big, seamed head. "Nup. She hit me a lick with the skillet. Tuk out part o' my ear. After, it tuk me the better part of an hour with tar soap to wash the last o' that hair grease offen my knuckles."

One bullet made the holes in his stomach, Kellet told Powers laconically while they were having a dip in a cold stream one afternoon.

"Carried a leetle pot-belly in them days," said Kellet. "Bullet went in one side and out t'other. I figgered fer a while they might's well rack me, stick me, bleed me, and smoke me fer fall. But I made it. Shore lost that pot-belly in th' gov'ment hospital though. They wouldn't feed me but custards and like that. My plumbin' was all mixed up an' cross-connected.

"Feller in th' next bed died one night. They used t'wake us up 'fore daylight with breakfast. He had prunes. I shore wanted them prunes. When I see he don't need 'em I ate 'em. Figgered nobody had to know." He chuckled.

Later, when they were dressed and mounted and following the fence, he added, "They found the prune stones in m'bandages."

But it was at night that Kellet told the other thing, the thing that grew on like a callus and went deeper than bullet scars.

Powers had been talking, for a change. Women. "They always got a out," he complained. He put an elbow out of his sleeping-bag and leaned on it. Affecting a gravelly soprano, he said, "I'd like you better, George, if you'd ack like a gentleman."

He pulled in the elbow and lay down with an eloquent thump. "I know what a gentleman is. It's whatever in the world you cain't be, not if you sprouted wings and wore a hello. *I* never seen one. I mean, I never seen a man yet where *some* woman, *some* time, couldn't tell him to ack like he was one."

The fire burned bright, and after a time it burned low. "I'm one," said Kellet.

Powers then sensed that thing, that heavy growth of memory. He said nothing. He was awake, and he knew that somehow Kellet knew it.

Kellet said, "Know the Pushmataha country? Nuh—you wouldn't. Crick up there called Kiamichi. Quit a outfit up Winding Stair way and was driftin'. Come up over this little rise and was well down t'ord th' crick when I see somethin' flash in the water. It's a woman in there. I pulled up pronto. I was that startled. She was mother-nekkid.

"Up she goes on t'other side 'til she's about knee-deep, an' shakes back her hair, and then she sees me. Makes a dive fer th' bank, slips, I reckon. Anyway, down she goes an' lays still.

"I tell you, man, I felt real bad. I don't like to cause a lady no upset. I'd as soon wheeled back an' fergot the whole thing. But what was I goin' to do—let her drown? Mebbe she was hurt.

"I hightailed right down there. Figured she'd ruther be alive an' embarrassed than at peace an' dead.

"She was hurt all right. Hit her head. Was a homestead downstream a hundred yards. Picked her up—she didn't weigh no more'n a buffalo calf—an' toted her down there. Yipped, but there wasn't no one around. Went in, found a bed, an' put her on it. Left her, whistled up my cayuse, an' got to me saddlebags. When I got back she was bleedin' pretty bad. Found a towel for under her head. Washed the cut with whiskey. Four-five inches long under the edge of her hair. She had that hair that's black, but blue when the sun's on it."

He was quiet for a long time. Powers found his pipe, filled it, rose, got a coal from the dying fire, lit up, and went back to his bedroll. He said nothing.

When he was ready, Kellet said, "She was alive, but out cold. I didn't know what the hell to do. The bleedin' stopped after a while, but I didn't know whether to rub her wrists or stand on m' head. I ain't no doctor. Finally I just set there near her to wait. Mebbe she'd wake up, mebbe somebuddy'd come. Mebbe I'd have my poke full o' trouble if somebuddy did come—I knowed that. But what was I goin' to do—ride off?

"When it got dark two-three hours later I got up an' lit a tallow-fat lamp an' a fire, an' made some coffee. Used my own Arbuckle. 'Bout got it brewed, heard a funny kind of squeak from t'other room. She's settin' bolt upright lookin' at me through the door, clutchin' the blanket to her so hard she like to push it through to t'other side, an' makin' her eyes round's a hitchin' ring. Went to her an' she squeaked ag'in an' scrambled away off into the corner an' tole' me not to touch her.

"Said, 'I won't, ma'am. Yo're hurt. You better take it easy.'

" 'Who are you?' she says. 'What you doin' here?' she says.

"I tol' her my name, says, 'Look, now, you're bleedin' ag'in. Just you lie down, now, an' let me fix it.'

"I don't know as she trusted me or she got faint. Anyway down she went, an' I put a cold cloth on the cut. She says, 'What happened?'

"Tole her, best I could. Up she comes ag'in. 'I was bathin'!' she says. 'I didn't have no—' and she don't get no further'n that, just squeaks some more.

"I says, straight out, 'Ma'am, you fell an' hurt yo're head. I don't recall a thing but that. I couldn't do nought but what I did. Reckon it was sort of my fault anyway. I don't mean you no harm. Soon's you git some help I'll leave. Where's your menfolks?'

"That quieted her down. She tole me about herself. She was homesteadin'. Had pre-emption rights an' eighteen months left t' finish th' term. Husband killed in a rock-slide. Swore to him she'd hold th' land. Didn't know what she'd do after, but spang shore she was a-goin' to do that first. Lot o' spunk."

Kellet was quiet again. The loom of the moon took black from the sky and gave it to the eastward ridge. Powers' pipe gurgled suddenly.

"Neighbor fourteen mile downstream was burned out the winter before. Feller eight mile 'tother way gone up to Winding Stair for a roundup, taken his wife. Be gone another

103

two months. This little gal sweat out corn and peas for dryin', had taters put by. Nobuddy ever come near, almost. Hot day, she just naturally bathed in the crick.

"Asked her what about drifters like me, but mebbe gunmen. She reached under the bed, drug out a derringer. Says, 'This's for sech trash.' An' a little pointy knife. 'This's for me,' she says, just like that. I tol' her to keep both of 'em by her. Was that sorry for her, liked her grit so, I felt half sick with it.

"Was goin' to turn in outside, by the shed. After we talked some an' I made her up some johnny-cake, she said I c'd bunk in th' kitchen if I wanted. Tol' her to lock her door. She locked it. Big wooden bar. I put down m'roll an' turned in."

The moon was a bead on the hill's haloed brow; a coronet, then a crown.

Powers put his pipe away.

"In the mornin'," said Kellett, "she couldn't get up. I just naturally kicked the door down when she wouldn't answer. Had a bad fever. Fast asleep an' couldn't wake up but for a half minute, an' then she'd slide off ag'in. Set by her 'most all day, 'cept where I saw to my hoss an' fixed some vittles. Did for her like you would for a kid. Kept washin' her face with cold water. Never done nothin' like that before; didn't know much what to do, done the best I could.

"Afternoon, she talked for a hour or so, real wild. Mostly to her man, like he was settin' there 'stead o' me. He was a lucky feller. She said . . .

"Be damned to you what she said. But I . . . tuk to answerin' her oncet in a while, just 'Yes, honey,' when she got to callin' hard for him. Man a full year dead, I don't think she really believed it, not all the way down. She said things to him like—like no woman ever thought to say to me. Anyway . . . when I answered thataway she'd talk quiet. If I didn't she'd just call and call, and git all roiled up, an' her head would bleed, so what else you expect me to do?

"Next day she was better, but weak's a starveling colt in a blowin' drought. Slept a lot. I found out where she'd been jerkin' venison, an' finished it up. Got some weeds outen her black-eye peas. Went back ever' now an' then to see she's all right. Remembered some red haw back over the ridge, rode over there and gathered some, fixed 'em to sun so's she'd have 'em for dried-apple pie come winter.

104

"Four-five days went by like that. Got a deer one day, skinned it an' jerked it. Done some carpenterin' in th' shed an' in th' house. Done what I could. Time I was fixin' the door to the kitchen I'd kicked down that first mornin', she lay a-watchin' me an' when I was done, she said I was good. 'Yo're good, Kellet,' she said. Don't sound like much to tell it. Was a whole lot."

Powers watched the moon rise and balance itself on the ridge, ready to float free. A single dead tree on the summit stood against it like a black-gloved hand held to a golden face.

Kellet said, "Just looka that ol' tree, so . . . strong-lookin' an' . . . so dead."

When the moon was adrift, Kellet said, "Fixed that door with a new beam an' good gudgeons. Man go to kick it down now'd have a job to do. She—"

Powers waited.

"—she never did use it. After she got well enough to get up an' around a bit, even. Just left it open. Mebbe she never thought about it. Mebbe she did, too. Nights, I'd stretch out in my bedroll, lay there, and wait. Pretty soon she'd call out, 'Good night, Kellet. Sleep good, now.' Thing like that, that's worth a passel o' farmin' an' carpenterin' . . .

"One night, ten-'leven days after I got there, woke up. She was cryin' there in the dark in t'other room. I called out what's the matter. She didn't say. Just kept a-bawlin'. Figgered mebbe her head hurt her. Got up, went to th' door. Asked her if she's all right. She just keeps a-cryin'—not loud, mind, but cryin' hard. Thing like that makes a man feel all tore up.

"Went on in. Called her name. She patted the side o' th' bed. I set down. Put my hand on her face to see if she was gettin' the fever ag'in. Face was cool. Wet, too. She tuk my hand in her two an' held it hard up ag'in her mouth. I didn't know she was so strong.

"Set there quiet for two-three minutes. Got m'hand loose. Says, 'What you bawlin' for, ma'am?'

"She says, 'It's good to have you here.'

"I stood up, says, 'You git back to yo're rest now, ma'am.' She—"

There were minutes between the words, but no change in his voice when he continued.

"—cried mebbe a hour. Stopped sudden, and altogether. Mebbe I slept after that, mebbe I didn't. Don't rightly recall.

105

"Next mornin' she's up bright an' early, fixin' chow. First time she's done it since she's hurt. Tole her, 'Whoa. Take it easy, ma'am. You don't want to tucker yo'reself out.'

"She says, 'I coulda done this three days ago.' Sounded mad. Don't rightly know who she's mad at. Fixed a powerful good breakfast.

"That day seemed the same, but it was 'way differ'nt. Other days we mostly didn't talk nothin' but business—caterpillars in th' tomato vines, fix a hole in th' smoke shed, an' like that. This day we talked the same things. Difference was, we had to try hard to keep the talk where it was. An' one more thing —didn't neither of us say one more word 'bout any work that might have to be done—tomorrow.

"Midday, I gathered up what was mine, an' packed my saddlebags. Brought my hoss up to th' shed an' watered him an' saddled him. Didn't see her much, but knowed she's watchin' me from inside th' house.

"All done, went to pat m'hoss once on the neck. Hit him so hard he shied. Right surprised m'self.

"She come out then. She stood a-lookin' at me. Says, 'Goodbye, Kellet. God bless you.'

"Says good-bye to her. Then didn't neither of us move for a minute. She says, 'You think I'm a bad woman.'

"Says, 'No sech a damn thing, ma'am! You was a sick one, an' powerful lonesome. You'll be all right now.'

"She says, 'I'm all right. I'll be all right long as I live,' she says, 'thanks to you, Kellet. Kellet,' she says, 'you had to think for both of us an' you did. Yo're a gentleman, Kellet,' she says.

"Mounted, then, an' rode off. On the rise, looked back, saw her still by the shed, lookin' at me. Waved m' hat. Rode on."

The night was a white night now, since the mood had shucked its buoyant gold for its travelling silver. Powers heard Kellet turn over, and knew he could speak now if he cared to. Somewhere a mouse screamed briefly under an owl's silent talons. Distantly, a coyote's hungry call built itself into the echoing loneliness.

Powers said, "So that's what a gentleman is. A man that c'n think for two people when the time comes for it?"

"Naw-w," drawled Kellet scornfully. "That's just what she come to believe because I never touched her."

Powers asked it, straight. "Why didn't you?"

A man will tell things, sometimes, things grown into him

106

like the calluses from his wire-cutters, things as much a part of him as, say, a notched ear or bullet scars in his belly; and his hearer should be a man who will not mention them after sun-up—perhaps not until his partner is dead—perhaps never.

Kellet said, "I caint."

RANSOME láy in the dark and smiled to himself, thinking about his hostess. Ransome was always in demand as a house guest, purely because of his phenomenal abilities as a raconteur. Said abilities were entirely due to his being so often a house guest, for it was the terse beauty of his word pictures of people and their opinions of people that made him the figure he was. And all those clipped ironies had to do with the people he had met last week-end. Staying a while at the Joneses, he could quietly insinuate the most scandalously hilarious things about the Joneses when he week-ended with the Browns the following fortnight. You think Mr. and Mrs. Jones resented that? Ah, no. You should hear the dirt on the Browns! And so it went, a two-dimensional spiral on the social plane.

This wasn't the Joneses or the Browns, though. This was Mrs. Benedetto's ménage; and to Ransome's somewhat jaded sense of humor, the widow Benedetto was a godsend. She lived in a world of her own, which was apparently set about with quasi-important ancestors and relatives exactly as her living room was cluttered up with perfectly unmentionable examples of Victorian rococo.

Mrs. Benedetto did not live alone. Far from it. Her very life, to paraphrase the lady herself, was wound about, was caught up in, was owned by and dedicated to her baby. Her baby was her beloved, her little beauty, her too darling my dear, and—so help me—her boobly wutsi-wutsikins. In himself he was quite a character. He answered to the name of Bubbles, which was inaccurate and offended his dignity. He had been christened Fluffy, but you know how it is with nicknames. He was large and he was sleek, that paragon among animals, a chastened alley-rabbit.

Wonderful things, cats. A cat is the only animal which can live like a parasite and maintain to the utmost its ability to take care of itself. You've heard of little lost dogs, but you never heard of a lost cat. Cats don't get lost, because cats don't belong anywhere. You wouldn't get Mrs. Benedetto to believe that. Mrs. Benedetto never thought of putting Fluffy's devotion to the test by declaring a ten-day moratorium on the canned salmon. If she had, she would have uncovered a sense of honor comparable with that of a bed-bug.

Knowing this—Ransome pardoned himself the pun—cate-gorically, Ransome found himself vastly amused. Mrs. Ben-edetto's ministrations to the phlegmatic Fluffy were posi-tively orgiastic. As he thought of it in detail, he began to feel that perhaps, after all, Fluffy was something of a feline phenomenon. A cat's ears are sensitive organs; any living being that could abide Mrs. Benedetto's constant flow of con-versation from dawn till dark, and then hear it subside in sleep only to be replaced by a nightshift of resounding snores; well, that *was* phenomenal. And Fluffy had stood it for four years. Cats are not renowned for their patience. They have, however, a very fine sense of values. Fluffy was getting some-thing out of it—worth considerably more to him than the discomforts he endured, too, for no cat likes to break even.

He lay still, marvelling at the carrying power of the widow's snores. He knew little of the late Mr. Benedetto, but he gathered now that he had been either a man of saintly patience, a masochist or a deaf-mute. A noise like that from just one stringy throat must be an impossibility, and yet, there it was. Ransome liked to imagine that the woman had calluses on her palate and tonsils, grown there from her conversation, and it was these rasping together that pro-duced the curious dry-leather quality of her snores. He tucked the idea away for future reference. He might use it next week-end. The snores were hardly the gentlest of lulla-bies, but any sound is soothing if it is repeated often enough.

There is an old story about a lighthouse tender whose lighthouse was equipped with an automatic cannon which fired every fifteen minutes, day and night. One night, when the old man was asleep, the gun failed to go off. Three seconds after its stated time, the old fellow was out of his bed and flailing around the room, shouting, "What was that?" And so it was with Ransome.

He couldn't tell whether it was an hour after he had fallen asleep, or whether he had not fallen asleep at all. But he found himself sitting on the edge of the bed, wide awake, straining every nerve for the source of the—what was it?—sound?—that had awakened him. The old house was as quiet as a city morgue after closing time, and he could see nothing in the tall, dark guestroom but the moon-silvered windows and the thick blacknesses that were drapes. Any old damn thing might be hiding behind those drapes, he thought comfortingly. He edged himself back on the bed and quickly snatched his feet off the floor. Not that anything was under the bed, but still—

A white object puffed along the floor, through the moonbeams, toward him. He made no sound, but tensed himself, ready to attack or defend, dodge or retreat. Ransome was by no means an admirable character, but he owed his reputation, and therefore his existence, to this particular trait, the ability to poise himself, invulnerable to surprise. Try arguing with a man like that sometime.

The white object paused to stare at him out of its yellow-green eyes. It was only Fluffy—Fluffy looking casual and easy-going and not at all in a mood to frighten people. In fact he looked up at Ransome's gradually relaxing bulk and raised a longhaired, quizzical eyebrow, as if he rather enjoyed the man's discomfiture.

Ransome withstood the cat's gaze with suavity, and stretched himself out on the bed with every bit of Fluffy's own easy grace. "Well," he said amusedly, "you gave me a jolt! Weren't you taught to knock before you entered a gentleman's boudoir?"

Fluffy raised a velvet paw and touched it pinkly with his tongue. "Do you take me for a barbarian?" he asked.

Ransome's lids seemed to get heavy, the only sign he ever gave of being taken aback. He didn't believe for a moment that the cat had really spoken, but there was something about the voice he had heard that was more than a little familiar. This was, of course, someone's idea of a joke.

Good God—it had to be a joke!

Well, he had to hear that voice again before he could place it. "You didn't say anything of course," he told the cat, "but if you did, what was it?"

"You heard me the first time," said the cat, and jumped up on the foot of his bed. Ransome inched back from the animal. "Yes," he said, "I—thought I did." Where on earth had he heard that voice before? "You know," he said, with an attempt at jocularity, "you should, under these circumstances, have written me a note before you knocked."

"I refuse to be burdened with the so-called social amenities," said Fluffy. His coat was spotlessly clean, and he looked like an advertising photograph for eiderdown, but he began to wash carefully. "I don't like you, Ransome."

110

"Thanks," chuckled Ransome, surprised. "I don't like you either."

"Why?" asked Fluffy.

Ransome told himself silently that he was damned. He had recognized the cat's voice, and it was a credit to his powers of observation that he had. It was his own voice. He held tight to a mind that would begin to reel on slight provocation, and, as usual when bemused, he flung out a smoke-screen of his own variety of glib chatter.

"Reasons for not liking you," he said, "are legion. They are all included in the one phrase—'You are a cat!'"

"I have heard you say that at least twice before," said Fluffy, "except that you have now substituted 'cat' for 'woman.'"

"Your attitude is offensive. Is any given truth any the less true for having been uttered more than once?"

"No," said the cat with equanimity. "But it is just that more clichéd."

Ransome laughed. "Quite aside from the fact that you can talk, I find you most refreshing. No one has ever criticized my particular variety of repartee before."

"No one was ever wise to you before," said the cat. "Why don't you like cats?"

A question like that was, to Ransome, the pressing of a button which released ordered phrases. "Cats," he said oratorically, "are without doubt the most self-centered, ungrateful, hypocritical creatures ôn this or any other earth. Spawned from a mésalliance between Lilith and Satan—"

Fluffy's eyes widened. "Ah! An antiquarian!" he whispered.

"—they have the worst traits of both. Their best qualities are their beauty of form and of motion, and even these breathe evil. Women are the ficklest of bipeds, but few women are as fickle as, by nature, any cat is. Cats are not true. They are impossibilities, as perfection is impossible. No other living creature moves with utterly perfect grace. Only the dead can so perfectly relax. And nothing—simply nothing at all—transcends a cat's incomparable insincerity."

Fluffy purred.

"Pussy! Sit-by-the-fire and sing!" spat Ransome. "Smiling up all toadying and yellow-eyed at the bearers of liver and salmon and catnip! Soft little puffball, bundle of joy, playing with a ball on a string; making children clap their soft hands

111

to see you, while your mean little brain is viciously alight with the pictures your play calls up for you. Bite it to make it bleed; hold it till it all but throttles; lay it down and step about it daintily; prod it with a gentle silken paw until it moves again, and then pounce. Clasp it in your talons then, lift it, roll over with it, sink your cruel teeth into it while you pump out its guts with your hind feet. Ball on a string! Play-actor!"

Fluffy fawned. "To quote you, that is the prettiest piece of emotional claptrap that these old ears have ever heard. A triumph in studied spontaneity. A symphony in cynicism. A poem in perception. The unqualified—"

Ransome grunted.

He deeply resented this flamboyant theft of all his pet phrases, but his lip twitched nevertheless. The cat was indeed an observant animal.

"—epitome of understatement," Fluffy finished smoothly. "To listen to you, one would think that you would like to slaughter earth's felinity."

"I would," gritted Ransome.

"It would be a favor to us," said the cat. "We would keep ourselves vastly amused, eluding you and laughing at the effort it cost you. Humans lack imagination."

"Superior creature," said Ransome ironically, "why don't you do away with the human race, if you find us a bore?"

"You think we couldn't?" responded Fluffy. "We can out-think, outrun and outbreed your kind. But why should we? As long as you act as you have for these last few thousand years, feeding us, sheltering us and asking nothing from us but our presence for purposes of admiration—why then, you may remain here."

Ransome guffawed. "Nice of you! But listen—stop your bland discussion of the abstract and tell me some things I want to know. How can you talk, and why did you pick me to talk to?"

Fluffy settled himself. "I shall answer the question socrati-cally. Socrates was a Greek, and so I shall begin with your last questions. What do you do for a living?"

"Why I—I have some investments and a small capital, and the interest—" Ransome stopped, for the first time fumbling for words. Fluffy was nodding knowingly.

"All right, all right. Come clean. You can speak freely."

Ransome grinned. "Well, if you must know—and you seem to—I am a practically permanent house guest. I have a considerable fund of stories and a flair for telling them; I look presentable and act as if I were a gentleman. I negotiate, at times, small loans—"

"A loan," said Fluffy authoritatively, "is something one intends to repay."

"We'll call them loans," said Ransome airily. "Also, at one time and another, I exact a reasonable fee for certain services rendered—"

"Blackmail," said the cat.

"Don't be crude. All in all, I find life a comfortable and engrossing thing."

"Q. E. D.," said Fluffy triumphantly. "You make your living being scintilliant, beautiful to look at. So do I. You help nobody but yourself; you help yourself to anything you want. So do I. No one likes you except those you bleed; everyone admires and envies you. So with me. Get the point?"

"I think so. Cat, you draw a mean parallel. In other words, you consider my behavior catlike."

"Precisely," said Fluffy through his whiskers. "And that is both why and how I can talk with you. You're so close to the feline in everything you do and think; your whole basic philosophy is that of a cat. You have a feline aura about you so intense that it contacts mine; hence we find each other intelligible."

"I don't understand that," said Ransome.

"Neither do I," returned Fluffy. "But there it is. Do you like Mrs. Benedetto?"

"No!" said Ransome immediately and with considerable emphasis. "She is absolutely insufferable. She bores me. She irritates me. She is the only woman in the world who can do both things to me at the same time. She talks too much. She reads too little. She thinks not at all. Her mind is hysterically hidebound. She has a face like the cover of a book that no one has ever wanted to read. She is built like a pinch-type whiskey bottle that never had any whiskey in it. Her voice is monotonous and unmusical. Her education was insufficient. Her family background is mediocre, she can't cook, and she doesn't brush her teeth often enough."

"My, my," said the cat, raising both paws in surprise. "I detect a ring of sincerity in all that. It pleases me. That is

113

exactly the way I have felt for some years. I have never found fault with her cooking, though; she buys special food for me. I am tired of it. I am tired of her. I am tired of her to an almost unbelievable extent. Almost as much as I hate you."

"Me?"

"Of course. You're an imitation. Your'e a phony. Your birth is against you, Ransome. No animal that sweats and shaves, that opens doors for women, that dresses itself in equally phony imitations of the skins of animals, can achieve the status of a cat. You are presumptuous."

"You're not?"

"I am different. I am a cat, and have a right to do as I please. I disliked you so intensely when I saw you this evening that I made up my mind to kill you."

"Why didn't you? Why—don't you?"

"I couldn't," said the cat coolly. "Not when you sleep like a cat . . . no, I thought of something far more amusing."

"Oh?"

"Oh yes." Fluffy stretched out a foreleg, extended his claws. Ransome noticed subconsciously how long and strong they seemed. The moon had gone its way, and the room was filling with slate-gray light.

"What woke you," said the cat, leaping to the window-sill, "just before I came in?"

"I don't know," said Ransome. "Some little noise, I imagine."

"No indeed," said Fluffy, curling his tail and grinning through his whiskers. "It was the stopping of a noise. Notice how quiet it is?"

It was indeed. There wasn't a sound in the house—oh yes, now he could hear the plodding footsteps of the maid on her way from the kitchen to Mrs. Benedetto's bedroom, and the soft clink of a teacup. But otherwise—suddenly he had it. "The old horse stopped snoring!"

"She did," said the cat. The door across the hall opened, there was the murmur of the maid's voice, a loud crash, the most horrible scream Ransome had ever heard, pounding footsteps rushing down the hall, a more distant scream, silence. Ransome bounced out of bed. "What the hell—"

"Just the maid," said Fluffy, washing between his toes, but keeping the corners of his eyes on Ransome. "She just found Mrs. Benedetto."

"Found—"

"Yes. I tore her throat out."

"Good—God! Why?"

Fluffy poised himself on the window-sill. "So you'd be blamed for it," he said, and laughing nastily, he leaped out and disappeared in the gray morning.

BUDGIE slid into the laboratory without knocking, as usual.

She was flushed and breathless, her eyes bright with speed and eagerness. "Whatcha got, Muley?"

Muhlenberg kicked the morgue door shut before Budgie could get in line with it. "Nothing," he said flatly, "and of all the people I don't want to see—and at the moment that means all the people there are—you head the list. Go away."

Budgie pulled off her gloves and stuffed them into an oversized shoulder-bag, which she hurled across the laboratory onto a work-surface. "Come on, Muley. I saw the meat-wagon outside. I know what it brought, too. That double murder in the park. Al told me."

"Al's jaw is one that needs more tying up than any of the stiffs he taxis around," said Muhlenberg bitterly. "Well, you're not getting near this pair."

She came over to him, stood very close. In spite of his annoyance, he couldn't help noticing how soft and full her lips were just then. *Just then*—and the sudden realization added to the annoyance. He had known for a long time that Budgie could turn on mechanisms that made every one of a man's ductless glands purse up its lips and blow like a trumpet. Every time he felt it he hated himself. "Get away from me," he growled. "It won't work."

"What won't, Muley?" she murmured.

Muhlenberg looked her straight in the eye and said something about his preference for raw liver over Budgie-times-twelve.

The softness went out of her lips, to be replaced by no particular hardness. She simply laughed good-naturedly. "All right, you're immune. I'll try logic."

"Nothing will work," he said. "You will not get in there to see those two, and you'll get no details from me for any of that *couche-con-carne* stew you call a newspaper story."

"Okay," she said surprisingly. She crossed the lab and picked up her handbag. She found a glove and began to pull it on. "Sorry I interrupted you, Muley. I do get the idea. You want to be alone."

His jaw was too slack to enunciate an answer. He watched her go out, watched the door close, watched it open again, heard her say in a very hurt tone, "But I do think you could tell me *why* you won't say anything about this murder."

He scratched his head. "As long as you behave yourself, I guess I do owe you that." He thought for a moment. "It's not your kind of a story. That's about the best way to put it."

"Not my kind of a story? A double murder in Lover's Lane? The maudlin mystery of the mugger, or mayhem in Maytime? No kidding, Muley—you're not serious!"

Budgie, this one isn't for fun. It's ugly. Very *damn* ugly. And it's serious. It's mysterious for a number of other reasons than the ones you want to siphon into your readers."

"What other reasons?"

"Medically. Biologically. Sociologically."

"My stories got biology. Sociology they got likewise; stodgy truisms about social trends is the way I dish up sex in the public prints, or didn't you know? So—that leaves medical. What's so strange medically about this case?"

"Good night, Budgie."

"Come on, Muley. You can't horrify *me*."

"That I know. You've trod more primrose pathology in your research than Krafft-Ebing plus eleven comic books. No, Budgie. No more."

"Dr. F. L. Muhlenberg, brilliant young biologist and special medical consultant to the City and State Police, intimated that these aspects of the case—the brutal murder and disfigurement of the embarrassed couple—were superficial compared with the unspeakable facts behind them. 'Medically mysterious', he was quoted as saying." She twinkled at him. "How's that sound?" She looked at her watch. "And I can make the early edition, too, with a head. Something like DOC SHOCKED SPEECHLESS—and a subhead: Lab Sleuth Suppresses Medical Details of Double Park Killing. Yeah, and your picture."

"If you dare to print anything of the sort," he raged, "I'll—"

"All right, all right," she said conciliatingly. "I won't. I really won't."

"Promise me?"

"I promise, Muley . . . if—"

"Why should I bargain?" he demanded suddenly. "Get out of here."

He began to close the door. "And something for the editorial page," she said. "Is a doctor within his rights in suppressing information concerning a murderous maniac and his methods?" She closed the door.

Muhlenberg bit his lower lip so hard he all but yelped. He ran to the door and snatched it open. "Wait!"

Budgie was leaning against the doorpost lighting a cigarette. "I *was* waiting," she said reasonably.

"Come in here," he grated. He snatched her arm and whirled her inside, slamming the door.

"You're a brute," she said rubbing her arm and smiling dazzlingly.

"The only way to muzzle you is to tell you the whole story. Right?"

"Right. If I get an exclusive when you're ready to break the story."

"There's probably a kicker in that, too," he said morosely. He glared at her. Then, "Sit down," he said.

She did. "I'm all yours."

"Don't change the subject," he said with a ghost of his natural humor. He lit a thoughtful cigarette. "What do you know about this case so far?"

"Too little," she said. "This couple were having a conversation without words in the park when some muggers jumped them and killed them, a little more gruesomely than usual. But instead of being delivered to the city morgue, they were brought straight to you on the orders of the ambulance interne after one quick look."

"How did you know about it?"

"Well, if you must know, I was in the park. There's a short-cut over by the museum, and I was about a hundred yards down the path when I . . ."

Muhlenberg waited as long as tact demanded, and a little longer. Her face was still, her gaze detached. "Go on."

". . . when I heard a scream," she said in the precise tone of voice which she had been using. Then she began to cry.

"Hey," he said. He knelt beside her, put a hand on her shoulder. She shoved it away angrily, and covered her face with a damp towel. When she took it down again she seemed to be laughing. She was doing it so badly that he turned away in very real embarrassment.

"Sorry," she said in a very shaken whisper. "It . . . was that kind of a scream. I've never heard anything like it. It did

118

something to me. It had more agony in it than a single sound should be able to have." She closed her eyes.

"Man or woman?"

She shook her head.

"So," he said matter-of-factly, "what did you do then?"

"Nothing. Nothing at all, for I don't know how long." She slammed a small fist down on the table. "I'm supposed to be a reporter!" she flared. "And there I stand like a dummy, like a wharf rat in concussion-shock!" She wet her lips. "When I came around I was standing by a rock wall with one hand on it." She showed him. "Broke two perfectly good fingernails, I was holding on so tight. I ran toward where I'd heard the sound. Just trampled brush, nothing else. I heard a crowd milling around on the avenue. I went up there. The meat-wagon was there, Al and that young sawbones Regal—Ruggles—"

"Regalio."

"Yeah, him. They'd just put those two bodies into the ambulance. They were covered with blankets. I asked what was up. Regalio waved a finger and said 'Not for school-girls' and gave me a real death-mask grin. He climbed aboard. I grabbed Al and asked him what was what. He said muggers had killed this couple, and it was pretty rugged. Said Regalio had told him to bring them here, even before he made a police report. They were both about as upset as they could get."

"I don't wonder," said Muhlenberg.

"Then I asked if I could ride and they said no and took off. I grabbed a cab when I found one to grab, which was all of fifteen minutes later, and here I am. Here I am," she repeated, "getting a story out of you in the damndest way yet. You're asking, I'm answering." She got up. "You write the feature, Muley. I'll go on into your icebox and do your work."

He caught her arm. "Nah! No you don't! Like the man said —it's not for school-girls."

"Anything you have in there *can't* be worse than my imagination!" she snapped.

"Sorry. It's what you get for barging in on me before I've had a chance to think something through. You see, this wasn't exactly two people."

"I know!" she said sarcastically. "Siamese twins."

He looked at her distantly. "Yes. 'Taint funny, kiddo."

119

For once she had nothing to say. She put one hand slowly up to her mouth and apparently forgot it, for there it stayed. "That's what's so ugly about this. Those two were . . . torn apart." He closed his eyes. "I can just see it. I wish I couldn't. Those thugs drifting through the park at night, out for anything they could get. They hear something . . . fall right over them . . . I don't know. Then—"

"All right, all right," she whispered hoarsely. "I can hear you."

"But, damn it," he said angrily, "I've been kicking around this field long enough to know every documented case of such a creature. And I just can't believe that one like this could exist without having been written up in some medical journal somewhere. Even if they were born in Soviet Russia, some translation of a report would've appeared somewhere."

"I know Siamese twins are rare. But surely such a birth wouldn't make international headlines!"

"This one would," he said positively. "For one thing, Siamese twins usually bear more anomalies than just the fact that they are attached. They're frequently fraternal rather than identical twins. More often than not one's born more fully developed than the other. Usually when they're born at all they don't live. But these—"

"What's so special?"

Muhlenberg spread his hands. "They're perfect. They're costally joined by a surprisingly small tissue-organ complex—"

"Wait, professor, 'Costally'—you mean at the chest?"

"That's right. And the link is—was—not major. I can't understand why they were never surgically separated. There may be a reason, of course, but that'll have to wait on the autopsy."

"Why wait?"

"It's all I can do to wait." He grinned suddenly. "You see, you're more of a help than you realize, Budge. I'm dying to get to work on them, but under the circumstances I have to wait until morning. Regalio reported to the police, and I know the coroner isn't going to come around this time of night, not if I could show him quintuplets in a chain like sausages. In addition, I don't have identities, I don't have relatives' releases—you know. So—a superficial examination, a lot of wild guesses, and a chance to sound off to you to keep myself from going nuts."

"You're *using* me!"

"That's bad?"

"Yes—when I don't get any fun out of it."

He laughed. "I love those incendiary statements of yours. m just not flammable."

She looked at him, up and a little sidewise. "Not at all?"

"Not now."

She considered that. She looked down at her hands, as if ey were the problems of Muhlenberg's susceptibility. She rned the hands over. "Sometimes," she said, "I really enjoy when we share something else besides twitches and moans. Iaybe we should be more inhibited."

"Do tell."

She said, "We have nothing in common. I mean, but othing. We're different to the core, to the bone. You hunt ut facts and so do I, but we could never share that because e don't use facts for the same things. You use facts only to nd more facts."

"What do you use them for?"

She smiled. "All sorts of things. A good reporter doesn't eport just what happens. He reports what he *sees*—in many ases a very different thing. Any way . . ."

"Wonder how these biological pressures affected our riends here," he mused, thumbing over his shoulder at the norgue.

"About the same, I'd judge, with certain important difficules. But wait—were they men or women, or one of each?"

"I didn't tell you, did I?" he said with real startlement.

"No," she said.

He opened his mouth to answer, but could not. The reason ame.

It came from downstairs, or outside, or perhaps from no-vhere or everywhere, or from a place without a name. It was ll around them, inside, behind them in time as well as space. t was the echo of their own first cry when they lost the first varmth and found loneliness, early, as everyone must. It was urt: some the pain of impact, some of fever and delirium, nd some the great pressure of beauty too beautiful to bear. ind like pain, it could not be remembered. It lasted as long s it was a sound, and perhaps a little longer, and the frozen ime after it died was immeasurable.

Muhlenberg became increasingly conscious of an ache in

his calves and in the trapezoid muscles of his back. They sen
him a gradual and completely intellectualized message o
strain, and very consciously he relieved it and sat down. Hi
movement carried Budgie's arm forward, and he looke
down at her hand, which was clamped around his forearm
She moved it away, opening it slowly, and he saw the angry
marks of her fingers, and knew they would be bruises in the
morning.

She said, "That was the scream. The one I heard. Wasn'
once enough?"

It was only then that he could look far enough out of him
self to see her face. It was pasty with shock, and wet, and he
lips were pale. He leapt to his feet. "Another one! *Come on!*"

He pulled her up and through the door. "Don't you under
stand?" he blazed. "Another one! It can't be, but somewher
out there it's happened again—"

She pulled back. "Are you sure it wasn't . . ." She nodde
at the closed door of the morgue.

"Don't be ridiculous," he snorted. *"They* couldn't be alive.*
He hurried her to the stairs.

It was very dark. Muhlenberg's office was in an agein
business building which boasted twenty-five-watt bulbs o
every other floor. They hurtled through the murk, past th
deepest doorways of the law firm, the doll factory, the import
export firm which imported and exported nothing but phon
calls, and all the other dim mosaics of enterprise. The build
ing seemed quite deserted, and but for the yellow-orang
glow of the landings and the pathetic little bulbs, there wer
no lights anywhere. And it was as quiet as it was almost dark
quiet as late night; quiet as death.

They burst out onto the old brownstone steps and stopped
afraid to look, wanting to look. There was nothing. Nothin
but the street, a lonesome light, a distant horn and, far up a
the corner, the distinct clicking of the relays in a traffic-ligh
standard as they changed an ignored string of emeralds to a
unnoticed ruby rope.

"Go up to the corner," he said, pointing. "I'll go down th
other way. That noise wasn't far away—"

"No," she said. "I'm coming with you."

"Good," he said, so glad he was amazed at himself. They
ran north to the corner. There was no one on the street withi

122

o blocks in any direction. There were cars, mostly parked,
e coming, but none leaving.

"Now what?" she asked.

For a moment he did not answer. She waited patiently
ile he listened to the small distant noises which made the
ght so quiet. Then, "Good night, Budge."

"Good—what!"

He waved a hand. "You can go home now."

"But what about the—"

"I'm tired," he said. "I'm bewildered. That scream wrung
e like a floor-mop and pulled me down too many stairs too
st. There's too much I don't know about this and not enough
an do about it. So go home."

"Aw, Muley . . ."

He sighed. "I know. Your story. Budgie, I faithfully prom-
e you I'll give you an exclusive as soon as I have facts I can
ust."

She looked carefully at his face in the dim light and nodded
what she saw there. "All right, Muley. The pressure's off.
all me?"

"I'll call you."

He stood watching her walk away. Quite a gal, he thought.
e wondered what had moved her to make that odd remark
out inhibitions. They'd certainly never bothered her be-
re. But—perhaps she had something there. Sometimes
en you take what is loosely called "everything," you have
a odd feeling that you haven't gotten much. He shrugged
d ambled back toward the laboratory, pondering morphol-
y, teratology, and a case where *monstra per defectum* could
exist with *monstra per fabricam alienam*.

Then he saw the light.

It flickered out over the street, soft and warm. He stopped
d looked up. The light showed in a third-story window. It
as orange and yellow, but with it was a flaring blue-white.
was pretty. It was also in his laboratory. No—not the
boratory. The morgue.

Muhlenberg groaned. After that he saved his breath. He
eeded it badly by the time he got back to the laboratory.

Muhlenberg dove for the heavy morgue door and snatched
open. A great pressure of heat punted a gout of smoke into
e lab. He slammed the door, ran to a closet, snatched out

a full-length lab smock, spun the faucets in the sink and soaked the smock. From another cabinet he snatched up two glass-globe fire extinguishers. He wrapped the wet cloth twice around his face and let the rest drop over his chest and back. Cradling the extinguishers in one bent forearm, he reached for the side of the door and grabbed the pump-type extinguisher racked there.

Now, suddenly not hurrying, he stepped up on the sill and stood on tiptoe, peering through a fold of the wet cloth. Then he crouched low and peered again. Satisfied, he stood up and carefully pegged the two glass extinguishers, one straight ahead, one to the right and down. Then he disappeared into the smoke, holding the third extinguisher at the ready.

There was a rising moan, and the smoke shook like a solid entity and rushed into the room and away. As it cleared Muhlenberg, head and shoulders wrapped in sooty linen, found himself leaning against the wall, gasping, with one hand on a knife-switch on the wall. A three-foot exhaust fan in the top sash of one window was making quick work of the smoke.

Racks of chemicals, sterilizers, and glass cabinets full of glittering surgeon's tools lined the left wall. Out on the floor were four massive tables, on each of which was a heavy marble top. The rest of the room was taken up by a chemist's bench, sinks, a partitioned-off darkroom with lightproof curtains, and a massive centrifuge.

On one of the tables was a mass of what looked like burned meat and melted animal fat. It smelled bad—not rotten bad but acrid and—and *wet*, if a smell can be described that way. Through it was the sharp, stinging odor of corrosive chemicals.

He unwound the ruined smock from his face and threw it into a corner. He walked to the table with the mess on it and stood looking bleakly at it for a time. Suddenly he put out a hand, and with thumb and forefinger pulled out a length of bone.

"What a job," he breathed at length.

He walked around the table, poked at something slumped there and snatched his hand away. He went to the bench and got a pair of forceps, which he used to pick up the lump. It looked like a piece of lava or slag. He turned on a hooded lamp and studied it closely.

"Thermite, by God," he breathed.

124

He stood quite still for a moment, clenching and unclenching his square jaw. He took a long slow turn around the seared horror on the morgue slab, then carefully picked up the forceps and hurled them furiously into a corner. Then he went out to the lab and picked up the phone. He dialled.

"Emergency," he said. "Hello, Sue. Regalio there? Muhlenberg. Thanks. . . . Hello, Doc. Are you sitting down? All right. Now get this. I'm fresh out of symmetrical teratomorphs. They're gone. . . . Shut up and I'll tell you! I was out in the lab talking to a reporter when I heard the damndest scream. We ran out and found nothing. I left the reporter outside and came back. I couldn't've been out more'n ten-twelve minutes. But somebody got in here, moved both stiffs onto one slab, incised them from the thorax to the pubis, rammed them full of iron oxide and granulated aluminum—have lots of that sort of stuff around here—fused 'em with a couple of rolls of magnesium foil and touched 'em off. Made a great big messey thermite bomb out of them. . . . No, dammit, of *course* there's nothing left of them! What would you think eight minutes at seven thousand degrees would do? . . . Oh, dry up, Regalio! I don't know who did it or why, and I'm too tired to think about it. I'll see you tomorrow morning. No—what would be the use of sending anyone down here? This wasn't done to fire the building; whoever did it just wanted to get rid of those bodies, and sure did a job. . . . The coroner? I don't know what I'll tell him. I'm going to get a drink and then I'm going to bed. I just wanted you to know. Don't tell the press. I'll head off that reporter who was here before. We can do without this kind of story. 'Mystery arsonist cremates evidence of double killing in lab of medical consultant.' A block from headquarters, yet. . . . Yeah, and get your driver to keep his trap shut, too. Okay, Regalio. Just wanted to let you know. . . . Well, you're no sorrier'n I am. We'll just have to wait another couple hundred years while something like that gets born again, I guess."

Muhlenberg hung up, sighed, went into the morgue. He turned off the fan and lights, locked the morgue door, washed up at the laboratory sink, and shut the place up for the night.

It was eleven blocks to his apartment—an awkward distance most of the time, for Muhlenberg was not of the fresh-air and deep-breathing fraternity. Eleven blocks was not far enough to justify a cab and not near enough to make walking a negligible detail. At the seventh block he was aware of an overwhelming thirst and a general sensation that somebody had pulled the plug out of his energy barrel. He was drawn as if by a vacuum into Rudy's, a Mexican bar with Yma Sumac and Villa-Lobos on the juke-box.

"*Olé, amigo*," said Rudy. "Tonight you don' smile."

Muhlenberg crawled wearily onto a stool. "*Deme una tequila* sour, and skip the cherry," he said in his bastard Spanish. "I don't know what I got to smile about." He froze, and his eyes bulged. "Come back here, Rudy."

Rudy put down the lemon he was slicing and came close. "I don't want to point, but who *is* that?"

Rudy glanced at the girl. "*Ay,*" he said rapturously. "*Que chuchin.*"

Muhlenberg remembered vaguely that *chuchin* was untranslatable, but that the closest English could manage with it was "cute." He shook his head. "That won't do." He held up his hand. "Don't try to find me a Spanish word for it. There isn't any word for it. Who is she?"

Rudy spread his hands. "*No sé.*"

"She by herself?"

"*Si.*"

Muhlenberg put his chin on his hand. "Make my drink. I want to think."

Rudy went, his mahogany cheeks drawn in and still in his version of a smile.

Muhlenberg looked at the girl in the booth again just as her gaze swept past his face to the bartender. "Rudy!" she called softly, "are you making a tequila sour?"

"*Si, senorita.*"

"Make me one too?"

Rudy beamed. He did not turn his head toward Muhlenberg, but his dark eyes slid over toward him, and Muhlenberg knew that he was intensely amused. Muhlenberg's face grew hot, and he felt like an idiot. He had a wild fantasy that his ears had turned forward and snapped shut, and that the cello-and-velvet sound of her voice, captured, was nestling down inside his head like a warm little animal.

He got off the bar stool, fumbled in his pocket for change and went to the juke-box. She was there before him, slipping a coin in, selecting a strange and wonderful recording called *Vene a Mi Casa*, which was a *borracho* version of "C'mon-a My House."

"I was just going to play that!" he said. He glanced at the juke-box. "Do you like Yma Sumac?"

"Oh, yes!"

"Do you like *lots* of Yma Sumac?" She smiled and, seeing it, he bit his tongue. He dropped in a quarter and punched out six sides of Sumac. When he looked up Rudy was standing by the booth with a little tray on which were two tequila sours. His face was utterly impassive and his head was tilted at the precise angle of inquiry as to where he should put Muhlenberg's drink. Muhlenberg met the girl's eyes, and whether she nodded ever so slightly or whether she did it with a single movement of her eyelids, he did not know, but it meant "yes." He slid into the booth opposite her.

Music came. Only some of it was from the records. He sat and listened to it all. Rudy came with a second drink before he said anything, and only then did he realize how much time had passed while he rested there, taking in her face as if it were quite a new painting by a favorite artist. She did nothing to draw his attention or to reject it. She did not stare rapturously into his eyes or avoid them. She did not even appear to be waiting, or expecting anything of him. She was neither remote nor intimate. She was close, and it was good.

He thought, in your most secret dreams you cut a niche in yourself, and it is finished early, and then you wait for someone to come along to fill it—but to fill it exactly, every cut, curve, hollow and plane of it. And people do come along, and one covers up the niche, and another rattles around inside it, and another is so surrounded by fog that for the longest time you don't know if she fits or not; but each of them hits you with a tremendous impact. And then one comes along and slips in so quietly that you don't know when it happened, and fits so well you almost can't feel anything at all. And that is it.

"What are you thinking about?" she asked him.

He told her, immediately and fully. She nodded as if he had been talking about cats or cathedrals or cam-shafts, or anything else beautiful and complex. She said, "That's right. It isn't all there, of course. It isn't even enough. But everything else isn't enough without it."

"What is 'everything else'?"

"You know," she said.

He thought he did. He wasn't sure. He put it aside for later. "Will you come home with me?"

"Oh, yes."

They got up. She stood by the door, her eyes full of him, while he went to the bar with his wallet.

"¿cuánto le debo?"

Rudy's eyes had a depth he had never noticed before. Perhaps it hadn't been there before. "Nada," said Rudy.

"On the house? Muchissimo gracias, amigo." He knew, profoundly, that he shouldn't protest.

They went to his apartment. While he was pouring brandy —brandy because, if it's good brandy, it marries well with tequila—she asked him if he knew of a place called Shank's, down in the warehouse district. He thought he did; he knew he could find it. "I want to meet you there tomorrow night at eight," she said. "I'll be there," he smiled. He turned to put the brandy carafe back, full of wordless pleasure in the knowledge that all day tomorrow he could look forward to being with her again.

He played records. He was part sheer technician, part delighted child when he could demonstrate his sound system. He had a copy of the Confucian "Analects" in a sandalwood box. It was printed on rice-paper and hand-illuminated. He had a Finnish dagger with intricate scrollwork which, piece by piece and as a whole, made many pictures. He had a clock made of four glass discs, the inner two each carrying one hand, and each being rim-driven from the base so it seemed to have no works at all.

She loved all these things. She sat in his biggest chair while he stared out at the blue dark hours and she read aloud to him from "The Crock of Gold" and from Thurber and Shakespeare for laughter, and from Shakespeare and William Morris for a good sadness.

She sang, once.

Finally she said, "It's bedtime. Go and get ready."

He got up and went into the bedroom and undressed. He showered and rubbed himself pink. Back in the bedroom, he could hear the music she had put on the phonograph. It was the second movement of Prokofiev's "Classical" Symphony, where the orchestra is asleep and the high strings tiptoe in. It was the third time she had played it. He sat down to wait until the record was over, and when it was, and she didn't come or speak to him, he went to the living-room door and looked in.

She was gone.

He stood absolutely still and looked around the room. The whole time she had been there she had unostentatiously put everything back after they had looked at it. The amplifier was still on. The phonograph was off, because it shut itself off. The record album of the Prokofiev, standing edge-up on the floor by the amplifier, was waiting to receive the record that was still on the turntable.

He stepped into the room and switched off the amplifier. He was suddenly conscious that in doing so he had removed half of what she had left there. He looked down at the record album; then, without touching it, he turned out the lights and went to bed.

You'll see her tomorrow, he thought.

He thought, you didn't so much as touch her hand. If it weren't for your eyes and ears, you'd have no way of knowing her.

A little later something deep within him turned over and sighed luxuriously. Muhlenberg, it said to him, do you realize that not once during that entire evening did you stop and think: this is an Occasion, this is a Great Day? Not once. The whole thing was easy as breathing.

As he fell asleep he remembered he hadn't even asked her her name.

He awoke profoundly rested, and looked with amazement at his alarm clock. It was only eight, and after what he had been through at the lab last night, plus what he had drunk, plus staying up so late, this feeling was a bonus indeed. He dressed quickly and got down to the lab early. The phone was already ringing. He told the coroner to bring Regalio and to come right down.

It was all very easy to explain in terms of effects; the burned morgue room took care of that. They beat causes around for an hour or so without any conclusion. Since Muhlenberg was so close to the Police Department, though not a member of it, they agreed to kill the story for the time being. If relatives or a carnival owner or somebody came along, that would be different. Meantime, they'd let it ride. It really wasn't so bad.

They went away, and Muhlenberg called the paper.

Budgie had not come to work or called. Perhaps she was out on a story, the switchboard suggested.

The day went fast. He got the morgue cleaned up and a lot done on his research project. He didn't begin to worry until the fourth time he called the paper—that was about five P.M.—and Budgie still hadn't come or called. He got her home phone number and called it. No; she wasn't there. She'd gone out early to work. Try her at the paper.

He went home and bathed and changed, looked up the address of Shank's and took a cab there. He was much too early. It was barely seven-fifteen.

Shank's was a corner bar of the old-fashioned type with plate-glass windows on its corner fronts and flyblown wainscoting behind them. The booths gave a view of the street corner which did the same for the booths. Except for the corner blaze of light, the rest of the place was in darkness, punctuated here and there by the unreal blues and greens of beer signs in neon script.

Muhlenberg glanced at his watch when he entered, and was appalled. He knew now that he had been artificially busier and busier as the day wore on, and that it was only a weak effort to push aside the thoughts of Budgie and what might have happened to her. His busyness had succeeded in getting him into a spot where he would have nothing to do but sit and wait, and think his worries through.

He chose a booth on the mutual margins of the cave-like darkness and the pallid light, and ordered a beer.

Somebody—let's be conventional and call him Mr. X—had gone 'way out of his way to destroy two bodies in his morgue. A very thorough operator. Of course, if Mr. X was really interested in suppressing information about the two pathetic halves of the murdered monster in the park, he'd only done part of the job. Regalio, Al, Budgie and Muhlenberg knew about it. Regalio and Al had been all right when he had seen them this morning, and certainly no attempts had been made on him. On the other hand, he had been in and around the precinct station and its immediate neighborhood all day, and about the same thing applied to the ambulance staff.

But Budgie . . .

Not only was she vulnerable, she wasn't even likely to be missed for hours by anyone since she was so frequently out on stories. Stories! Why—as a reporter she presented the greatest menace of all to anyone who wanted to hide information!

With that thought came its corollary: Budgie was missing, and if she had been taken care of he, Muhlenberg, was next on the list. Had to be. He was the only one who had been able to take a good long look at the bodies. He was the one who had given the information to the reporter and the one who still had it to give. In other words, if Budgie had been taken care of, he could expect some sort of attack too, and quickly.

He looked around the place with narrowing eyes. This was a rugged section of town. Why was he here?

He had a lurching sense of shock and pain. The girl he'd met last night—that couldn't be a part of this thing. It mustn't be. And yet because of her he found himself here, like a sitting duck.

He suddenly understood his unwillingness to think about the significance of Budgie's disappearance.

"Oh, no" he said aloud.

Should he run?

Should he—and perhaps be wrong? He visualized the girl coming there, waiting for him, perhaps getting in some trouble in this dingy place, just because he'd gotten the wind up over his own fantasies.

He couldn't leave. Not until after eight anyway. What else then? If they got him, who would be next? Regalio, certainly. Then Al. Then the coroner himself.

Warn Regalio. That at least he might do, before it was too late. He jumped up.

There was, of course, someone in the phone booth. A woman. He swore and pulled the door open.

"Budgie!"

He reached in almost hysterically, pulled her out. She spun limply into his arms, and for an awful split second his thoughts were indescribable. Then she moved. She squeezed him, looked up incredulously, squeezed him again. "Muley! Oh, Muley, I'm so glad it's you!"

"Budgie, you lunkhead—where've you been?"

"Oh, I've had the most awful—the most wonderful—"

"Hey, yesterday you cried. Isn't that your quota for the year?"

"Oh, shut up. Muley, Muley, no one could get mixed up more than I've been!"

"Oh," he said reflectively, "I dunno. Come on over here. Sit down. Bartender! Two double whiskey sodas!" Inwardly, he smiled at the difference in a man's attitude toward the world when he has something to protect. "Tell me." He cupped

131

her chin. "First of all, where have you been? You had me scared half to death."

She looked up at him, at each of his eyes in turn. There was a beseeching expression in her whole pose. "You won't laugh at me, Muley?"

"Some of this business is real un-funny."

"Can I *really* talk to you? I never tried." She said, as if there were no change of subject, "You don't know who I am."

"Talk then, so I'll know."

"Well," she began, "it was this morning. When I woke up. It was such a beautiful day! I went down to the corner to get the bus. I said to the man at the newsstand, "Post?" and dropped my nickel in his cup, and right in chorus with me was this man . . ."

"This man," he prompted.

"Yes. Well, he was a young man, about—oh, I don't know how old. Just right, anyway. And the newsdealer didn't know who to give the paper to because he had only one left. We looked at each other, this fellow and I, and laughed out loud. The newsy heard my voice loudest, I guess, or was being chivalrous, and he handed the paper to me. The bus came along then and we got in, and the fellow, the young one, I mean, he was going to take a seat by himself but I said come on— help me read the paper—you helped me buy it."

She paused while the one-eyed bartender brought the drinks.

"We never did look at the paper. We sort of . . . talked. I never met anyone I could talk to like that. Not even you, Muley, even now when I'm trying so. The things that came out . . . as if I'd known him all my—no," she said, shaking her head violently, "not even like that. I don't know. I can't say. It was fine.

"We crossed the bridge and the bus ran alongside the meadow, out there between the park and the fairgrounds. The grass was too green and the sky was too blue and there was something in me that just wanted to explode. But good, I mean, good. I said I was going to play hookey. I didn't say I'd like to, or I felt like it. I said I was going to. And he said let's, as if I'd asked him, and I didn't question that, not one bit. I don't know where he was going or what he was giving up, but we pulled the cord and the bus stopped and we got out and headed cross country."

"What did you do all day?" Muhlenberg asked as she sipped.

"Chased rabbits. Ran. Lay in the sun. Fed ducks. Laughed a lot. Talked. Talked a *whole* lot." Her eyes came back to the present, back to Muhlenberg. "Gosh, I don't know, Muley. I tried to tell myself all about it after he left me. I couldn't. Not so I'd believe it if I listened."

"And all this wound up in a crummy telephone booth?" She sobered instantly. "I was supposed to meet him here. I couldn't just wait around home. I couldn't stomach the first faint thought of the office. So I just came here.

"I sat down to wait. I don't know why he asked me to meet him in a place like—what on earth is the matter with you?"

"Nothing," choked Muhlenberg. "I was having an original thought called 'It's a small world.' " He waved her forthcoming questions away. "Don't let me interrupt. You first, then me. There's something weird and wonderful going on here."

"Where was I? Oh. Well, I sat here waiting and feeling happy, and gradually the feeling went away and the gloom began to seep in. Then I thought about you, and the murder in the park, and that fantastic business at your lab last night, and I began to get scared. I didn't know what to do. I was going to run from here, and then I had a reaction, and wondered if I was just scaring myself. Suppose he came and I wasn't here? I couldn't bear that. Then I got scared again and —wondered if he was part of the whole thing, the Siamese-twin murder and all. And I hated myself for even thinking such a thing. I went into a real hassle. At last I squared myself away and figured the only thing to do was to call you up. And you weren't at the lab. And the coroner didn't know where you'd gone and—oh-h-h, *Muley!*"

"It meant that much?"

She nodded.

"Fickle bitch! Minutes after leaving your lover-boy—"

She put her hand over his mouth. "Watch what you say," she said fiercely. "This was no gay escapade, Muley. This was like—like nothing I've ever heard of. He didn't touch me, or act as if he wanted to. He didn't have to; it wasn't called for. The whole thing *was* the whole thing, and not a preliminary to anything else. It was—it was—oh, *damn* this language!"

Muhlenberg thought about the Prokofiev album standing upright by his amplifier. Damn it indeed, he thought. "What was his name?" he asked gently.

"His—" She snapped her head up, turned slowly to him. She whispered, "I never asked him. . . ." and her eyes went quite round.

"I thought not." Why did I say that? he asked himself. I almost know. . . .

He said, suddenly, "Budgie, do you love him?"

Her face showed surprise. "I hadn't thought about it. Maybe I don't know what love is. I thought I knew. But it was less than this." She frowned. "It was more than this, though, some ways."

"Tell me something. When he left you, even after a day like that, did you feel . . . that you'd lost something?"

She thought about it. "Why . . . no. No, I didn't. I was full up to here, and what he gave me he left with me. That's the big difference. No love's like that. Can you beat that? I didn't *lose* anything!"

He nodded. "Neither did I," he said.

"You *what?*"

But he wasn't listening. He was rising slowly, his eyes on the door.

The girl was there. She was dressed differently, she looked trim and balanced. Her face was the same, though, and her incredible eyes. She wore blue jeans, loafers, a heavy, rather loose sweater, and two soft-collar points gleamed against her neck and chin. Her hair hardly longer than his own, but beautiful, beautiful. . . .

He looked down, as he would have looked away from a great light. He saw his watch. It was eight o'clock. And he became aware of Budgie looking fixedly at the figure in the door, her face radiant. "Muley, come on. Come on, Muley! There he is!"

The girl in the doorway saw him then and smiled. She waved and pointed at the corner booth, the one with windows on two streets. Muhlenberg and Budgie went to her.

She sat down as they came to her. "Hello. Sit there. Both of you."

Side by side they sat opposite her. Budgie stared in open admiration. Muhlenberg stared too, and something in the back of his mind began to grow, and grow, and— "No," he said, incredulously.

134

"Yes," she said, directly to him. "It's true." She looked at Budgie. "She doesn't know yet, does she?"

Muhlenberg shook his head. "I hadn't time to tell her."

"Perhaps you shouldn't," said the girl.

Budgie turned excitedly to Muhlenberg. "You know him!"

Muhlenberg said, with difficulty, "I know . . . know—"

The girl laughed aloud. "You're looking for a pronoun."

Budgie said, "Muley, what's he mean? Let me in on it."

"An autopsy would have shown it, wouldn't it?" he demanded.

The girl nodded. "Very readily. That was a close call."

Budgie looked from one to the other. "Will somebody tell me what in blazes this is all about?"

Muhlenberg met the girl's gaze. She nodded. He put an arm around Budgie. "Listen, girl reporter. Our—our friend here's something . . . something new and different."

"Not new," said the girl. "We've been around for thousands of years."

"Have you now!" He paused to digest that, while Budgie squirmed and protested, "But—but—but—"

"Shush, you," said Muhlenberg, and squeezed her shoulders gently. "What you spent the afternoon with isn't a man, Budgie, any more than what I spent most of the night with was a woman. Right?"

"Right," the girl said.

"And the Siamese twins weren't Siamese twins, but two of our friend's kind who—who—"

"They were in syzygy." An inexpressible sadness was in the smooth, almost contralto, all but tenor voice.

"In what?" asked Budgie.

Muhlenberg spelled it for her. "In some forms of life," he started to explain, "well, the microscopic animal called paramecium's a good example—reproduction is accomplished by fission. The creature elongates, and so does its nucleus. Then the nucleus breaks in two, and one half goes to each end of the animal. Then the rest of the animal breaks, and presto—two paramecia."

"But you—he—"

"Shaddup," he said. "I'm lecturing. The only trouble with reproduction by fission is that it affords no variation of strains. A single line of paramecium would continue to reproduce that way until, by the law of averages, its dominant traits would all be nonsurvival ones, and bang—no more paramecia. So they have another process to take care of that difficulty. One paramecium rests beside another, and gradually their contacting side walls begin to fuse. The nuclei gravitate toward that point. The side walls then break down, so that the nuclei then have access to one another. The nuclei flow together, mix and mingle, and after a time they separate and half goes into each animal. Then the side walls close the opening, break away from one another, and each animal goes its way.

"That is syzygy. It is in no sense a sexual process, because paramecia have no sex. It has no direct bearing on reproduction either—that can happen with or without syzygy." He turned to their companion. "But I'd never hear of syzygy in the higher forms."

The faintest of smiles. "It's unique with us, on this plane anyway."

"What's the rest of it?" he demanded.

"Our reproduction? We're parthenogenetic females."

"Y-you're a female?" breathed Budgie.

"A term of convenience," said Muhlenberg. "Each individual has both kinds of sex organs. They're self-fertilizing."

"That's a—a what do you call it?—a hermaphrodite," said Budgie. "Excuse me," she added in a small voice.

Muhlenberg and the girl laughed uproariously; and the magic of that creature was that the laughter couldn't hurt. "It's a very different thing," said Muhlenberg. "Hermaphrodites are human. She—our friend there—isn't."

"You're the humanest thing I ever met in my whole life," said Budgie ardently.

The girl reached across the table and touched Budgie's arm. Muhlenberg suspected that that was the very first physical contact either he or Budgie had yet received from the creature and that it was a rare thing and a great compliment.

"Thank you," the girl said softly. "Thank you very much for saying that." She nodded to Muhlenberg. "Go on."

"Technically—though I know of no case where it has actually been possible—hermaphrodites can have contact with either sex. But parthenogenetic females won't, can't, and wouldn't. They don't need to. Humans cross strains along with the reproductive process. Parthenogenesis separates the two acts completely." He turned to the girl. "Tell me, how often do you reproduce?"

"As often as we wish to."

"And syzygy?"

"As often as we must. Then—we must."

"And that is—"

"It's difficult. It's like the paramecia's, essentially, but it's infinitely more complex. There's cell meeting and interflow, but in tens and then dozens, hundreds, then thousands of millions of cells. The join begins here—" she put her hand at the approximate location of the human heart—"and extends. But you saw it in those whom I burned. You are one of the few human beings who ever have."

"That isn't what I saw," he reminded her gently.

She nodded, and again there was that deep sadness. "That murder was such a stupid, incredible, unexpected thing!"

"Why were they in the park?" he asked, his voice thick with pity. "Why, out there, in the open, where some such human slugs could find them?"

"They took a chance, because it was important to them," she said wearily. She looked up, and her eyes were luminous. "We love the outdoors. We love the earth, the feel and smell of it, what lives from it and in it. Especially then. It was such a deep thicket, such an isolated pocket. It was the merest accident that those—those men found them there. They couldn't move. They were—well, medically you could call it unconscious. Actually, there—there never was a consciousness like the one which comes with syzygy."

"Can you describe it?"

She shook her head slowly, and it was no violation of her complete frankness. "Do you know, you couldn't describe sexuality to me so that I could understand it? I have no—no comparison, no analogies. It—" she looked from one to the other—"it amazes me. In some ways I envy it. I know it is a strife, which we avoid, for we are very gentle. But you have a capacity for enjoying strife, and all the pain, all the misery and poverty and cruelty which you suffer, is the cornerstone of everything you build. And you build more than anyone or anything in the known universe."

Budgie was wide-eyed. "You envy *us*. *You?*"

She smiled. "Don't you think the things you admire me for are rather commonplace among my own kind? It's just that they're rare in humans."

Muhlenberg said slowly, "Just what is your relationship to humanity?"

"It's symbiotic, of course."

"Symbiotic? You live with us, and us with you, like the cellulose-digesting microbes in a termite? Like the yucca moth, which can eat only nectar from the yucca cactus, which can spread its pollen only through the yucca moth?"

She nodded. "It's purely symbiotic. But it isn't easy to explain. We live on that part of humans which makes them different from animals."

"And in turn—"

"We cultivate it in humans."

"I don't understand that," said Budgie flatly.

"Look into your legends. We're mentioned often enough there. Who were the sexless angels? Who is the streamlined fat boy on your Valentine's Day cards? Where does inspiration come from? Who knows three notes of a composer's new symphony, and whistles the next phrase as he walks by the composer's house? And—most important to you two—who really understands that part of love between humans which is not sexual—because we can understand no other kind? Read your history, and you'll see where we've been. And in exchange we get the building—bridges, yes, and aircraft and soon, now, space-ships. But other kinds of building too. Songs and poetry and this new thing, this increasing sense of the oneness of all your species. And now it is fumbling toward a United Nations, and later it will grope for the stars; and where it builds, we thrive."

"Can you name this thing you get from us—this thing that is the difference between men and the rest of the animals?"

"No. But call it a sense of achievement. Where you feel that most, you feed us most. And you feel it most when others of your kind enjoy what you build."

"Why do you keep yourselves hidden?" Budgie suddenly asked. "Why?" She wrung her hands on the edge of the table. "You're so beautiful!"

"We have to hide," the other said gently. "You still kill anything that's . . . different."

Muhlenberg looked at that open, lovely face and felt a sickness, and he could have cried. He said, "Don't you ever kill anything?" and then hung his head, because it sounded like a defense for the murdering part of humanity. Because it was.

"Yes," she said very softly, "we do."

"You can *hate* something?"

It isn't hate. Anyone who hates, hates himself as well as the object of his hate. There's another emotion called righteous anger. That makes us kill."

"I can't conceive of such a thing."

"What time is it?"

"Almost eight-forty."

She raised herself from her booth and looked out to the corner. It was dark now, and the usual crowd of youths had gathered under the street-lights.

"I made appointments with three more people this evening," she said. "They are murderers. Just watch." Her eyes seemed to blaze.

Under the light, two of the youths were arguing. The crowd, but for a prodding yelp or two, had fallen silent and was beginning to form a ring. Inside the ring, but apart from the two who were arguing, was a third—smaller, heavier and, compared with the sharp-creased, bright-tied arguers, much more poorly dressed, in an Eisenhower jacket with one sleeve tattered up to the elbow.

What happened then happened with frightening speed. One of the arguers smashed the other across the mouth. Spitting blood, the other staggered back, made a lightning move into his coat pocket. The blade looked for all the world like a golden fan as it moved in the cyclic pulsations of the street-lamp. There was a bubbling scream, a deep animal grunt, and two bodies lay tangled and twitching on the sidewalk while blood gouted and seeped and defied the sharpness of creases and the colors of ties.

Far up the block a man shouted and a whistle shrilled. Then the street corner seemed to become a great repulsing pole for humans. People ran outward, rayed outward, until, from above, they must have looked like a great splash in mud, reaching out and out until the growing ring broke and the particles scattered and were gone. And then there were only the bleeding bodies and the third one, the one with the tattered jacket, who hovered and stepped and waited and did not know which way to go. There was the sound of a single pair of running feet, after the others had all run off to silence, and these feet belonged to a man who ran fast and ran closer and breathed heavily through a shrieking police whistle.

The youth in the jacket finally turned and ran away, and the policeman shouted once around his whistle, and then there were two sharp reports and the youth, running hard, threw up his hands and fell without trying to turn his face away, and skidded on it and lay still with one foot turned in and the other turned out.

The girl in the dark sweater and blue jeans turned away from the windows and sank back into her seat, looking levelly into the drawn faces across the table. "Those were the men who killed those two in the park," she said in a low voice, "and that is how we kill."

"A little like us," said Muhlenberg weakly. He found his handkerchief and wiped off his upper lip. "Three of them for two of you."

"Oh, you don't understand," she said, and there was pity in her voice. "It wasn't because they killed those two. It was because they pulled them apart."

Gradually, the meaning of this crept into Muhlenberg's awed mind, and the awe grew with it. For here was a race which separated insemination from the mixing of strains, and apart from them, in clean-lined definition, was a third component, a psychic interflow. Just a touch of it had given him a magic night and Budgie an enchanted day; hours without strife, without mixed motives or misinterpretations.

If a human, with all his grossly efficient combination of functions, could be led to appreciate one light touch to that degree, what must it mean to have that third component, pure and in essence, torn apart in its fullest flow? This was worse than any crime could be to a human; and yet, where humans can claim clear consciences while jailing a man for a year for stealing a pair of shoes, these people repay the cruelest sacrilege of all with a quick clean blow. It was removal, not punishment. Punishment was alien and inconceivable to them.

He slowly raised his face to the calm, candid eyes of the girl. "Why have you shown us all this?"

"You needed me," she said simply.

"But you came up to destroy those bodies so no one would know—"

"And I found you two, each needing what the other had, and blind to it. No, not blind. I remember you said that if you ever could really share something, you could be very close." She laughed. "Remember your niche, the one that's finished early and never exactly filled? I told you at the time

140

that it wouldn't be enough by itself if it *were* filled, and anyone completely without it wouldn't have enough either. And you—" She smiled at Budgie. "You never made any secret about what you wanted. And there the two of you were, each taking what you already had, and ignoring what you needed."

"Headline!" said Budgie, "Common Share Takes Stock."

"Subhead!" grinned Muhlenberg, "Man With A Niche Meets Girl With An Itch."

The girl slid out of the booth. "You'll do," she said.

"Wait! You're not going to leave us! Aren't we ever going to see you again?"

"Not knowingly. You won't remember me, or any of this."

"How can you take away—"

"Shush, Muley. You know she can."

"Yes, I guess she—wait though—wait! You give us all this knowledge just so we'll understand—and then you take it all away again. What good will that do us?"

She turned toward them. It may have been because they were still seated and she was standing, but she seemed to tower over them. In a split second of fugue, he had the feeling that he was looking at a great light on a mountain.

"Why, you poor things—didn't you know? Knowledge and understanding aren't props for one another. Knowledge is a pile of bricks, and understanding is a way of building. Build for me!"

They were in a joint called Shank's. After the triple killing, and the wild scramble to get the story phoned in, they started home.

"Muley," she asked suddenly, "what's syzygy?"

"What on earth made you ask me that?"

"It just popped into my head. What is it?"

"A non-sexual interflow between the nuclei of two animals."

"I never tried that," she said thoughtfully.

"Well, don't until we're married," he said. They began to hold hands while they walked.

I FINALLY killed Lutch Crawford with a pair of bolt-cutters. And there was Lutch—all of him, all his music, his jump, his public and his pride, in the palm of my hand. Literally in the palm of my hand—three pinkish slugs with horn at one end and blood at the other. I tossed 'em, caught 'em, put 'em in my pocket and walked off whistling *Daboo Dabay,* which had been Lutch's theme. It was the first time in eight years I had heard that music and enjoyed it. Sometimes it takes a long while to kill a man.

I'd tried it twice before. I tried it smart, and failed. I tried it sneak, and failed. Now it's done.

Whistling it, I can hear the whole band—the brass background: "Hoo Ha Hoo Ha" (how he used to stage that on the stand, the skunk—Lutch, I mean, with the sliphorns and trumpets turning in their chairs, blowing the "hoo" to the right with cap-mutes, swinging around, blowing the "ha" at the left, open) and then Lutch's clarinet a third above Skid Portly's gimmicked-up guitar: "Daboo, dabay, dabay daboo . . ." You know, Spotlights on Lutch, a bright overflow of light on Skid and his guitar, light bronzing and scything from the swinging bells of the trombones here and the trumpets over there . . . the customers ate it up, they loved it, they loved him, the bubbleheaded bunch of bastiches . . . and Fawn at the piano, white glow from the spot running to her, gold flashes lighting up her face when the brasses swung, lighting up the way she cocked her head to one side, half smiling at Lutch, stroking the keyboard as if it was his face, loving him more than anybody there.

And up in back, in the dark, out of sight but altogether needed, like a heart, there was always Crispin, crouching over the skins, his bass a thing you felt with your belly rather than heard, but the real beat coming through his hands, pushing out one crushed ruff for each beat, shifting from center to edge—not much—matching the "hoo ha" of the brass. You couldn't see Crispin, but you could feel what he made. They loved it. He made love with the skins. He was loving Fawn with the pedal, with the sticks, there in the dark.

And I'd be out front, off to one side, seeing it all, and I can see it now, just whistling the theme. It was all there—Lutch,

142

everything about Lutch, everything that Lutch was. There was the swinging brass, and Crispin loving Fawn, and Fawn loving Lutch, and Lutch giving theme solo to Skid's guitar, taking the foolish obbligato for himself. And there was Fluke, and that's me. Sure, in the dark. Always keep Fluke in the dark; don't show them Fluke's face. Fluke has a face that kept him out of the United States Army, didn't you know? Fluke has a mouth only as big as your two thumbnails, and all his teeth are pointed.

I was as much a part of it as any of them, but I didn't make anything. I just worked there. I was the guy who waited for ten bars of theme, and then came in with the beat, holding the microphone just off my cheek like a whisper-singer, saying "Lutch is here, Lutch is gone, man, gone." Lutch used to say old Fluke had a voice like an alto-horn with a split reed. He called it a dirty voice. It was a compliment. "Gone, man, gone," I'd say, and then talk up: "Top o' the morn from the top o' the heap, Kizd. This is the Fluke, the fin of the fish, the tail of the whale, bringin' you much of Lutch and such . . . Lutch Crawford and his Gone Geese, ladies and gentlemen, from the Ruby Room of the Hotel Halpern in . . ." (or the Rainbow, or the Angel, or wherever). That was me, Fluke. I hadn't wanted the buildup, all that jive about "fin and the fish." That was Lutch's idea. That was Lutch, like giving his theme solo to Skid's guitar instead of taking it himself. He even hauled me into his recording dates— you know that. That was the thing about that band; it was a machine; and some will drive a machine, and some will ride it, and Lutch, he rode.

I *had* to kill him.

I'll tell you about the time I tried it smart.

Five years ago, it was. We had an ivory man who was pretty good. Name was Hinkle. He arranged a lot—he was the one who styled the band the way you know it. You can forget him; he was killed. Went down to a dance pitch in the South Side to hear a bass-player who was getting famous, and some drunk started an argument and pulled a gun and missed the cat he aimed at and hit Hinkle. It was none of Hinkle's argument—he didn't even know anybody there. Anyway, he got iced and we had to play a date without a piano. We got along, strictly ho-hum.

Then about eleven o'clock this baby shuffles up to the stand, all big eyes and timidity. She pulled Lutch's swallow-

143

tail between numbers, dropped it like it was hot, and stood there blushing like a radish. She was only about seventeen, cute-fat, with long black hair and pink lips like your kid sister. It took her three tries to lay out what she wanted, but the idea was she played a little piano and thought she might fill out a number for us.

Lutch was always an easy fall for anyone who looked like he wanted something real hard. He didn't think five seconds. He waved her over to the ivory, and called for "Blue Prelude," which had enough reed, soon enough, that we could cover the piano if it soured.

We didn't cover up a thing. The kid played Hinkle, perfect, pure and easy; close your eyes and Hinkle was there, walking bass and third-runs, large as life.

The rest of the date turned over to the kid, far as the band was concerned. She pulled out a bag of tricks that I'll never forget. She had style, and good wrists. She read like lightning and memorized better, and she had a touch. Hell, I don't have to tell you about Fawn Amory . . . anyhow, we had a powwow, and Lutch had dinner with her folks. Fawn had every disk Lutch Crawford had ever waxed—that was how she knew Hinkle's style—and she'd been playing piano since she was a pup. Lutch hired her with her daddy's blessing, and we had us a piano again.

We began to get big about then. It wasn't so much Fawn's playing—she wasn't brilliant, she was just terrific—but it was what she was to the band. The music business is full of round-heels and thrushes who feed on seed; this kid was from fresh air. She made the band worth staying with. Turnover just stopped, except for a couple of times when a side-man would carry too much altitude and make a pass. That never happened more than once per man. Then one or the other of us would happily pull the wolf's teeth. Once Skid busted a four hundred dollar guitar over a guy's head for that. (A good thing in the long run; he went into electrics seriously after that; but the electric guitar comes later.) And once I gave a spare lip to a trumpet man, pushing three teeth out under his nose, when his right hand forgot what his left was hired for.

She had this wide-eyed yen for Lutch when she joined us, and it was there for anyone to see. But clean, dig me? Lutch, he treated her like the rest of the sides. He kept it just like it was, and we went places. I don't think I was the only one

ho lost sleep. As long as no one made a move, everything
tayed the same and the band as a whole jatoed. We rose,
ack.

It was Fawn who made the break. Looking back, I guess
could've been expected. We were all pretty wise; we did
hat we did because we thought it out. But she was just a
id. She'd been eating her heart out for too long, I guess, and
he had no muscles for a pitch like that. We were in Boulder
ity that night, taking fifteen about two in the morning at a
oadhouse. There was all kinds of moon. I was in a wild
assle with myself. Fawn was under my skin clear down to
e marrow by then. I went into the bar and slurped up a
oilermaker—they always make me sick, and I wanted a
mall trouble to concentrate on. I left the rest of the sides
w-jamming around a table and walked outside. There was
gravel path, the kind that gives a dry belch under your feet.
stayed off it. I walked on the grass and looked at the moon,
hich was bad for me, and felt the boilermaker seething
nder my low ribs, and felt but rugged. You know.

It wasn't only Fawn. I realized that. It was something to
o with Lutch. He was so—sure of himself. Hell. I never
ould be that. Never until now, when I've got what was
oming to me. Now I'm damn sure where I'm going, and I
id it with my own hands. Not everybody can say that. But
utch, he could. He had talent, see—big talent. He was a real
usician. But he didn't use it, only to guide with his finger-
ps. He styled Hinkle still, and another man soloed his
eme. He was like that. He was so sure of himself that he
idn't have to hog anything. He didn't even have to reach
ut and pick up anything that he knew he could have. Now
e, I never could know till I tried. There shouldn't be guys
ke Lutch Crawford, guys that never have to wonder or
orry. Them as has, gits, they say. There can't be any honest
ompetition with a guy like that. He'll win out, or you will.
: he does, he'll do it easy as breathing. If you do, it's only
ecause he let you. Guys like that shouldn't be born. If they
re, they ought to be killed. Things are tough enough with
n even break. Lutch, he had a pet name for the band. He
alled it the unit. That doesn't sound like a pet name but it
as. Fluke was his barker, and part of the unit . . . it didn't
atter that the band would be just as good without me. Any
ne of us could be dropped or replaced, and it would still be
utch Crawford's Gone Geese. But Fluke was in, and Skid,

145

and Crispin and the rest, and that's the way he wanted
to stay. I was in the bucks, with a future—thanks to hi
Thank you very much to him for every damn thing.

So I was standing on the grass looking at the moon a
feeling all this, when I heard Fawn sob. Just once. I we
that way, walking on the grass, sliding my feet so that l
shoe wouldn't squeak.

She was standing at the corner of the building with Lutc
She was facing the moon. She was crying without maki
any more noise and without covering her face. It was wet a
sort of pulled down and sidewards as if I saw it through
wavy glass.

She said, "I can't help it, Lutch, I love you."

And he said, "I love you too. I love everybody. It's nothi
to get sick over."

"It isn't . . ." The way she said that, it was a questi
and a whole flood of detail about how sick you can get. "I
me kiss you, Lutch," she whispered. "I won't ever ask y
again. Let me this once. Once, I got to, Lutch, I got to, I ca
go on much longer like this . . ."

Now, I hated him, and I think I hated her a little, for
second, but you know, I'd of kicked him clear to Pensaco
if he hadn't done what she said. I never had a feeling like t
before. Never. I don't want it again.

Well, he did. Then he went back inside and got his clari
and hit a blue lick or two to call us back in, the same as
ways. He left her out there, and me too, though he did
know I was there. Difference was, he left me alone . . .

We finished the date somehow, Crispin and his heartbe
drums, and Skid throwing that famous gliss all over t
finger-board—he could really glissando with that new guit
that Crispin helped him design, but I'm coming to that—a
the horns and Fluke. Yeak, Fluke, real smooth: "Sweet S
now, kizd, the sweetest Sue we ever blew, featuring Fa
Amory, the breeze on keys . . ." And Fawn ripples into
intro, and I give her a board-fade on the p.a. system, a
sigh in with, "Oh kizd, ain't we got Fawn . . ." and cut ba
to full volume on the piano mike. And I kept spooning t
corn back and back to myself, "Ain't we got Fawn, ain't
got—"

Crispin was a big blond guy who was a graduate electri

gineer. He earned his way through school playing drums,
d after he graduated went right on playing. If he'd gone
to electronics the way he'd planned, he'd of kept on play-
g drums. By the same token nothing could keep him from
essing with electronics while he was a trap man. He was
rever rehashing our p.a. system, and Skid's git-box was like
eanuts to him; he kept coming back for more. Skid was am-
ified when he started with us—a guitar's pretty nowhere
thout a pickup in a band nowadays—but all he had was a
mple magnetic pickup clamped onto a regular concert
itar. He had a few gimmicks too—a pedal volume control
d a tone-switch on the box that gave him a snarl when he
anted it. Trouble was, at high volumes that pickup picked
everything—the note and the scratch of the plectrum and
e peculiar squeak of Skid's calloused left fingers when he
d them on the wound strings, so that a guitar solo always
d a background of pops and crackles and a bunch of guys
histling for taxicabs.

Crispin, he fixed that. He was a big, good-natured cat that
erybody liked on sight, and sometimes when we went into
new town Crispin would go down to Radio Row and talk
me repairman into the use of his shop for a couple days.
rispin would drag in Skid's guitar amplifier and haul its
ts out and attach tone generators and oscilloscopes and all
e that, and after that would spend good sleeping time
lling Skid how to run the thing. After a couple of years
id had an instrument that would sit up and typewrite. He
d a warble-vibrato on it, and a trick tailpiece that he
erated with his elbow that would raise a six-string chord
halftone while he held it, and some jazz called an at-
nuator that let him hit a note that wouldn't fade, just like it
as blown out of an organ. Skid had a panel beside him with
ore buttons, switches, and controls on it than a custom-
ilt accordion has stops. He used to say that the instrument
as earning his keep—any three-chord man from a hill-billy
nd could take his spot if he got that instrument. I thought
was right. For years I thought he was right when he said
at.

It was before rehearsal the next day, that time in Boulder
ty, that Crispin came to me and talked like with my mouth.
was in the sunporch thinking about that moon last night

and all that went with it, about Lutch and the way ever
thing came so easy to him, he never had to make up his min
Crispin lounged up next to me and said,

"Fluke, did you ever see the time when Lutch could
make up his mind?"

I said, "Brother," and he knew I meant no.

He looked at his thumb, threw it out of joint. "Cat g
everything he wants without asking for it. Never has to thi
of asking for it."

"You're so right," I said. I didn't feel like talking.

He said, "He rates it. I'm glad." He was, too.

I said, "I'm glad too." I wasn't. "What brings up all t
jive, Crispin?"

He waited a long time. "Well, he just asked me somethir
He was all— all— ah, he was like a square at the Savoy, sh
fling his feet and blushing."

"Lutch?" I demanded. Lutch usually came on like col
all steam, no smoke. "What was it?"

"It was about Fawn," he said.

I felt something the size and weight of a cueball drop in
my stomach. "What's with Fawn?"

"He wanted to know what the sides would think if he a
Fawn got married."

"What'd you tell him?"

"What could I tell him? I said it would be fine. I said
didn't have to make any difference. It might even be better

"Better," I said. "Sure." Much better. Even if it was o
of your reach, at least you could dream. You could hope f
some break, some way. Lutch and Fawn . . . they would
fool around with this marriage kick, now. They'd do it
right.

"I knew you'd think the same way," he said. He sound
as if there was a load off his mind. He slapped my back—
hate that—and walked off whistling Daboo Dabay.

That was when I made up my mind to kill Lutch. Not f
Fawn. She was just part of it—the biggest part, yes; but
couldn't stand this one more trip his way of the silver platt
I remember once when I was a kid hitch-hiking. It was co
and I'd been at a crossroads near Mineola for a long tin
I began to wish real hard, hard like praying. A long ti
later I remembered what it was I wished for so hard. N
for a ride. Not for some guy with a heater in his car to st
What I wished for was a whole bunch of cars to come alo

I could thumb them. Dig me? The biggest break I ever wanted was to have the odds raised for me, so I could make my own way easier. That's all anyone should have. Lutch, born talented, good-looking, walking through life picking up old pieces . . . people like that shouldn't live. Every minute they live, a guy like us gets his nose rubbed in it.

For a second there I thought I'd quit, walk off, get clear. And then I remembered the radio, the jukes, people humming in front of elevator doors—and I knew I'd never get away from him. If he was dead it would be different; I could be glad when I heard that jive. No, I had to kill him.

But I'd play it smart.

For a couple of days I thought about it. I didn't think about much else. I thought of all the ways I'd ever heard about, and all the tricks they use in the whodunits to catch up on all the ways. I had about decided on an auto accident —he was all the time driving, either with the band or on quick trips for mail or spare reeds or music and all like that, and the law of averages was in my favor; he never had accidents. I was actually out casing the roads around there in Lutch's car when I had one of those fantastically unexpected pieces of luck that you dream about if you've got a good imagination.

I'd just turned into the highway from the Shinnebago side road when I heard sirens. I pulled over right away. A maroon Town-and-Country came roaring around the bend of the highway at about eighty. There were bullet holes in the windshield and the driver was hunched low. There were two rats in the back blasting away with automatics. Behind them came a State Police car, gaining. I didn't wait and watch; I was out and under before I knew what I was doing. Peering around the rear of my machine, I looked up just as one of the men in the Town-and-Country straightened up, holding his right forearm. Just then the driver hauled the car into the road I'd just left. It couldn't be done at that speed but he did it, the tires screaming from Dizzy Gillespie; and the man who was hit went sling-shotting out of the car. First he bounced and then he slid. I thought he'd never stop sliding. About the time he hit the road, the police car flashed by me with the right front tire flat. It was crabbing left and crabbing right, and this time the tires were from Stan Kenton.

The important thing is that that cat's gun flew straight up in the air when he was hit and landed in the weeds not twenty feet from me. I had it before those cops got their car stopped.

They never saw me. They were busy, then with the car, afte ward with the stiff. I walked down there and talked to then Seems these characters had been robbing gas stations an motorists. They'd already killed two. One of the cops growle about these war souvenir guns, and he'd be glad when all th foreign ammo was used up. They said they'd get the guy who'd gotten away soon enough; just a matter of time. I sai sure. Then I got back in Lutch's machine and drove awa real thoughtful. I knew I'd never have another chance lik this.

The next afternoon I told Lutch I'd go in town with hin He was picking up the mail and I said I had to go to the dru store. He didn't think anything about it. I went and got th gun and stuck it into the sleeve of my jacket, under my arn pit. It stayed there fine. It was a big Belgian automatic. had four shots left in it.

I felt all right. I thought I was doing okay until Lutc looked over at me—he was driving—and asked me if I felt a right. Then I realized I had sweat on my upper lip. I looke in the rear view mirror. I could see maybe two miles—w were out on the flats—and there wasn't a car in sight. I looke ahead. There was a truck. It passed. Then the road wa clear.

I said, "Pull over to the side, Lutch. I want to talk to you

He looked at me, surprised. "I can listen and drive, Fluk Shoot."

Shoot, he said. I almost laughed. "Pull over, Lutch." meant to sound normal but it came out as a hoarse whispe

"Don't be silly," he said. He had that big easy open-hande way about him, Lutch had. "Go on, Fluke, get it off yo chest."

I took out the gun and kicked off the safeties and poked into his ribs. "Pull over to the side, Lutch."

He pulled up his arm and looked down under it at th gun. "Why, sure," he said, and pulled over and stopped. H switched off, leaned back into the angle of the seat and th door so he half faced me, and said, "Lay it on me, Fluke. Yo fixing to kill me with that?" He didn't sound scared, and tha was because he wasn't. He really wasn't. Nothing like th had ever happened to him, so nothing ever could. He wasn prodding me, either. He was talking to me like at rehearsa Lutch was a very relaxed cat.

150

"Yes, I am," I told him.

He looked at it curiously. "Where'd you get it?"

I told him that too. If he'd only started to sweat and cry, I'd have shot him then. I hated him too much to just shoot him easy. I told him all about it. "They haven't caught those jokers yet," I said. "The cops'll dig one of these slugs out of you and it'll be the same as the ones in those other killings. They'll think those hoods did it."

"They will? What about you?"

"I'll have one of the slugs too. In the arm. It'll be worth it. Anything else you want to know?"

"Yes. Why? Fluke, *why?* Is it—Fawn?"

"That's right."

He sort of shook his head. "I hate to say this, Fluke, but I don't think killing me will help your chances any. I mean, even if she never finds out."

I said, "I know that, Lutch. But I'll have an even break; that's all I ever want. I can't get it with you around."

His face was sorry for me, and that's absolutely all. "Go on, then," he told me.

I pulled the trigger. The gun bucked in my hand. I saw him spin, and then everything went black, like I was under a baby spot and the fuse blew.

When I came to my eyes wouldn't straighten out. The whole world was full of dazzly black speckles and something globular was growing out of the back of my head.

I was still in the front seat of the car. Something was scratching and chafing at my wrist. I pulled it away and put my head in my hands and groaned.

"How you doing?" Lutch said. He bent forward, peering anxiously into my face.

I got my handkerchief out and put it behind my head and looked at it. There was blood—just a speck. "What happened, Lutch?"

He grinned. It was a little puckered, but still a grin. "You'll never make a gunman, Fluke. I've seen you twice with the gang in shooting galleries. You're afraid of guns."

"How did you know that?"

"You always close your eyes real tight, screw 'em down, before you pull a trigger. I was half-turned toward you as it was, and it was easy to twist aside. Turning made the gun ride around and slip back under my arm. Then I hit you with my shoulder and ran your head back against the door post. Does it hurt much?"

"I didn't shoot you."

"You tore hell out of my shirt."

"God damn you, Lutch," I said quietly.

He sat back with the arms folded, watching me, for a long time, until I asked, "What are we waiting for?"

"For you to feel well enough to drive."

"Then what?"

"Back to the club."

"Come on, Lutch; lay it on me. What are you going to do?"

"Think," said Lutch. He opened the door and got out and walked around the car. "Shove over," he said. He was carrying the gun. He wasn't pointing it, but he was holding it ready to use. I shoved over.

I drove slowly. Lutch wouldn't talk. I didn't dig him at all. He was doing just what he said—thinking. Once I took a hand off the wheel. His eyes were on me immediately. I just felt the lump on my head and put the hand back. For the time being I was hogtied.

When we stopped in front of the club he said, "Go on up to my room." (We had quarters over the hall.) "I'll be right behind you with the gun in my side pocket. If anyone stops you don't stall. Shake 'em naturally and go on up. I'm not afraid of guns and I'll shoot you if you don't do what I say. Do I mean it?"

I looked at his face. He meant it. "Well, all reet," I said, and got out.

No one stopped us. When we were in his room he said, "Get in that closet."

I opened my mouth to say something but decided not to. I got in the closet and closed and locked the door. It was dark.

"Can you hear me?" he said.

"Yup."

In a much softer voice he said, "Can you hear me now?"

"I can hear you."

"Then get this. I want you to listen to every word that is said out here until I open the door again. If you make a noise I'll kill you. Understand?"

"You're in, Jack," I said. My head hurt.

A long time—maybe two or three minutes—passed. From

far away I heard him calling, but couldn't make out what he was saying. I think he was on the stair landing. I heard him come in and shut the door. He was whistling between his teeth. *Daboo, Dabay.* Then there was a light knock on the door.

"Come in!"

It was Fawn. "What's cookin', good-lookin'?" she sang.

"Sit down, chicken."

The chair was wicker. I could hear it plain.

Lutch Crawford always talked straight to the point. That's how he got so much work done. "Fawn, about the other night, with all that moon. How do you feel now?"

"I feel the same way," she said tightly.

Lutch had a little habit of catching his lower lip with his teeth and letting it go when he was thinking hard. There was a pause about long enough to do this. Then he said, "You been hearing rumors around about you and me?"

"Well I—" She caught her breath. "Oh, Lutch—"I heard the wicker, sharp and crisp, as she came up out of it.

"Hold on!" Lutch snapped. "There's nothing to it, Fawn. Forget it."

I heard the wicker again, slow, the front part, the back part. She didn't say anything.

"There's some things too big for one or two people to fool with, honey," he said gently. "This band's one of 'em. For whatever it's worth, it's bigger than you and me. It's going good and it'll go better. It's about as perfect as a group can get. It's a unit. Tight. So tight that one wrong move'll blow out all its seams. You and me, now—that'd be a wrong move."

"How do you know? What do you mean?"

"Call it a hunch. Mostly, I know that things have been swell up to now, and I know that if you—we—anyway, we can't risk a change in the good old status quo."

"But—what about me?" she wailed.

"Tough on you?" I'd known Lutch a long time, and this was the first time his voice didn't come full and easy. "Fawn, there's fourteen cats in this aggregation and they all feel the same way about you as you do about me. You have no monopoly. Things are tough all over. Think of that next time you feel spring fever coming on." I think he bit at his lower lip again. In a voice soft like Skid's guitar with the bass stop, he said, I'm sorry, kid."

"Don't call me *kid!*" she blazed.

"You better go practice your scales," he said thickly.

The door slammed.

After a bit he let me out. He went and sat by the window, looking out.

"Now what did you do that for?" I wanted to know.

"For the unit," he said, still looking out the window.

"You're crazy. Don't you want her?"

What I could see of his face answered that question. I don't think I'd realized before how much he wanted her. I don't think I'd thought about it. He said, "I don't want her so badly I'd commit murder for an even chance at her. You do. If anyone wants her worse than I do, I don't want her enough. That's the way I see it."

I could of told him then that it wasn't only him and Fawn that bothered me; that that was just part of it. Somehow it didn't seem to make no never mind just then. If he wanted to play the square he was welcome to it. "I'll go pack," I said.

He jumped up. "You'll do no such a damn thing!" he roared. "Listen, hipster; you've seen how far I'll go to keep this unit the way it is. You taught me something today, the hard way, and by the Lord you're not going to kick over this group just when you've taught it to me!" He walked over and stood close; I had to crease the back of my neck to see his face. He jabbed his fingers at my nose. "If you walk out on the unit now, so help me, I'll track you down and hound you to death. Now get out of here."

"All right," I told him. "But listen. I'll take a raincheck on that last. You're riding a high riff right now. Think it over quiet, and tell me tonight if you want me to stay. I'll do what you say."

He grinned the old grin again. "Good, Fluke. See ya."

It's hard to hate a joe like that. But if you can make it, you can do a job.

I made it.

So. That was the time I tried it smart. Next time I tried it sneaky.

We played the Coast, up and back. We did two rushes in feature pictures and thirteen shorts. We guested on some of the biggest radio shows going. We came back East after a lick at Chicago, where there was a regular Old Home Week with Fawn's folks, and we got three consecutive weeks at the Paramount. We played 'em sleek, and had the old folks

154

smiling into each others' eyes. We played 'em frantic, and blew the roof. You know.

And every dollar that fell into our laps, and every roar of applause, and every line of print in the colyums that drooled over us, I hated, and there was plenty to hate. The Geese played so many different kinds of music there was no getting away from it anywhere. I once saw a juke-box with seven Crawford plates in it at once! There was Lutch with the world throwing itself at his head because he was a nice guy. And here I was in the gravy because he was good to me. And the whole world was full of the skunk and his music, and there'd never be any rest from it anywhere. (Did you hear the Hot Club of France's recording of *Daboo Dabay?*) A great big silk-lined prison for old Fluke; a padded cell. Lutch Crawford built a padded cell and was keeping old Fluke in it.

Fawn got a little haggard, after that time in Boulder City, but she gradually pulled up out of it. She was learning, the way the rest of us had learned, to feel one way and act another. Well, isn't that the rock-bottom starting point for anyone in show business? She was the better for it . . .

We started West again, and South, and the time I tried it sneaky was in Baton Rouge.

It was a road club again, real razzle, with curved glass and acoustic ceilings and all that jazz. I can't say that anything particular keyed me off—it was just that I'd made up my mind a long time ago how I was going to do it and I needed a spot near running water. Baton Rouge has a fair-sized creek running past its front door, and Old Man River, he don't say nothin'.

It was very simple—it's surprising how simple some things can be, even things you've been eating your heart out over for years, when they get fixed up at last . . . Lutch got a letter. The hat-check girl at the club turned away to hang up a coat and when she turned back the letter was there by the tip-plate. There were plenty of people in and out through the lobby. I was, myself. The powder-room was downstairs; I was sick that night. Everyone knew about it; they were laughing at old Fluke. I am allergic to shrimps, and here I had to go and gulp up a pound or more of New Orleans fried shrimp and rice: I had hives that grease-paint would barely cover, and could just about navigate, and I had to take a trip down below every twenty minutes or so. Sometimes I stayed a long while . . .

Lutch got the letter. It was sealed, addressed with a type-writer. No return address. The hat-check girl gave it to the head-waiter who gave it to Lutch. Lutch read it, told Crispin and Fawn he'd be back, he didn't know when, put on his hat and left. I don't know what he thought about on the way. The letter, I guess. It said

> Dear Lutch,
>
> First, don't show this to anyone or tell anyone about it yet. Make sure no one is looking over your shoulder or anything like that.
>
> Lutch, I'm half out of my mind over something I've heard. I think a serious danger threatens my daughter Fawn, and I must talk to you. I am in Baton Rouge. I don't want Fawn to know it yet.
>
> Maybe there is nothing in this business but it is best to play it safe. I am waiting for you near a warehouse above Morrero—that is just down-river from Baton Rouge. The warehouse has LE CLERC ET FILS painted on the street side. I am in the office out near the end of the wharf. I think you might be followed. Take a cab to the depot at Mor-rero and walk to the river. You can't miss it. But watch for a shadow, you can't be too careful. I hope all this turns out to be for nothing.
>
> Bring this with you. If what I fear is true it would not be safe even to burn it at the club. Please hurry.
>
> Anxiously,
> JOHN AMORY.

I'm proud of that letter. Fawn's pop and Lutch were real buddy-buddy, and the old man would never ask a favor unless it was important. The letter was the only evidence there was, and Lutch brought it with him. A nice job, if I do say so myself.

No one saw Lutch. The cab-driver didn't know who he was, or if he did he never mentioned it later. Lutch came as soon as he could, knocked at the door of the office. There was a dim light inside. No one answered. He came in and closed the door behind him. He called out, softly, "Mr. Amory!"

I whispered, from inside the warehouse, "In here."

Lutch went to the inner door, stepped into the warehouse,

and stopped, with the light from the office showing up the strip of skin between his collar and his hair just fine. I hit him there with a piece of pipe. He never made a sound. This time I wasn't going to talk it over with him.

I caught him before he hit the floor and carried him over to the long table beside the sink. The sink was already full of water, and I had seen to it that it was river water, just in case. I put the pipe where I could reach it in case I had to hit him again, and spread him out on the table with his head over the sink. Then I dunked it, and held it under.

Like I thought, it revived him and he began to kick and squirm. The burlap sacks I had laid on the table muffled that all right, and I had him pretty firmly around the shoulders, with my elbow at the back of his neck forcing his head under. I had one leg hooked under the sink support. He didn't have a chance, though it was hard work for a few minutes.

When he was quiet again, and with five minutes or so over for good measure, I got the small-boat anchor chain—an old rusty one it was—and wound it around him secure but careless-like; it could be by accident. I got the letter out of his pocket and burned it, grinding all the ashes down on a small piece of roofing tin which I dropped into the river. I rolled Lutch in after it. There was quite a current running—he started downstream almost before he was under the surface. I said, "So long, superman," straightened myself, locked up the warehouse after turning the light out, emptying the sink and all like that, and, picking up the car I'd parked two blocks away, drove back to the club. It was easy to climb in the basement window into the stall of the men's room I'd left locked, and to come back upstairs without being noticed. The whole thing had taken just forty-three minutes.

I was happy about the whole thing. The chain would hold him under, that and the mud, and the catfish would make quick work of him. But if, by some fluke, the body should be found, well, the chain could be an accident, and he certainly died of drowning. In river water. The bump on the back of his neck—that was nothing.

But Lutch Crawford was hard to kill.

I don't have to tell you about the next month or so, with the headlines and all that jive that went on. The band went right ahead; Lutch's hand was always so light on it that his absence made almost no difference. The sides worried some about him, but it took them three days to get really panicked. By that time my mind was easy. No amount of police work and private detective shenanigans could do a thing about it. The whole band alibied me, and the hat-check girl too, with my hives. Matter of fact, no one even thought to ask me any questions, specially. No one remembered exactly what time Lutch left the club; there had been nothing to call it to anyone's attention. A clean job.

The next thing I wanted to do was to get clear of the whole aggregation and go live by myself. I was careful, though, and made no move until someone else did it first.

It came to a head six weeks after Lutch disappeared. We'd moved on to Fort Worth, Texas. Fawn and Crispin hadn't wanted to leave Baton Rouge, but finally decided that Lutch, wherever he was, knew our schedule as well as we did and would come back when he was ready to.

We had a big powwow in Fort Worth. Crispin took the floor. Everyone was there.

Fawn still looked bad. She'd lost a lot of weight. Skid Portly looked five years older.

Crispin came to the point as quick as Lutch used to.

"Gang," he said, "don't get your hops up; I didn't call you because I have any new ideas about Lutch or where he might be. There's no word.

"What brings this up is that after two weeks at Brownsville and a week at Santa Monica, this tour is over. We have our pick of several offers—I'll go over them with you later—and we've got to decide right now what we're going to do. Lutch isn't here and there's no way of knowing when he will show. We can either take a vacation after the Santa Monica date, and hang up the fiddle until Lutch shows up, or we can go on. What do you say?"

"I could use a rest," I said.

"We could all use a rest," said Crispin. "But what has us tuckered out is this business of Lutch. If it wasn't for that we wouldn't think of a break until next summer."

Fawn said, "What would Lutch want us to do?"

Moff—Lew Moffatt, that was, the reed man—said, "I don't reckon there's any doubt about that."

There was a general numble of agreement. Lutch would have gone on.

"Then we go on?"

Everybody said yes but me. I didn't say. No one noticed.

Crispin nodded. "That leaves a big question. As far as performances are concerned, we can get along. But someone has to take over booking, contracts, a lot of the arranging, hotel accommodations, and so on."

"What do you mean some*one?*" asked Skid. "Lutch did four men's work."

"I know," said Crispin. "Well, do you think we can make it? How about the arrangements? Skid, you and Fawn used to help him the most."

Skid nodded. Fawn said, "We can do it."

Crispin said, "I'll handle the business, if it's okay with you." It was. "Now, how about billing? We can't phony it up; Lutch's dis—uh—absence has had a flock of publicity, and if Lutch doesn't come back before we start, we can't bill him. The customers wouldn't like it."

They chewed that over. Finally Skid said. "Why'n't you take it, Crisp?"

"Me? I don't want it."

The rest of them all started talking at once. Lutch and Crispin had worked very close together. The general idea was that they wanted him to do it.

Crispin had been lounging back against a long table. Now he stood up straight. He said,

"All right, all right. But listen. This band is Lutch Crawford's Gone Geese, and if it's all the same to you it'll stay that way. We can bill as Don Crispin and Lutch Crawford's Gone Geese if you like; but I want it so that wherever Lutch is, he'll know that it's still his band. That means, too, that any new arrangement or novelty or what have you, is going to be done the way Lutch would do it, to the very best of our ability. If any one of you hears something in the band that doesn't sound like Lutch, speak up. I want it so that when Lutch comes back—damn it, I won't say *if*—when Lutch comes back he can pick up the baton in the middle of a number and take over from there. Are you with it?"

They were. After the fuss had died down Koko deCamp, the hot trumpet man, spoke up sort of timid. "Crispin," he said, "I don't want to cause any hard feelings, but I have a standing offer with the King combo. My contract with Lutch is up at the end of this tour, and I think I could do myself more good with the King. That's only—" he added quickly, "if Lutch don't come back."

Crispin frowned and scratched his head. He looked over at

Fawn. She said again. "What would Lutch want him to do?"

Crispin said, "There it is. Lutch would let you do whatever you thought you wanted. He never stopped anyone who wanted to leave."

I could of told him. I didn't.

Crispin went on, "There's the code word, kizd, 'What would Lutch want?' Start from there. Anyone else want out? There'll be no hard feelings."

The bass man—we'd only had him a couple of months—said he thought he'd go. Then I spoke up.

Fawn said, "Oh, no!"

"Why, Fluke?" asked Crispin. They all stared at me.

I spread my hands. "I want out, that's all. Do I have to fill out a questionnaire?"

"There won't be any 'Gone Geese' without Fluke," said Skid.

He was so right. The way they billed it was "Don Crispin and the Lutch Crawford Orchestra." Crispin and Fawn did their best to make me stay with it, but no. Oh no. I was over, out and clear. I think Fawn figured it that it hurt me to stay close to the band, after Lutch had been so good to me. Hell. I wanted to laugh, that was all, and I couldn't do that where the band could see me.

We broke up at Santa Monica after the date there. I thought I'd take it easy for a year or so and look around, but what should drop into my lap but a gold-plated offer from a radio station in Seattle, for a night record-jockey stand. That was made to order. My voice and delivery and savvy of the sharps and the flats were perfect for it, and best of all, I could work where people didn't have to look at my face. Sometimes I think if I had been in radio from the start, I wouldn't of—I might not have become the kind of cat who—ah, that's useless chatter now.

I got twenty-six weeks with options and could have upped the ante if I'd wanted to argue, which I didn't. Crispin and the rest of Lutch's sidemen went all out for me, sending me telegrams during my show, giving me personal appearances, and plugging me in their clubs. Seemed like, dead or alive, Lutch kept on being kind. I didn't let it get me. I'd lived long enough to know you can't break clean from any close contact with a human being. Quit a job, get a divorce, leave a home town, it drags on in shreds and tatters that haunt you. I held tight to laughing. Lutch was dead.

Then one night I got that advance shipment of Mecca records. Six sides of Crispin-Crawford.

I gave it a big hello in the old Fluke style: "Aha, lil kizd—a clump of jump for bacon to crisp-in; Crispin and Crawford, and six new plates for gates. Just like old times for Fluke the Juke. . . . This spinner's a winner: old *Deep Purple* in the Crispin crunchy style."

I played it off. I hadn't heard any of these plates yet, though they were cleared for broadcast; they'd been delivered just before air time. *Deep Purple* was the old bandstand arrangement that Lutch had done himself. Moff was playing Lutch's clarinet, and there wasn't enough difference to matter. In the double-time ride in the third chorus, Skid slipped in a lick on guitar that I hadn't heard before, but it was well inside the Crawford tradition. The other platters showed up the same way; Crispin took a long drum solo in *Lady Be Good* that was new, but strictly Crawford. I held out the two new ones until last.

I mean new. There was a blow-top novelty called *One Foot in the Groove* that I had never heard; the by-line was Moff and Skid Portly. The other one was an arrangement of *Tuxedo Junction*. We'd always used a stock arrangement for that one; this was something totally new. In the first place it let in some bop sequences, and in the second place it really exploited an echo chamber—the first time that had been done on a Crawford record. I listened to it bug-eyed.

It was good. It was *very* good. But the thing that tore me all apart was that it was Lutch Crawford, through and through. Lutch had never used an echo before. But he would —he *would*, because it was a new trend. Just like the be-bop continuities. I could imagine the powwow before the recording session, and Fawn saying "What would Lutch want?"

Listening to it, I saw Lutch, wide shoulders, long hands, pushing the brass this way, that way, reaching up and over to haul the sound of the drums up and then crush them down, down to a whispering cymbal. I could see him hold it down there with his right hand flat in the air in front of him as if he had it on a table, long enough for him to catch his lower lip between his teeth and pull it loose, and suddenly, then, like a flash-bulb going off, dazzle the people with an explosion of scream-trumpet and high volume guitar.

The turntable beside me went quietly about its work, with the sound-head pulsing a little like a blood-pressure gauge.

It hypnotized me, I guess. Next thing I knew my engineer was waving frantically at me through the plateglass, giving me a 'dead-air' sign, and I realized that the record had been finished for seconds. I drew a thick rattling breath and said the only thing in the world that there was—a thing bigger than me, clearer than my scriptsheets or the mike in front of me or anything else. I said stupidly, "That was Lutch. That was Lutch Crawford. He isn't dead. *He isn't dead . . .*"

Something in front of my eyes began bobbing up and down. It was the engineer again, signalling. I had been staring straight at him without seeing him. I was seeing Lutch. The engineer pointed downward, waggled his finger round and round. That meant play a record. I nodded and put on a Crosby plate, and sat back as if I'd been lanced in the gut with a vaulting pole.

My phone light flashed. I took calls on the show; the phones were equipped with lights instead of bells so they wouldn't crowd the mike. I picked up the receiver, saying automatically, "Fluke the Juke."

"One moment please." An operator. Then, "Fluke? Oh, Fluke . . ." Fawn. It was Fawn Amory.

"Fluke," she said, her words tumbling over each other the way notes did on her keyboard, "Oh Fluke, darling, we heard you, we all heard you. We're in Denver. We cut a date to catch your show. Fluke honey, you said it, Fluke, you said it!"

"Fawn—"

"You said he isn't dead. We know that, Fluke—we all do. But the way you said it; you don't know how much that means to us! We did it, you see? *Tuxedo Junction*—we worked and worked—something that would be new and would be Lutch too. Lutch can't die as long as we can do that, don't you see?"

"But I—"

"We're going to do more, Fluke. More Lutch, more real Lutch Crawford. Will you come back, Fluke? We want to do more 'Gone Geese' records and we can't without you. Won't you please, Fluke? We *need* you!" There was a murmuring in her background. Then,

"Fluke? This is Crispin. I want to double that, boy. Come on back."

"Not me, Crispin. I'm done," I managed to say.

"I know how you feel," said Crispin quickly. He knew I was about to hang up on him. "I won't push you, hipster. But think it over, will you? We're going to keep on, whatever happens, and wherever Lutch is, alive or—wherever he is, he'll have a band, and as long as he has a band, he's here."

"You're doing fine," I croaked.

"Just think it over. We can do twice as well if you'll come back. Keep in touch. Here's Fawn again."

I hung up.

I'll never know how I got through that show. I know why I did. I did because I was going to make my own way. That was why I had wanted to kill Lutch. Come sick, come ça, as the man said, this was my kick—making my own way without Lutch Crawford.

Six o'clock was closing time for me, and I imagine I got through the routines all right; no one said anything to me about it. And if I didn't answer the phone, and ignored requests, and played all the long stuff I could get my hands on so I wouldn't have to talk, well, they took it the way any outfit will take guff from a guy they pay too highly.

I walked, I don't know where. I suppose I frightened a lot of kids on their way to school with that face of mine, and got a lot of queer looks from women scrubbing their porch steps. I wouldn't know. *Lutch isn't dead* was the only thing that made. I can't tell you all the things I went through; there was a time of fear, when I thought Lutch was after me for what I'd done, and a time of calm, when I thought it couldn't matter less—I could just go on minding my own business and let Lutch die altogether, the way everybody has to. And there was a time of cold fury, when I heard that new *Tuxedo Junction* with the echoing guitar, and knew that Crispin would keep turning new Lutch out—real Lutch, that no one else in the music business could imitate. Lutch, he was talented like three or four people, and there happened to be three or four people with just those talents in his band. Anyway, it's all a haze.

About ten o'clock it all clicked into the clear. I found myself on Elliott Avenue away out near Kinnear Park—I must've walked miles—and everything was squared away. *I hate Lutch Crawford*—I was left with that, the old familiar feeling. And I still had to do something about it because Lutch wasn't dead.

I walked into a telegraph office and wired Crispin.

They started by giving me something I didn't want—but wasn't that the whole trouble? This time it was a sort of surprise party and testimonial dinner. I guess I was a little sour.

They didn't understand. Crispin, he tried to make me feel better by guaranteeing that he'd see to it I was paid twice over for breaking my radio contract. Fawn—well, Fawn shouldn't have been so sweet to me. That was a huge mistake. Anyway, there was a dinner and some drinks and Crispin and Skid and Moff and them got up one by one and said what a fine cat I was. Then they all sat around playing "remember when" and passing side remarks to the empty chair at the head of the table where Lutch's clarinet was. It was a fine party.

After that I went to work. What they saw me doing was "Is coming up a sizzle-swizzle for *Rum and Coca Cola*, featuring the Id-kid, Skid, and his supercharged git-fiddle, so look out!" And "We got a dream-scheme, kizd, all soft and lofty, smooth, forsooth, but full of nerve-verve. Hey Moff, stroke these quiet cats with *Velvet Paws* . . ." So—I helped them.

What I was doing was trying to find Lutch so's I could kill him. You should have been a fly on the wall to hear those slave-sessions. Take a tune, find old Lutch, mix 'em up, make 'em be something new that's styled like something they wouldn't let be dead. So—they helped me.

I could have killed Lutch by killing the lot of them. I never did discard that idea. But maybe I'm lazy. Somewhere in that aggregation was the essence of what was Lutch. If I could smoke that out and kill it, he'd be dead. I knew that. It was just a matter of finding out what it was. It shouldn't have been much trouble. Hell, I knew that outfit inside out—performers, arrangements, even what they liked to eat. I told you—there was damn little turnover there. And in the music business people show up real soon for what they are.

But it wasn't easy.

That outfit was like a machine made for a very special purpose—but made all out of standard parts you could buy on the open market. That isn't to say that some of the parts weren't strictly upper-bracket; all of them were machined to a millionth. But I couldn't believe that what Lutch called "unit" was the thing that made that group an individual, great one. If Lutch had been around, you could've said that Lutch made the difference between a good machine and something alive. But Lutch wasn't around, and the thing still lived. Lutch had put the life in it, by choosing the right pieces and giving them the right push. After that the thing ran under its own power—the power of life—and Lutch Crawford wouldn't be dead until that life was gone. It was going to be him or me.

164

So I helped them. We had club and hotel dates, and we made records, and in keeping Lutch alive, I helped them.

And they helped me. Every time a new tune started climbing the top ten, every time someone came up with a number that looked like a winner, we'd arrange it for the band; and in those sessions the band and the workings of every least part were torn down and inspected and argued over. I never missed a word of this, so—they helped me.

It was hell for me. If you've got guts enough to kill a man, you've got to finish the job. Lutch was alive. It was bad away from the band, with every radio and juke-box in the whole world blasting out Crawford creations. It was bad with the band—sometimes you could *see* him!

Theme time at a club, and the lights the way they always were, and the band the same, except that now Crispin's luggage was front and center. The swinging bells of the brass and their "hoo ha" and then Skid's solo *Daboo, Dabay* with Moff taking the obbligato on the clarinet. Moff never stood out front to play, though. He was out of sight like Crispin used to be. Crispin, crushing the beat, whisper-drumming, stared up and out the way he used to when he was in the blackness, and Skid was no different, watching his fingers . . . all the books say a good guitarist never watches his fingers but I guess Skid never read them . . . but you could see he was following *someone*, and it wasn't Crispin, from under his pulled-down eyebrows. But Lutch was there most of all for Fawn, Fawn with the flickering golden light touching and leaving her face, and her head tilted to one side so the heavy hair swung forward past her round bare shoulder; and on her face that look, that half-smile, half-hungry look—hungry like Lutch was there looking at her, not like he was away.

Daboo dabay . . . it hypnotized those cats. We always opened with it, and sometimes we had as many as three half-hour network spots, and that meant theme opening and closing. It was always the same. I often wondered if the customers who faithfully spattered out their applause at the drop of a *hoo ha* had any idea that this was different, this was a—a resurrection, maybe eight times a night.

First I was sure it was the brass—the low brass, where that peculiar vitality came from. You see, that was my protection—Lutch was strong in everything we did, but you couldn't *see* him in anything but the theme. When we did the theme I concentrated on what I heard, not on what it meant. Anyway, night after night I waited for the theme, and cut out everything but that low brass as I listened. It wasn't notes I was listening for, but tone—style—*Lutch*. After a week or so I pinned it down to the second trumpet and a trombone. I was sure I was right; the Crawford quality was somewhere down there where the tone was low and full.

I got a break on it. So did Karpis and Heintz, the sliphorn and trumpet men I'd singled out. See, they roomed together in a hotel we used during Convention Week in Spokane. So one night they didn't get to the club in time to open. The hotel was an old firetrap—no escapes. The only way out of their room was through the door. No phone. Small transom, and that jammed and painted over. Locking the door from outside, putting a twist of coat-hanger wire in the key so it couldn't turn, that was easy. It was forty minutes before a bellhop let them out.

I heard the theme twice without those two sides. Crispin put it in a nutshell when I asked him about it later. "Thin," he said, "but it's still Lutch." That was what I thought.

No one found out who had locked those boys in, of course. I don't operate so I can be found out. No one knew who was responsible when two trumpets and a reed man got left miles behind us when we went to St. Louis. We'd hired a bus and a couple of cars—we had a quartet and two vocalists by then. And one of the cars just quit back there in the fog. Who watered the gasoline? Some shmoe at a gas station, and let's forget it.

The theme wasn't the theme on that date. I hadn't knocked out the thing that was Lutch—I'd knocked out the orchestra by pulling those men; we were just nothing. That was no answer. I had to find the heart of Lutch, and stop it, stop it so it could never beat again.

Somebody slugged Stormy, the bass, while he was asleep the second afternoon in St. Louis. He went to the hospital and they got another man quick. He wasn't Stormy, but he was good. You could hear that the bass was different—but the orchestra was still Lutch.

How long can you keep it up? Sometimes I thought I'd go crazy. Actually. Sometimes I wanted to run out into the tables and smash the customers around, because I thought maybe they knew what I was looking for. I was so close to it. That thing that was Lutch could cut in and cut out during a number, and I'd never notice it, being so busy listening to one instrument or combo. Someone out there could know, right in the same room with me, and I wouldn't. Sometimes I thought I was going out of my mind.

I even got us a new piano player for a night. I had to come out in the open for that, but it was safe. I hung around the conservatory until I latched on to a kid who was all starry-eyed about Lutch Crawford. I made like a talent scout. The kid was good-looking, with pimples. A jack-rabbit right hand, like Art Tatum, or it would be in a few years. I told Fawn about the boy, and said he was pining away. I laid it on. You know. You know how old Fluke. And Fawn, her and her soft heart! she not only agreed to let the kid in, but persuaded Crispin to let him take a one-night stand!

He did. He was good. He read like crazy, and he played every note that was on the paper and played 'em right; and he played a lot more he dreamed up, and they were right too. But he wasn't for the Geese. Now, here's a funny thing. It's aside from the business of killing Lutch. This kid was wrong for us, but so good Crispin spoke to Forway, the tour manager, and today that kid's making records that sell three quarters of a million each. All because of the break I got him by way of getting Fawn off the ivory for a night. Now what do you think of that?

I found out that night, though, that Fawn wasn't the "Lutch" thing that I was hunting. The band sounded like Lutch Crawford with the wrong piano, that's all. It wasn't wrong enough to keep Lutch from being there, somewhere in the sharps and flats. I wanted to run up to the stand and rip the music apart with my hands and yell, "Come out of there, you yellow skunk! Come out and let me get to you!"

I was glad it wasn't Fawn. I'd have stopped her, if it was, but I wouldn't have liked doing it much . . .

And I *found* him. I found him!

He had been right there all the time, looking at me, me looking at him, and I hadn't wits enough to see him.

Virus X and I found him. Virus X is something like flu, and something like dysentery, and it's no fun. It swept through us like a strong wind. I got it first, and it only lasted a couple of days. Moff, now, he was out two weeks. We only had to close for two nights, though. We made it the rest of the time, sometimes with something like a full band, sometimes with a skeleton. One of the short-timers was the guy who played guitar—Skid Portly.

Skid always said that any hill-billy could do what he did, given his guitar. I believed him. Why not? I'd diddled around with the instrument myself. Put your finger behind a fret, pluck the string. With a pedal you could make it louder or softer. With push-buttons you could make it warble or snarl or *whuff!* out with a velvet sound. With a switch you could make it sound exactly like a harpsichord or an organ. With a lever under your arm you could make all six strings rise in pitch like six fire sirens rising together, to almost a full tone. You didn't play it. You operated it.

Skid came down with Virus X, and we called in a character called Sylviro Giondonato, a glossy-haired, olive-skinned cat from East St. Louis. He was bugeyed at the chance, like the pianist I'd found. He played a whole mess of guitar, and when he got his hands on Skid's instrument I thought he was going to cry. He spent ten hours in Skid's hotel room learning the gimmicks on that box, with Skid, who was feeling rotten, coaching him every step of the way. I know he did things on that guitar that Skid wouldn't dare to do. Giondonato had one of those crazy ears like Rheinhardt or Eddie South—not that Eddie plays guitar.

The band played that night without Lutch.

Gionni—Johnny, we called him—was a star. The customers all but clawed down the ceiling-beams. A big hit. But it wasn't Lutch.

Crispin ripped off a momma-daddy on the tom after a while, our signal to take fifteen. I don't think I heard it. I was crouching at the corner of the stand thinking over and over, *No Lutch! No Lutch!* and trying not to laugh. It had been a long time.

When Crispin touched my shoulder I almost jumped out from behind my teeth. "No Lutch!" I said. I couldn't help it.

"Hey," said Crispin. "Level off, Fluke. So you noticed it too?"

"Brother."

"You wouldn't think one man's work would make that much difference, would you?"

"I don't get it," I said. I meant that. "Johnny's a hell of a guitar player. Man, I think he's *better* than Skid."

"He is," Crispin said. "But—I think I know why Lutch

168

doesn't show when he plays. Johnny plays terrific guitar. Skid plays terrific electric guitar. Dig me? The two are played pretty much the same—and so are a cello and a viola. But the attack is 'way different. Johnny exploits guitar as good as I've heard it anywhere so far. But Skid plays that instrument out there."

"What's that to do with Lutch?"

"Think back, Fluke. When Skid came with us, he was amplified, period. Look what he's got now—and look where we are now. You know how much we've depended on him."

"I thought we were depending on his guitar."

Crispin shook his big, straight-nosed head. "It's Skid. I don't think I realized it myself until now."

"Thanks," I told him.

He looked at me curiously. "For what?"

I threw up my hands. "For—well, I feel better now, that's all."

"You're a large charge of strange change, Fluke," he said.

I said, "Everybody knows that."

Three nights later I slugged Skid Portly from behind. I killed Lutch Crawford with a pair of bolt-cutters. And there was Lutch—all of him, all his music, all his jump, his public and his pride, in the palm of my hand. Literally in the palm of my hand—three pinkish slugs with horn at one end and blood at the other. I tossed 'em, caught 'em, put 'em in my pocket and walked off whistling *Daboo Dabay*. It was the first time in eight years I had heard that music and enjoyed it. Sometimes it takes a long time to kill a man.

Rehearsal next day was pretty dismal.

Crispin had everything set up. When we were all there, sort of milling around, he got up on the lower tier of the stand. Everyone shut up, except me, but then, I wasn't laughing out loud.

Crispin's mouth was tight. "I asked Fawn what to do," he said abruptly, "just like Lutch used to. She said, 'What would Lutch do?' I think Lutch would first see if we could make it the way we are—find out how bad we're hurt. Right?"

Everybody uh-huhed. That's what Lutch would do. Someone said, "How's Skid?"

Crispin barked, "You play trumpet. How'd you feel if someone sliced off your lip?" Then he said, "I'm sorry, Riff."

Riff said, "Gosh, that's okay."

They took their places. Fawn looked like the first week after Baton Rouge. Giondonato started for the guitar. Crispin waved him back. "Stand by, Johnny." He glanced at the guitar. It was ready to go, resting neck upward on the seat of Skid's chair. Crispin touched it, straightened it up a bit, lovingly. He bent and shifted the speaker outward a little. Then he went to his luggage. "Theme," he said. He looked over at me. I picked up my mike, puffed into it, adjusted the gain.

Crispin gave a silent one-two. Fawn stroked a chord. The brasses swung right: *Hoo*

And left: *Ha*

Fawn crowded the beat with her chord. I looked at her. For the very first time she wasn't looking at that spot on the floor in front of the band. She was looking at Crispin.

Hoo Ha

Moff raised his clarinet, tongued it, laid his lips around the mouthpiece, filliped the stops nervously, and then blew.

And with the first note of the clarinet, shockingly, came the full, vibrato voice of Skid's guitar: *Daboo, Dabay, Dabay, Daboo . . .*

And right on top of it there was a thunderous, animal, coughing gasp, and a great voice screaming, screaming, sobbing like peals of laughter. The sound was huge, and crazy, and it dwindled to an echoing, "He isn't dead, he isn't dead . . ."

And then I had to breathe, and I realized that the sounds had come from me, that I was standing frozen, staring at Skid's glittering guitar, with the mike pressed close to my cheek. I began to cry. I couldn't help it. I threw down the microphone—it made a noise like thunder—and I took the rolled-up handkerchief out of my pocket and hurled it at the guitar, which was playing on and on and on, Lutch's theme, the way Lutch wanted it played, by somebody else. The handkerchief opened in the air. Two of them hit the instrument and made it thrum. One stuck to the cloth and went cometing under the chair.

Moff ran over there. I was screaming, "Use these, damn you!" Moff bent as if to pick something up, drew back. "Crispin—it's the—the fingers . . ." and then he folded up and slumped down between the chairs.

Crispin made a noise almost like the first one I had blown

170

into the mike. Then he rushed me. He caught me by the front of the coat and the belt and lifted me high in the air. I heard Fawn scream, *"Don!"* and then he threw me on the floor. I screamed louder than Fawn did.

I must have blacked out for a moment. When I opened my eyes I was lying on the floor. My left arm had two elbows. I couldn't feel it yet. Crispin was standing over me, one foot on each side. He was shoving the rest of them back. They were growling like dogs. Crispin looked a mile high.

"Why did you do that to Skid?" Crispin asked. His voice was quiet; his eyes were not. I said, "My arm . . ." and Crispin kicked me.

"Don! Don, let me—" and people began to jostle and push, and Fawn broke through. She went to her knees beside me. "Hello, Fluke," she said, surprisingly.

I began to cry again. "The poor thing's out of his mind," she said.

"The poor thing?" roared Stormy. "Why, he—"

"Fluke, why did you do it?"

"He wouldn't die," I said.

"Who wouldn't, Fluke? Skid?"

They made me sore. They were so dumb. "Lutch," I said. "He wouldn't be dead."

"What do you know about Lutch?" gritted Crispin.

"Leave him alone," she blazed. "Go on, Fluke."

"Lutch was living in Skid's guitar," I said patiently, "and I had to let him out."

Crispin swore. I really didn't know he ever did that. My arm began to hurt then. Fawn got up slowly. "Don . . ."

Crispin grunted. Fawn said, "Don, Lutch used to worry all the time about Fluke. He always wanted Fluke to know he was wanted for himself. Fluke had something that no one else had, but he wouldn't believe it. He always thought Lutch and the rest of us were sorry for him."

The guitar was still playing. It rose in crescendo. I twitched. "Skid—" I yelled.

"Moff, turn that thing off," said Crispin. A second later the guitar stopped. "I knew it would trap somebody," he said to me, "but I never thought it would be you. That's a recording played through the guitar amplifier. I made hundreds of 'em when I was running tests on Skid's guitar. I've been worried for a long time about the luck we've been having—a choir missing this night, a side missing that night, a combo out the next night. The more I thought of it the more it took a pattern. Someone was doing it, and when that happened to Skid, I had an idea that someone'd give himself away, if only for a second, when that guitar began to play. I never expected *this!*"

"Leave him alone," said Fawn tiredly. "He can't understand you." She was crying.

Crispin turned on her. "What do you want to do with him? Kiss and make up?"

"I want to kill him!" she shrieked back at him. She held out her polished nails, crooked, like claws. "With these! Don't you know that?"

Crispin stepped back, stunned.

"But that doesn't matter," she went on in a low voice. "We can't stop saying it now, of all times— What would Lutch want?"

It got very quiet in there.

"Do you know why he was rejected from the army during the war?" she asked.

Nobody said anything.

Fawn said, "Extreme ugliness of face. That was a ground for deferment. Look it up if you don't believe me." She shook her head slowly and looked at me. "Lutch was always so careful of his feelings, and so were we all. Lutch wanted him to have his face made over, but he didn't know how to suggest it to Fluke—Fluke was psychopathically sensitive about it. Well, he waited too long, and I waited too long, and now look. I say let's have it done now, and save what little is left of the— creature."

Stormy said, "This good-for-evil kick can go just so far." The rest of them growled.

Fawn raised her hands and let them fall. "What would Lutch do?"

"I killed Lutch," I said.

"Shut up, you," said Crispin. "All right, Fawn. But listen. After he gets out of the hospital, I don't care if he looks like Hedy Lamarr—he stays out of my way or by God I'll strap him down and take him apart with a blunt nailfile."

At long, long last I blacked out.

There was a time of lying still and watching the white, curve-edged ceiling stream past, and a time of peeping through holes in the bandages. I never said another word, and very little was said to me. The world was full of strangers who knew what they were doing, and that was okay with me.

They took the bandage off this morning and gave me a mirror. I didn't say anything. They went away. I looked myself over.

I'm no bargain. But by the Lord I can cite you hundreds of people now who are uglier than I am. That's a change from not knowing a single one.

So I killed Lutch Crawford?

Who was the downy-clown, the wise-eyes, the smarty-party, the gook with a book and his jaws full of saws, who said, "The evil that men do lives after them . . ."? He didn't know Lutch Crawford. Lutch did good.

Look at the guy in the mirror. Lutch did that.

Lutch isn't dead. I never killed anybody.

I told you and told you and told you that I want to make my own damn way! I don't want this face! And now that I have this all written down I'm going out. You couldn't make me a big guy too, could you, Lutch? I'm going out through the top sash. I can get through. And then six floors, face first.

Fawn—

THEY say, "Ever been in jail?" and people laugh. People make jokes about jail. It's bad, being in jail. Particularly if you're in for something you didn't do. It's worse if you did do it; makes you feel like such a damn fool for getting caught. It's still worse if you have a cellmate like Crawley. Jail's a place for keeping cons out of the way a while. A guy isn't supposed to go nuts in one.

Crawley was his name and crawly he was. A middle-sized guy with a brown face. Spindly arms and legs. Stringy neck. But the biggest chest I ever did see on a man his size. I don't care what kind of a shirt they put on him. The bigger it was, the farther the cuffs hung past his hands and the tighter it was over his chest. I never seen anything like it. He was the kind of a lookin' thing that stops traffic wherever he goes. Sort of a humpback with the hump in front. I'm not in the cell two weeks when I get this freak for a jail buddy. I'm a lucky guy. I'm the kind of lug that slips and breaks his neck on the way up to collect a jackpot playing Screeno in the movies. I find hundred-dollar bills on the street and the man with the net scoops me up for passing counterfeits. I get human spiders like Crawley for cellmates.

He talked like a man having his toenails pulled out. He breathed all the time so you could hear it. He made you wish he'd stop it. He made you feel like stopping it. It whistled.

Two guards brought him in. One guard was enough for most cons, but I guess that chest scared them. No telling what a man built like that might be able to do. Matter of fact he was so weak he couldn't lift a bar of soap even. Hadn't, anyway, from the looks of him. A man couldn't get that crummy in a nice clean jail like ours without leaving soap alone right from the time they deloused him when they booked him in. So I said, "What'smatter, bull, I ain't lonely," and the guard said, "Shut the face. This thing's got his rent paid in advance an' a reservation here," and he pushed the freak into the cell. I said, "Upper bunk, friend," and turned my face to the wall. The guards went away and for a long time nothing happened.

After a while I heard him scratching himself. That was all right in itself but I never heard a man scratch himself before o it echoed. I mean inside him; it was as if that huge chest was a box and sounding board. I rolled over and looked at him. He'd stripped off the shirt and was burrowing his fingers into his chest. As soon as he caught my eye he stopped, and in spite of his swarthy skin, I could see him blush.

"What the hell are you doing?" I asked.

He grinned and shook his head. His teeth were very clean and strong. He looked very stupid. I said, "Cut it out, then."

It was about eight o'clock, and the radio in the area below the tiers of cell-blocks was blaring out a soap opera about a woman's trials and tribs with her second marriage. I didn't like it, but the guard did, so we heard it every night. You get used to things like that and after a week or so begin to follow them. So I rolled out of the bunk and went to the gratings to listen. Crawley was a hulk over in the corner; he'd been here about twenty minutes now and still had nothing to say, which was all right with me.

The radio play dragged on and wound up as usual with another crisis in the life of the heroine, and who the hell really cared, but you'd tune in tomorrow night just to see if it would really be as dopey as you figured. Anyway, that was 8:45, and the lights would go out at nine. I moved back to my bunk, laid out a blanket, and began washing my face at the little sink by the door. At ten minutes to, I was ready to turn in, and Crawley still hadn't moved. I said:

"Figurin' to stay up all night?"

He started. "I—I—no, but I couldn't possibly get into that upper bunk."

I looked him over. His toothpick arms and legs looked too spindly to support a sparrow's weight, let alone the tremendous barrel of a chest. The chest looked powerful enough to push the rest of him through a twenty-foot wall. I just didn't know.

"You mean you can't climb up?"

He shook his head. So did I. I turned in. "What are you going to do? The guard'll look in in a minute. If you ain't in your bunk you'll get solitary. I been there, fella. You wouldn't like it. All by yourself. Dark. Stinks. No radio; no one to talk to; no nothin'. Better try to get into that bunk." I turned over.

A minute later he said, without moving, "No use trying. I couldn't make it anyway."

Nothing happened until three minutes to nine when the lights blinked. I said "Hell!" and swung into the upper bunk, being careful to put my lucky bone elephant under the mattress first. Without saying a word—and "thanks" was noticeably the word he didn't say—he got into the lower just as we heard footsteps of the guard coming along our deck. I went to sleep wondering why I ever did a thing like that for a homely looking thing like Crawley.

The bell in the morning didn't wake him; I had to. Sure, I should've let him sleep. What was he to me? Why not let the guard pitch icewater on him and massage his feet with a night-stick? Well, that's me. Sucker. I broke a man's cheekbone once for kicking a cur-dog. The dog turned around and bit me afterwards. Anyway, I hopped out of my bunk—almost killed myself; forgot for a minute it was an upper—and, seeing Crawley lying there whistling away out of his lungs, I put out a hand to shake him. But the hand stopped cold. I saw something.

His chest was open a little. No, not cut. Open, like it was hinged—open like a clam in a fish market. Like a clam, too, it closed while I watched, a little more with each breath he took. I saw a man pulled out of the river one time in the fall. He'd drowned in the summer. That was awful. This was worse. I was shaking all over. I was sweating. I wiped my upper lip with my wrist and moved down and grabbed his feet and twisted them so he rolled off the bunk and fell on the floor. He squeaked and I said, "Hear that bell? That means you're through sleeping; remember?" Then I went and stuck my head under the faucet. That made me feel better. I saw I'd been afraid of this Crawley feller for a minute. I was just sore now. I just didn't like him.

He got up off the floor very slowly, working hard to get his feet under him. He always moved like that, like a man with nothing in his stomach and two hundred pounds on his back. He had to sort of coil his legs under him and then hand-over-hand up the bunk supports. He was weak as a duck. He wheezed for a minute and then sat down to put on his pants. A man has to be sick or lazy to do that. I stood drying my face and looking at him through the rag towel.

"You sick?" He looked up and said no.

"What's the matter with you?"

"Nothing. I told you that last night. What do you care anyway?"

"Mind your mouth, cellmate. They used to call me Killer back home. I tore a guy's arm off one time and beat him over the head with the bloody end of it. He was a little freak like you. He didn't excuse himself when he walked in front of me."

Crawley took all this noise calmly enough. He just sat there looking up at me with muddy eyes and didn't say anything. It made me sore. I said, "I don't think I like you. See that crack on the floor? That one there. You stay on this side of it. Cross that line and I pop you. See?"

Now that was a dirty trick; the running water was on "my" side of the line, and so was the cell door, where he'd have to go to get his eats. So was the bunk. He got up off the bunk clumsy-like, and crossed over to the window and stood with his back to it, looking at me. He didn't look scared and he didn't look sore and he didn't look sorry. He just watched me, quiet, obedient like a hound-dog, but all patient and hatred inside like a fat tabby-cat. I snorted and turned my back to him, grasping the grating, waiting for chow. Prison rules were that if a man didn't want to eat he didn't have to. If he didn't want to eat he wouldn't show up at the grating when the mess wagon came along his deck. If he was sick, there was a sick-call at ten o'clock. That was none of the trusty's business, the guy who pushed the wagon. He fed whoever was reaching through the bars with his square messkit and his tin cup and spoon.

So I hung out there, and Crawley was backed up against the other wall and I could feel his eyes on my back. My mind was clicking right along. Funny, though. Like—well, like this:

"I oughta get paid for having to bunk with a sideshow. By God I will get paid, too. I got two messkits, his and mine. *I can feel them eyes*. Here's one time I get four prunes and four pieces of bread and by golly enough prune-juice to really sweeten that lousy coffee. Hot dam—tomorrow's Wednesday. Two eggs instead of one! I'll starve the — until he gets so weak an' sick they'll ship him out of here. Oh, boy—wait'll Sunday! Wait'll that misshapen cockroach has to watch me eatin' two lumps of ice cream! An' if he squeals I'll break his neck an' stuff it under his belt. *I can feel—two sets of eyes!*"

The wagon came. I stuck out one kit. A spoon of oatmeal and a dribble of watered, canned milk in one side; two prunes and juice in the other. Coffee in the cup. Two hunks of bread on the cup. I quickly stuck out the other kit. The trusty didn't even look. He filled up again and moved on. I backed away with a kit in each fist. I was afraid to turn around. There was one guy behind me and I could feel two pairs of eyes on my back. I spilled a couple of drops of coffee from my left hand and saw I was shaking. I stood there like a damn fool because I was afraid to turn around.

I said to myself, what the hell, he could not pull his finger out of a tub of lard and he's got you on the run. Put down the grub and walk on him. If you don't like his eyes, close 'em. Close all—I gulped—*four of them.*

Aw, this was silly. I went over to him and said, "Here," and gave him his messkit. I spooned a little oatmeal into his dish. I told him to go and sit on his bunk and eat. I showed him how to sweeten his coffee with prune-juice. I don't know why I did it. I don't know why I never reminded him again about the line. He didn't say a damn thing. Not even thanks.

I ate and washed my kit before he was half through. He chewed enough for two people. I guess I knew from the start that there was more to him than just one guy. When he was done he sat there looking at me again. He put his kit on the floor beside him and then went and stood by the window. I was going to say something to him about it, but I figured I'd let him be.

It was raining, gloomy outside. That was lousy. On a clear day they let us in the yard for an hour in the afternoon. Rainy days we had a half-hour in the area under the cell-blocks. If you had money you could get candy and smokes and magazines. If you didn't have money you did without. I still had twenty cents. I was rolling my own, stretching it. Wasn't nobody going to bring me cash money. I was doing a little sixty-day stretch for something that doesn't matter very much, and if I watched it I could keep smoking until I was done here.

Well, anyway, on rainy days there's not much to do. You make your bunk. If you have a break, you can usually drag up something interesting to talk about with your cellmate. As long as your cell is halfway clean looking, it's okay, but they're all scrubbed bone-white and chrome-shiny because that's all there is to do. After I'd sat for an hour and a half smoking more than I could afford and trying to find something new to think about, I grabbed the bucket and brush and began to polish the floor. I made up my mind to do just half of it. That was a bright idea. When the guards came around inspecting for dirty cells at ten-thirty, one-half of this one would look crummy because the other half would be really scrubbed. That and Crawley's dirty messkit would get him into a nice jam. The guards knew by this time how I kept my cell.

Feeling almost happy at the idea, I turned to and began wearing out my knees and knuckles. I really bore down. When I came to the middle of the cell I went back and started over. I worked right up to Crawley's messkit. I stopped there. I picked it up and washed it and put it away. Crawley moved over to the clean half. I finished washing the floor. It certainly looked well. All over. Ah, don't ask me why.

I put the gear away and sat down for a while. I tried to kid myself that I felt good because I'd shown that lazy monstrosity up. Then I realized I didn't feel good at all. What was he doing; pushing me around? I looked up and glared at him. He didn't say anything. I went on sitting. Hell with him. This was the pay-off. Why, I wouldn't even talk to him. Let him sit there and rot, the worthless accident.

After a while I said, "What's the rap?"

He looked up at me inquiringly. "What are you in for?" I asked again.

"Vag."

"No visible means of support, or no address?"

"Visible."

"What'd the man in black soak you?"

"I ain't seen him. I don't know how much it's good for."

"Oh; waiting trial, huh?"

"Yeah. Friday noon. I got to get out of here before that." I laughed. "Got a lawyer?"

He shook his head.

"Listen," I told him, "you're not in here on somebody's complaint, you know. The county put you here and the county'll prosecute. They won't retract the charge to spring you. What's your bail?"

"Three hundred."

"Have you got it?" I asked. He shook his head.

"Can you get it?"

"Not a chance."

"An' you 'got to get out of here'."

"I will."

"Not before Friday."

"Uh-huh. Before Friday. Tomorrow. Stick around; you'll see."

I looked at him, his toothpick arms and legs. "Nobody ever broke this jail and it's forty-two years old. I'm six foot three an' two-twenty soaking wet, an' I wouldn't try it. What chance you got?"

He said again, "Stick around."

I sat and thought about that for a while. I could hardly believe it. The man couldn't lift his own weight off the floor. He had no more punch than a bedbug, and a lot less courage. And he was going to break this jail, with its twelve-foot walls and its case-hardened steel bars! Sure, I'd stick around.

"You're as dumb as you look," I said. "In the first place, it's dumb to even dream about cracking this bastille. In the second place, it's dumb not to wait for your trial, take your rap—it won't be more than sixty—and then you get out of here clean."

"You're wrong," he said. There was an urgency about his strange, groaning voice. "I'm waiting trial. They haven't mugged me or printed me or given me an examination. If they convict me—and they will if I ever go to court—they'll give me a physical. Any doc—even a prison doc—would give his eyeteeth to X-ray me." He tapped his monstrous chest. "I'll never get away from them if they see the plates."

"What's your trouble?"

"It's no trouble. It's the way I am."

"How are you?"

"Fine. How are you?"

Okay, so it was none of my business. I shut up. But I was astonished at that long spiel of his. I didn't know he could talk that much.

Lunch came and went, and he got his share, in spite of myself, a little more. Nothing much was said; Crawley just didn't seem to be interested in anything that went on around him. You'd think a guy whose trial is coming up would worry about it. You'd think a guy who was planning a jail-break would worry about it. Not Crawley. He just sat and waited for the time to come. Damn if I didn't do all his fretting for him!

At two o'clock the bolts shot back. I said, "Come on, Crawley. We got a chance to stretch our legs in the area. If you got any money you can buy something to read or smoke."

Crawley said, "I'm okay here. Besides, I got no money. They sell candy?"

"Yeah."

"You got money?"

"Yep. Twenty cents. Tobacco for me for another two weeks at the rate of two or three home-made cigarettes per day. There ain't one penny for anyone or anything else."

"Hell with that. Bring back four candy bars. Two marshmallow, one coconut, one fudge."

I laughed in his face and went out, thinking that here was one time when I'd have a story to tell the rest of the boys that would keep a lifer laughing. But somehow I never did get a chance to say anything to anybody about Crawley. I couldn't tell you how it happened. I started to talk to one fellow and the guard called him over. I said howdy to another and he told me to dry up, he had some blues he wanted to soak in. It just didn't work out. Once I really thought I had a start—one of the stoolies, this time; but just as I said, "Hey, you ought to get a load of my cellmate," the bell rang for us to get back in the cells. I just had time to get to the prison store before the shutter banged down over the counter. I went back up to my deck and into my cell. I pitched Crawley his candy bars. He took them without saying aye, yes, or no—or thanks.

Hardly a word passed between us until long after supper. He wanted to know how to fix one blanket so it felt like two. I showed him. Then I hopped into the upper bunk and said:

"Try sleepin' tonight."

He said, "What's the matter with you?"

"You was talking in your sleep last night."

"I wasn't talking to myself," he said defensively.

"You sure wasn't talking to me."

"I was talking to—my brother," said Crawley, and he laughed. My God, what a laugh that was. It was sort of dragged out of him, and it was grating and high-pitched and muffled and it went on and on. I looked over the edge of the bunk, thinking maybe he wasn't laughing, maybe he was having a fit. His face was strained, his eyes were screwed shut. All right, but his mouth was shut. His lips were clamped tight together. *His mouth was shut* and he went on laughing! He was laughing from inside somewhere, from his chest, some way I never even heard of before. I couldn't stand it. If that laughing didn't stop right away I'd have to stop breathing. My heart would stop breathing. My life was squirting out through my pores, turning to sweat. The laughter went higher and higher, just as loud, just as shrill, and I knew I could hear it and

Crawley could, but no one else. It went up and up until I stopped hearing it, but even then I knew it was still going on and up, and though I couldn't hear it any more, I knew when it stopped. My back teeth ached from the way my jaws had driven them into the gums. I think I passed out, and then slept afterward. I don't remember the lights going out at nine, or the guards checking up.

I been slugged before, many a time, and I know what it's like to come to after being knocked out. But when I came out of this it was more like waking up, so I must have slept. Anyway, it wasn't morning. Must have been about three or four, before the sun came up. There was a weak moon hanging around outside the old walls, poking a gray finger in at us, me and Crawley. I didn't move for a few minutes, and I heard Crawley talking. And I heard someone else answering.

Crawley was saying something about money. "We got to get money, Bub. This is a hell of a jam. We thought we didn't need it. We could get anything we wanted without it. See what happened? Just because I'm no beauty winner a cop asks us questions. They stick us in here. Now we've got to break it. Oh, we can do it; but if we get some money it don't have to happen again. You can figure something, can't you, Bub?"

And then came the answering voice. It was the grating one that had been laughing before. That wasn't Crawley's voice! That belonged to somebody else. Aw, that was foolish. Two men to a cell. One man to a bunk. But here were two men talking, and I wasn't saying anything. I suddenly had a feeling my brains were bubbling like an egg frying in too much grease.

The voice shrilled, "Oh, sure. Money's no trouble to get. Not the way we work, Crawley! He, he!" They laughed together. My blood felt so cold I was afraid to move in case my veins broke. The voice went on. "About this break; you know just what we're going to do?"

"Yeh," said Crawley. "Gee, Bub, I'd sure be wuthless without you. Man, what a brain, what a brain!"

The voice said, "You don't have to do without me! Heh! Just you try and get rid of me!"

I took a deep, quiet breath and slowly raised up and hung my head over the edge of the bunk so I could see. I couldn't be scared any more. I couldn't be shocked any more. After seeing that, I was through. A guy lives all his life for a certain moment. Like that little old doc that delivered the quints.

He never did anything like it before. He never did again. From then on he was through. Like a detective in a book solving a crime. It all leads up to one thing—who done it? When the dick finds that out, he's through. The book's finished. Like me; I was finished when I saw Crawley's brother. That was the high point.

Yeah, it was his brother. Crawley was twins. Like them Siamese twins, but one was big and the other was small. Like a baby. There was only the top part of him, and he was growing out of Crawley's chest. But that oversize chest was just built for the little one to hide in. It folded around the little one. It was hinged like I said before, something like a clamshell. My God!

I said it was like a baby. I meant just small like that. It wasn't baby stuff, aside from that. The head was shaggy, tight-curled. The face was long and lean with smooth, heavy eyebrows. The skin was very dark, and there was little crooked fangs on each side of the mouth, two up, two down. The ears were just a little pointed. That thing had sense of its own, and it was bad clear through. I mean really bad. That thing was all Crawley's crime-brains. Crawley was just a smart mule to that thing. He carried it around with him and he did what it wanted him to do. Crawley obeyed that brother of his—and so did *everybody else!* I did. My tobacco money; cleaning the cell; seeing that Crawley got fed—that was all the little twin's doing, all of it. It wasn't my fault. Nobody *ever* pushed me around like that before!

Then it saw me. It had thrown its hideous little head back to laugh, and it flung up a withered arm and piped, "You! Go to sleep! *Now!*" So—I did.

I don't know how it happened. If I'd slept all that time the bulls would have taken me to the ward. But so help me, from that time until two o'clock I don't know what happened. The Crawley twins kept me fogged, I guess. But I must have gotten dressed and washed; I must have eaten, and I'll guarantee that the Crawleys didn't wash no messkits. Anyhow, the next thing I remember is the bolt shooting back on the cell door. Crawley came up behind me as I stood there looking at it, and I felt his eyes on my back. Four eyes. He said:

"Go on. What are you waiting for?"

I said: "You've done something to me. What is it?"

He just said, "Get going."

We walked out together, out along the deck and down two

183

long flights of iron stairs to the area. We took maybe fifteen, maybe twenty steps, and then Crawley whispered, *"Now!"*

I was loaded with H. E. I was primed and capped, and the firing pin of his voice stung me. I went off like that. There were two guards in front of me. I took them by their necks and cracked their heads together so powerfully that their skulls seemed soft. I screamed and turned and bounded up the stairs, laughing and shouting. Prisoners scattered. A guard grabbed at me on the first landing. I picked him up and threw him over my shoulder and ran upward. A gun blammed twice, and each bullet went *thuck!* as it bored into the body of the bull I carried. He snatched at the railing as I ran and I heard the bones in his wrist crackle. I pitched him over the rail and he landed on another guard down there in the area. The other guard was drawing a bead on me and when the body struck him his gun went off. The slug ricocheted from the steps and flew into the mouth of a prisoner on the second deck. I was screaming much louder than he was. I reached the third deck and ran around the cell-block chattering and giggling. I slid to a stop and threw my legs over the railing and sat there swinging my feet. Two cops opened fire on me. Their aim was lousy because only three out of the twelve bullets hit me. I stood on the lower rail and leaned my calves against the upper one and spread out my arms and shouted at them, cursing them with my mouth full of blood. The prisoners were being herded six and eight to a cell, down on the area level. The guards in the area suddenly stood aside, making way like courtiers for the royalty of a man with a submachine gun. The gun began singing to me. It was a serenade to a giant on a balcony, by a grizzled troubadour with a deep-toned instrument. I couldn't resist that music for more than a moment, so I came down to the area, turning over and over in the air, laughing and coughing and sobbing as I fell.

You watched me, didn't you, you flatfooted blockheads? You got out your guns and ran from the doors, from the series of searching rooms, booking rooms, desk rooms, bull-pens? You left the doors open when you ran? Crawley's out in the street now. No hurry for Crawley. Crawley gives the orders wherever he is. There'll be others—like me.

I've done work for Crawley. See me now? And—Crawley didn't even say, "Thanks."

I'LL have to start with an anecdote or two that you may have heard from me before, but they'll bear repeating, since it's Kelley we're talking about.

I shipped out with Kelley when I was a kid. Tankships, mostly coastwise: load somewhere in the oil country—New Orleans, Aransas Pass, Port Arthur, or some such—and unload at ports north of Hatteras. Eight days out, eighteen hours in, give or take a day or six hours. Kelley was ordinary seaman on my watch, which was a laugh; he knew more about the sea than anyone aft of the galley. But he never ribbed me, stumbling around the place with my blue A.B. ticket. He had a sense of humor in his peculiar quiet way, but he never gratified it by proofs of the obvious—that he was twice the seaman I could ever be.

There were a lot of unsual things about Kelley, the way he looked, the way he moved; but most unusual was the way he thought. He was like one of those extra-terrestrials you read about, who can think as well as a human being but not *like* a human being.

Just for example, there was that night in Port Arthur. I was sitting in a honkytonk up over a bar with a red-headed girl called Red, trying to mind my own business while watching a chick known as Boots, who sat alone over by the juke-box. This girl Boots was watching the door and grinding her teeth, and I knew why, and I was worried. See, Kelley had been seeing her pretty regularly, but this trip he'd made the break and word was around that he was romancing a girl in Pete's place—a very unpopular kind of rumor for Boots to be chewing on. I also knew that Kelley would be along any minute because he'd promised to meet me here.

And in he came, running up that long straight flight of steps easy as a cat, and when he got in the door everybody just hushed, except the juke-box, and it sounded scared.

Now, just above Boots' shoulder on a little shelf was an electric fan. It had sixteen-inch blades and no guard. The very second Kelley's face showed in the doorway Boots rose up like a snake out of a basket, reached behind her, snatched that fan off the shelf and threw it.

It might as well have been done with a slow-motion camera

as far as Kelley was concerned. He didn't move his feet at all. He bent sideways, just a little, from the waist, and turned his wide shoulders. Very clearly I heard three of those whining blade-tips touch a button on his shirt *bip-bip-bip!* and then the fan hit the doorpost.

Even the juke-box shut up then. It was *so* quiet. Kelley didn't say anything and neither did anyone else.

Now, if you believe in do-as-you-get-done-to, and someone heaves an infernal machine at you, you'll pick it right up and heave it back. But Kelley doesn't think like you. He didn't look at the fan. He just watched Boots, and she was white and crazed-looking, waiting for whatever he might have in mind.

He went across the room to her, fast but not really hurrying, and he picked her out from behind that table, and he threw her.

He threw her at the fan.

She hit the floor and slid, sweeping up the fan where it lay, hitting the doorjamb with her head, spinning out into the stairway. Kelley walked after her, stepped over her, went on downstairs and back to the ship.

And there was the time we shipped a new main spur gear for the starboard winch. The deck engineer used up the whole morning watch trying to get the old gear-wheel off its shaft. He heated the hub. He pounded it. He put in wedges. He hooked on with a handybilly—that's a four-sheave block-and-tackle to you—and all he did with that was break a U-bolt.

Then Kelley came on deck, rubbing sleep out of his eyes, and took one brief look. He walked over to the winch, snatched up a crescent wrench, and relieved the four bolts that held the housing tight around the shaft. He then picked up a twelve-pound maul, hefted it, and swung it just once. The maul hit the end of the shaft and the shaft shot out of the other side of the machine like a torpedo out of its tube. The gearwheel fell down on the deck. Kelley went forward to take the helm and thought no more about it, while the deck crew stared after him, wall-eyed. You see what I mean? Problem: Get a wheel off a shaft. But in Kelly's book it's: Get the shaft out of the wheel.

I kibitzed him at poker one time and saw him discard two pair and draw a winning straight flush. Why that discard?

Because he'd just realized the deck was stacked. Why the flush? God knows. All Kelley did was pick up the pot—a big one—grin at the sharper, and leave.

I have plenty more yarns like that, but you get the idea. The guy had a special way of thinking, that's all, and it never failed him.

I lost track of Kelley. I came to regret that now and then; he made a huge impression on me, and sometimes I used to think about him when I had a tough problem to solve. What would Kelley do? And sometimes it helped, and sometimes it didn't; and when it didn't, I guess it was because I'm not Kelley.

I came ashore and got married and did all sorts of other things, and the years went by, and a war came and went, and one warm spring evening I went into a place I know on West 48th St. because I felt like drinking *tequila* and I can always get it there. And who should be sitting in a booth finishing up a big Mexican dinner but—no, not Kelley.

It was Milton. He looks like a college sophomore with money. His suits are always cut just so, but quiet; and when he's relaxed he looks as if he's just been tagged for a fraternity and it matters to him, and when he's worried you want to ask him has he been cutting classes again. It happens he's a damn good doctor.

He was worried, but he gave me a good hello and waved me into the booth while he finished up. We had small talk and I tried to buy him a drink. He looked real wistful and then shook his head. "Patient in ten minutes," he said, looking at his watch.

"Then it's nearby. Come back afterward."

"Better yet," he said, getting up, "come with me. This might interest you, come to think of it."

He got his hat and paid Rudy, and I said, *"Luego,"* and Rudy grinned and slapped the *tequila* bottle. Nice place, Rudy's.

"What about the patient?" I asked as we turned up the avenue. I thought for a while he hadn't heard me, but at last he said, "Four busted ribs and a compound femoral. Minor internal hemorrhage which might or might not be a ruptured spleen. Necrosis of the oral frenum—or was while there was any frenum left."

"What's a frenum?"

187

"That little strip of tissue under your tongue."

"Ongk," I said, trying to reach it with the tip of my tongue. "What a healthy fellow."

"Pulmonary adhesions," Milton ruminated. "Not serious, certainly not tubercular. But they hurt and they bleed and I don't like 'em. And acne rosacea."

"That's the nose like a stop light, isn't it?"

"It isn't as funny as that to the guy that has it."

I was quelled. "What was it—a goon-squad?"

He shook his head.

"A truck?"

"No."

"He fell off something."

Milton stopped and turned and looked me straight in the eye. "No," he said. "Nothing like anything. Nothing," he said, walking again, "at all."

I said nothing to that because there was nothing to say.

"He just went to bed," said Milton thoughtfully, "because he felt off his oats. And one by one these things happened to him."

"In *bed?*"

"Well," said Milton, in a to-be-absolutely-accurate tone, "when the ribs broke he was on his way back from the bathroom."

"You're kidding."

"No I'm not."

"He's lying."

Milton said, "I believe him."

I know Milton. There's no doubt that he believed the man. I said, "I keep reading things about psychosomatic disorders. But a broken—what did you say it was?"

"Femur. Thigh, that is. Compound. Oh, it's rare, all right. But it can happen, has happened. These muscles are pretty powerful, you know. They deliver two-fifty, three hundred pound thrusts every time you walk up stairs. In certain spastic hysteriae, they'll break bones easily enough."

"What about all those other things?"

"Functional disorders, every one of 'em. No germ disease."

"Now this boy," I said, "*really* has something on his mind."

"Yes, he has."

But I didn't ask what. I could hear the discussion closing as if it had a spring latch on it.

We went into a door tucked between store fronts and

climbed three flights. Milton put out his hand to a bell-push and then dropped it without ringing. There was a paper tacked to the door.

DOC I WENT FOR SHOTS COME ON IN.

It was unsigned. Milton turned the knob and we went in.

The first thing that hit me was the smell. Not too strong, but not the kind of thing you ever forget if you ever had to dig a slit trench through last week's burial pit. "That's the necrosis," muttered Milton. "Damn it." He gestured. "Hang your hat over there. Sit down. I'll be out soon." He went into an inner room, saying, "Hi, Hal," at the doorway. From inside came an answering rumble, and something twisted in my throat to hear it, for no voice which is that tired should sound that cheerful.

I sat watching the wallpaper and laboriously un-listening those clinical grunts and the gay-weary responses in the other room. The wall-paper was awful. I remember a night-club act where Reginald Gardiner used to give sound-effect renditions of wallpaper designs. This one, I decided, would run "Body to *weep* . . . yawp, yawp; body to weep . . . yawp, yawp," very faintly, with the final syllable a straining retch. I had just reached a particularly clumsy join where the paper utterly demolished its own rhythm and went "Yawp yawp body to *weep*" when the outer door opened and I leaped to my feet with the rush of utter guilt one feels when caught in an unlikely place with no curt and lucid explanation.

He was two long strides into the room, tall and soft-footed, his face and long green eyes quite at rest, when he saw me. He stopped as if on leaf springs and shock absorbers, not suddenly, completely controlled, and asked, "Who are you?"

"I'll be damned," I answered. "Kelley!"

He peered at me with precisely the expression I had seen so many times when he watched the little square windows on the one-arm bandits we used to play together. I could almost hear the tumblers, see the drums; not lemon . . . cherry . . . cherry . . . and *click!* this time but tankship . . . Texas . . . him! . . . and *click!* "I be god dam," he drawled, to indicate that he was even more surprised than I was. He transferred the small package he carried from his right hand to his left and shook hands. His hand went once and a half times around mine with enough left over to tie a half-hitch. "Where in time you been keepin' yourse'f? How'd you smoke me out?"

"I never," I said. (Saying it, I was aware that I always fell into the idiom of people who impressed me, to the exact degree of that impression. So I always found myself talking more like Kelley than Kelley's shaving mirror.) I was grinning so wide my face hurt. "I'm glad to see you." I shook hands with him again, foolishly. "I came with the doctor."

"You a doctor now?" he said, his tone prepared for wonders.

"I'm a writer," I said deprecatingly.

"Yeah, I heard," he reminded himself. His eyes narrowed; as of old, it had the effect of sharp-focussing a searchlight beam. "I heard!" he repeated, with deeper interest. "Stories. Gremlins and flyin' saucers an' all like that." I nodded. He said, without insult, "Hell of a way to make a living."

"What about you?"

"Ships. Some drydock. Tank cleaning. Compass 'djustin'. For a while had a job holdin' a insurance inspector's head. You know."

I glanced at the big hands that could weld or steer or compute certainly with the excellence I used to know, and marvelled that he found himself so unremarkable. I pulled myself back to here and now and nodded toward the inner room. "I'm holding you up."

"No you ain't. Milton, he knows what he's doin'. He wants me, he'll holler."

"Who's sick?"

His face darkened like the sea in scud-weather, abruptly and deep down. "My brother." He looked at me searchingly. "He's . . ." Then he seemed to check himself. "He's sick," he said unnecessarily, and added quickly, "He's going to be all right, though."

"Sure," I said quickly.

I had the feeling that we were both lying and that neither of us knew why.

Milton came out, laughing a laugh that cut off as soon as he was out of range of the sick man. Kelley turned to him slowly, as if slowness were the only alternative to leaping on the doctor, pounding the news out of him. "Hello, Kelley. Heard you come in."

"How is he, Doc?"

Milton looked up quickly, his bright round eyes clashing with Kelley's slitted fierce ones. "You got to take it easy, Kelley. What'll happen to him if you crack up?"

"Nobody's cracking up. What do you want me to do?"

Milton saw the package on the table. He picked it up and opened it. There was a leather case and two phials. "Ever use one of these before?"

"He was a pre-med before he went to sea," I said suddenly.

Milton stared at me. "You two know each other?"

I looked at Kelley. "Sometimes I think I invented him."

Kelley snorted and thumped my shoulder. Happily I had one hand on a built-in china shelf. His big hand continued the motion and took the hypodermic case from the doctor. "Sterilize the shaft and needle," he said sleepily, as if reading. "Assemble without touching needle with fingers. To fill, puncture diaphragm and withdraw plunger. Squirt upward to remove air an' prevent embolism. Locate major vein in—"

Milton laughed. "Okay, okay. But forget the vein. Any place will do—it's subcutaneous, that's all. I've written the exact amounts to be used for exactly the symptoms you can expect. Don't jump the gun, Kelley. And remember how you salt your stew. Just because a little is good, it doesn't figure that a lot has to be better."

Kelley was wearing that sleepy inattention which, I remembered, meant only that he was taking in every single word like a tape recorder. He tossed the leather case gently, caught it. "Now?" he said.

"Not now," the doctor said positively. "Only when you have to."

Kelley seemed frustrated. I suddenly understood that he wanted to do something, build something, fight something. Anything but sit and wait for therapy to bring results. I said, "Kelley, any brother of yours is a—well, you know. I'd like to say hello, if it's all—"

Immediately and together Kelley and the doctor said loudly, "Sure, when he's on his feet," and "Better not just now, I've just given him a sedat—" And together they stopped awkwardly.

"Let's go get that drink," I said before they could flounder any more.

"Now you're talking. You too, Kelley. It'll do you good."

"Not me," said Kelley. "Hal—"

"I knocked him out," said the doctor bluntly. "You'll cluck around scratching for worms and looking for hawks till you wake him up, and he needs his sleep. Come on."

Painfully I had to add to my many mental images of Kelley the very first one in which he was indecisive. I hated it.

"Well," said Kelley, "let me go see."

He disappeared. I looked at Milton's face, and turned quickly away. I was sure he wouldn't want me to see that expression of sick pity and bafflement.

Kelley came out, moving silently as always. "Yeah, asleep," he said. "For how long?"

"I'd say four hours at least."

"Well all right." From the old-fashioned clothes tree he took a battered black engineer's cap with a shiny, crazed patent leather visor. I laughed. Both men turned to me, with annoyance, I thought.

On the landing outside I explained. "The hat," I said. "Remember? Tampico?"

"Oh," he grunted. He thwacked it against his forearm.

"He left it on the bar of this ginmill," I told Milton. "We got back to the gangplank and he missed it. Nothing would do but he has to go back for it, so I went with him."

"You was wearin' a *tequila* label on your face," Kelley said. "Kept tryin' to tell the taxi man you was a bottle."

"He didn't speak English."

Kelley flashed something like his old grin. "He got the idea."

"Anyway," I told Milton, "the place was closed when we got there. We tried the front door and the side doors and they were locked like Alcatraz. We made so much racket I guess if anyone was inside they were afraid to open up. We could see Kelley's hat in there on the bar. Nobody's *about* to steal that hat."

"It's a good hat," he said in an injured tone.

"Kelley goes into action," I said. "Kelley don't think like other people, you know, Milt. He squints through the window at the other wall, goes around the building, sets one foot against the corner stud, gets his fingers under the edge of that corrugated iron siding they use. 'I'll pry this out a bit,' he says. 'You slide in and get my hat.'"

"Corrugated was only nailed on one-by-twos," said Kelley.

"He gives one almighty pull," I chuckled, "and the whole damn side falls out of the building, I mean the second floor too. You never heard such a clap-o'-thunder in your life."

"I got my hat," said Kelley. He uttered two syllables of a laugh. "Whole second floor was a cathouse, an' the one single stairway come out with the wall."

"Taxi driver just took off. But he left his taxi. Kelley drove back. I couldn't. I was laughing."

"You was drunk."

"Well, *some*," I said.

We walked together quietly, happily. Out of Kelley's sight, Milton thumped me gently on the ribs. It was eloquent and it pleased me. It said that it was a long time since Kelley had laughed. It was a long time since he had thought about anything but Hal.

I guess we felt it equally when, with no trace of humor . . . more as if he had let my episode just blow itself out until he could be heard . . . Kelley said, "Doc, what's with the hand?"

"It'll be all right," Milton said.

"You put splints."

Milton sighed. "All right, all right. Three fractures. Two on the middle finger and one on the ring."

Kelley said, "I saw they were swollen."

I looked at Kelley's face and I looked at Milton's, and I didn't like either, and I wished to God I were somewhere else, in a uranium mine maybe, or making out my income tax. I said, "Here we are. Ever been to Rudy's, Kelley?"

He looked up at the little yellow-and-red marquee. "No."

"Come on," I said. "*Tequila.*"

We went in and got a booth. Kelley ordered beer. I got mad then and started to call him some things I'd picked up on waterfronts from here to Tierra del Fuego. Milton stared wall-eyed at me and Kelley stared at his hands. After a while Milton began to jot some of it down on a prescription pad he took from his pocket. I was pretty proud.

Kelley gradually got the idea. If I wanted to pick up the tab and he wouldn't let me, his habits were those of *uno puñeto sin cojones* (which a Spanish dictionary will reliably misinform you means "a weakling without eggs"), and his affections for his forebears were powerful but irreverent. I won, and soon he was lapping up a huge combination plate of beef *tostadas,* chicken *enchiladas,* and pork *tacos.* He endeared himself to Rudy by demanding salt and lemon with his *tequila* and dispatching same with flawless ritual: hold the lemon between left thumb and forefinger, lick the back of the left hand, sprinkle salt on the wet spot, lift the *tequila* with the right, lick the salt, drink the *tequila,* bite the lemon. Soon he was imitating the German second mate we shipped out of Puerto Barrios one night, who ate fourteen green bananas and lost them and all his teeth over the side, in gummed gutturals which had us roaring.

But after that question about fractured fingers back there in the street, Milton and I weren't fooled any more, and though everyone tried hard and it was a fine try, none of the laughter went deep enough or stayed long enough, and I wanted to cry.

We all had a huge hunk of the nesselrode pie made by Rudy's beautiful blond wife—pie you can blow off your plate by flapping a napkin . . . sweet smoke with calories. And then Kelley demanded to know what time it was and cussed and stood up.

"It's only been two hours," Milton said.

"I just as soon head home all the same," said Kelley. "Thanks."

"Wait," I said. I got a scrap of paper out of my wallet and wrote on it. "Here's my phone. I want to see you some more. I'm working for myself these days; my time's my own. I don't sleep much, so call me any time you feel like it."

He took the paper. "You're no good," he said. "You never were no good." The way he said it, I felt fine.

"On the corner is a newsstand," I told him. "There's a magazine called *Amazing* with one of my lousy stories in it."

"They print it on a roll?" he demanded. He waved at us, nodded to Rudy, and went out.

I swept up some spilled sugar on the table top and pushed it around until it was a perfect square. After a while I shoved in the sides until it was a lozenge. Milton didn't say anything either. Rudy, as is his way, had sense enough to stay away from us.

"Well, that did him some good," Milton said after a while.

"You know better than that," I said bitterly.

Milton said patiently. "Kelley thinks *we* think it did him some good. And thinking that does him good."

I had to smile at that contortion, and after that it was easier to talk. "The kid going to live?"

Milton waited, as if some other answer might spring from somewhere, but it didn't. He said, "No."

"Fine doctor."

"Don't kid like that!" he snapped. He looked up at me. "Look, if this was one of those—well, say pleurisy cases on the critical list, without the will to live, why I'd know what to do. Usually those depressed cases have such a violent desire to be reassured, down deep, that you can snap 'em right

194

out of it if only you can think of the right thing to say. And you usually can. But Hal's not one of those. He wants to live. If he didn't want so much to live he'd've been dead three weeks ago. What's killing him is sheer somatic trauma—one broken bone after another, one failing or inflamed internal organ after another."

"Who's doing it?"

"Damn it, *no*body's doing it!" He caught me biting my lip. "If either one of us should say Kelley's doing it, the other one will punch him in the mouth. Right?"

"Right."

"Just so that doesn't have to happen," said Milton carefully, "I'll tell you what you're bound to ask me in a minute: why isn't he in a hospital?"

"Okay, why?"

"He was. For weeks. And all the time he was there these things kept on happening to him, only worse. More, and more often. I got him home as soon as it was safe to get him out of traction for that broken thigh. He's much better off with Kelley. Kelley keeps him cheered up, cooks for him, medicates him—the works. It's all Kelley does these days."

"I figured. It must be getting tough."

"It is. I wish I had your ability with invective. You can't lend that man anything, give him anything . . . proud? God!"

"Don't take this personally, but have you had consultations?"

He shrugged. "Six ways from the middle. And nine-tenths of it behind Kelley's back, which isn't easy. The lies I've told him! Hal's just *got* to have a special kind of Persian melon that someone is receiving in a little store in Yonkers. Out Kelley goes, and in the meantime I have to corral two or three doctors and whip 'em in to see Hal and out again before Kelley gets back. Or Hal has to have a special prescription, and I fix up with the druggist to take a good two hours compounding it. Hal saw Grundage, the osteo man, that way, but poor old Ancelowics the pharmacist got punched in the chops for the delay."

"Milton, you're all right."

He snarled at me, and then went on quietly, "None of it's done any good. I've learned a whole encyclopedia full of wise words and some therapeutic tricks I didn't know existed. But . . ." He shook his head. "Do you know why Kelley and I wouldn't let you meet Hal?" He wet his lips and cast about for an example. "Remember the pictures of Mussolini's corpse after the mob got through with it?"

I shuddered. "I saw 'em."

"Well, that's what he looks like, only he's alive, which doesn't make it any prettier. Hal doesn't know how bad it is, and neither Kelley nor I would run the risk of having him see it reflected in someone else's face. I wouldn't send a wooden Indian into that room."

I began to pound the table, barely touching it, hitting it harder and harder until Milton caught my wrist. I froze then, unhappily conscious of the eyes of everyone in the place looking at me. Gradually the normal sound of the restaurant resumed. "Sorry."

"It's all right."

"There's got to be some sort of reason!"

His lips twitched in a small acid smile. "That's what you get down to at last, isn't it? There's always a reason for everything, and if we don't know it, we can find it out. But just one single example of real unreason is enough to shake our belief in everything. And then the fear gets bigger than the case at hand and extends to a whole universe of concepts labelled 'unproven.' Shows you how little we believe in anything, basically."

"That's a miserable piece of philosophy!"

"Sure. If you have another arrival point for a case like this, I'll buy it with a bonus. Meantime I'll just go on worrying at this one and feeling more scared than I ought to."

"Let's get drunk."

"A wonderful idea."

Neither of us ordered. We just sat there looking at the lozenge of sugar I'd made on the table top. After a while I said, "Hasn't Kelley any idea of what's wrong?"

"You know Kelley. If he had an idea he'd be working on it. All he's doing is sitting by watching his brother's body stew and swell like yeast in a vat."

"What about Hal?"

"He isn't lucid much any more. Not if I can help it."

"But maybe he—"

"Look," said Milton, "I don't want to sound cranky or anything, but I can't hold still for a lot of questions like . . ." He stopped, took out his display handkerchief, looked at it, put it away. "I'm sorry. You don't seem to understand that I didn't take this case yesterday afternoon. I've been sweating it out for nearly three months now. I've already thought of everything you're going to think of. Yes, I questioned Hal, back and forth and sideways. Nothing. N-n-nothing."

That last word trailed off in such a peculiar way that I looked up abruptly. "Tell me," I demanded.

"Tell you what?" Suddenly he looked at his watch. I covered it with my hand. "Come on, Milt."

"I don't know what you're—damn it, leave me alone, will you? If it was anything important, I'd've chased it down long ago."

"Tell me the unimportant something."

"No."

"Tell me why you won't tell me."

"Damn you, I'll do that. It's because you're a crackpot. You're a nice guy and I like you, but you're a crackpot." He laughed suddenly, and it hit me like the flare of a flashbulb. "I didn't know you could look so astonished!" he said. "Now take it easy and listen to me. A guy comes out of a steak house and steps on a rusty nail, and ups and dies of tetanus. But your crackpot vegetarian will swear up and down that the man would still be alive if he hadn't poisoned his system with meat, and uses the death to prove his point. The perennial Dry will call the same casualty a victim of John Barleycorn if he knows the man had a beer with his steak. This one death can be ardently and whole-heartedly blamed on the man's divorce, his religion, his political affiliations or on a hereditary taint from his great-great-grandfather who worked for Oliver Cromwell. You're a nice guy and I like you," he said again, "and I am not going to sit across from you and watch you do the crackpot act."

"I do not know," I said slowly and distinctly, "what the hell you are talking about. And now you *have* to tell me."

"I suppose so," he said sadly. He drew a deep breath. "You believe what you write. No," he said quickly, "I'm not asking you, I'm telling you. You grind out all this fantasy and horror stuff and you believe every word of it. More basically, you'd rather believe in the *outré* and the so-called 'unknowable' than in what I'd call *real* things. You think I'm talking through my hat."

"I do," I said, "but go ahead."

"If I called you up tomorrow and told you with great joy that they'd isolated a virus for Hal's condition and a serum was on the way, you'd be just as happy about it as I would be, but way down deep you'd wonder if that was what was really wrong with him, or if the serum is what really cured him. If on the other hand I admitted to you that I'd found two small punctures on Hal's throat and a wisp of fog slipping out of the room—by God! see what I mean? You have a gleam in your eye already!"

I covered my eyes. "Don't let me stop you now," I said coldly. "Since you are not going to admit Dracula's punctures, what are you going to admit?"

"A year ago Kelley gave his brother a present. An ugly little brute of a Haitian doll. Hal kept it around to make faces at for a while and then gave it to a girl. He had bad trouble with the girl. She hates him—really hates him. As far as anyone knows she still has the doll. Are you happy now?"

"Happy," I said disgustedly. "But Milt—you're not just ignoring this doll thing. Why, that could easily be the whole basis of . . . hey, sit down! Where are you going?"

"I told you I wouldn't sit across from a damn hobbyist. Enter hobbies, exit reason." He recoiled. "Wait—*you* sit down now."

I gathered up a handful of his well-cut lapels. "We'll both sit down," I said gently, "or I'll prove to your heart's desire that I've reached the end of reason."

"Yessir," he said good-naturedly, and sat down. I felt like a damn fool. The twinkle left his eyes and he leaned forward. "Perhaps now you'll listen instead of riding off like that. I suppose you know that in many cases the voodoo doll does work, and you know why?"

"Well, yes. I didn't think you'd admit it." I got no response from his stony gaze, and at last realized that a fantasist's pose of authority on such matters is bound to sit ill with a serious and progressive physician. A lot less positively, I said, "It comes down to a matter of subjective reality, or what some people call faith. If you believe firmly that the mutilation of a doll with which you identify yourself will result in your own mutilation, well, that's what will happen."

"That, and a lot of things even a horror story writer could find out if he researched anywhere else except in his projective imagination. For example, there are Arabs in North Africa today whom you dare not insult in any way really important to them. If they feel injured, they'll threaten to die,

198

and if you call the bluff they'll sit down, cover their heads, and damn well *die*. There are psychosomatic phenomena like the stigmata, or wounds of the cross, which appear from time to time on the hands, feet and breasts of exceptionally devout people. I know you know a lot of this," he added abruptly, apparently reading something in my expression, "but I'm not going to get my knee out of your chest until you'll admit I'm at least capable of taking a thing like this into consideration and tracking it down."

"I never saw you before in my life," I said, and in an important way I meant it.

"Good," he said, with considerable relief. "Now I'll tell you what I did. I jumped at this doll episode almost as wildly as you did. It came late in the questioning because apparently it *really didn't matter* to Hal."

"Oh, well, but the subconscious—"

"Shaddup!" He stuck a surprisingly sharp forefinger into my collarbone. "I'm telling you; you're not telling me. I won't disallow that a deep belief in voodoo might be hidden in Hal's subconscious, but if it is, it's where sodium amytal and word association and light and profound hypnosis and a half-dozen other therapies give not a smidgin of evidence. I'll take that as proof that he carries no such conviction. I guess from the looks of you I'll have to remind you again that I've dug into this thing in more ways for longer and with more tools than you have—and I doubt that it means any less to me than it does to you."

"You know, I'm just going to shut up," I said plaintively.

"High time," he said, and grinned. "No, in every case of voodoo damage or death, there has to be that element of devout belief in the powers of the witch or wizard, and through it a complete sense of identification with the doll. In addition, it helps if the victim knows what sort of damage the doll is sustaining—crushing, or pins sticking into it, or what. And you can take my word for it that no such news has reached Hal."

"What about the doll? Just to be absolutely sure, shouldn't we get it back?"

"I thought of that. But there's no way I know of getting it back without making it look valuable to the woman. And if she thinks it's valuable to Hal, we'll *never* see it."

"Hm. Who is she, and what's her royal gripe?"

"She's as nasty a piece of fluff as they come. She got involved with Hal for a little while—nothing serious, certainly not on his part. He was . . . he's a big good-natured kid who thinks the only evil people around are the ones who get killed at the end of the movie. Kelley was at sea at the time and he blew in to find this little vampire taking Hal for everything she could, first by sympathy, then by threats. The old badger game. Hal was just bewildered. Kelley got his word that nothing had occurred between them, and then forced Hal to lower the boom. She called his bluff and it went to court. They forced a physical examination on her and she got laughed out of court. She wasn't the mother of anyone's unborn child. She never will be. She swore to get even with him. She's without brains or education or resources, but that doesn't stop her from being pathological. She sure can hate."

"Oh. You've seen her."

Milton shuddered. "I've seen her. I tried to get all Hal's gifts back from her. I had to say all because I didn't dare itemize. All I wanted, it might surprise you to know, was that damned doll. Just in case, you know . . . although I'm morally convinced that the thing has nothing to do with it. Now do you see what I mean about a single example of unreason?"

" 'Fraid I do." I felt upset and quelled and sat upon and I wasn't fond of the feeling. I've read too many stories where the scientist just hasn't the imagination to solve a haunt. It had been great, feeling superior to a bright guy like Milton.

We walked out of there and for the first time I felt the mood of a night without feeling that an author was ramming it down my throat for story purposes. I looked at the clean-swept, star-reaching cubism of the Radio City area and its living snakes of neon, and I suddenly thought of an Evelyn Smith story the general idea of which was "After they found out the atom bomb was magic, the rest of the magicians who enchanted refrigerators and washing machines and the telephone system came out into the open." I felt a breath of wind and wondered what it was that had breathed. I heard the snoring of the city and for an awesome second felt it would roll over, open its eyes, and . . . *speak*.

On the corner I said to Milton, "Thanks. You've given me a thumping around. I guess I needed it." I looked at him. "By the Lord I'd like to find some place where you've been stupid in this thing."

"I'd be happy if you could," he said seriously.

I whacked him on the shoulder. "See? You take all the fun out of it."

He got a cab and I started to walk. I walked a whole lot that night, just anywhere. I thought about a lot of things. When I got home the phone was ringing. It was Kelley.

I'm not going to give you a blow-by-blow of that talk with Kelley. It was in that small front room of his place—an apartment he'd rented after Hal got sick, and not the one Hal used to have—and we talked the night away. All I'm withholding is Kelley's expression of things you already know: that he was deeply attached to his brother, that he had no hope left for him, that he would find who or what was responsible and deal with it his way. It is a strong man's right to break down if he must, with whom and where he chooses, and such an occasion is only an expression of strength. But when it happens in a quiet sick place, where he must keep the command of hope strongly in the air; when a chest heaves and a throat must be held wide open to sob silently so that the dying one shall not know; these things are not pleasant to describe in detail. Whatever my ultimate feeling for Kelley, his emotions and the expressions of them are for him to keep.

He did, however, know the name of the girl and where she was. He did not hold her responsible. I thought he might have a suspicion, but it turned out to be only a certainty that this was no disease, no subjective internal disorder. If a great hate and a great determination could solve the problem, Kelley would solve it. If research and logic could solve it, Milton would do it. If I could do it, I would.

She was checking hats in a sleazy club out where Brooklyn and Queens, in a remote meeting, agree to be known as Long Island. The contact was easy to make. I gave her my spring coat with the label outward. It's a good label. When she turned away with it I called her back and drunkenly asked her for the bill in the right-hand pocket. She found it and handed it to me. It was a hundred. "Damn taxis never got change," I mumbled and took it before her astonishment turned to sleight-of-hand. I got out my wallet, crowded the crumpled note into it clumsily enough to display the two other C-notes there, shoved it into the front of my jacket so that it missed the pocket and fell to the floor, and walked off. I walked back before she could lift the hinged counter and

201

skin out after it. I picked it up and smiled foolishly at her. "Lose more business cards that way," I said. Then I brought her into focus. "Hey, you know, you're cute."

I suppose "cute" is one of the four-letter words that describe her. "What's your name?"

"Charity," she said. "But don't get ideas." She was wearing so much pancake makeup that I couldn't tell what her complexion was. She leaned so far over the counter that I could see lipstick stains on her brassiere.

"I don't have a favorite charity yet," I said. "You work here alla time?"

"I go home once in a while," she said.

"What time?"

"One o'clock."

"Tell you what," I confided, "let's both be in front of this place at a quarter after and see who stands who up, okay?" Without waiting for an answer I stuck the wallet into my back pocket so that my jacket hung on it. All the way into the dining room I could feel her eyes on it like two hot, glistening, broiled mushrooms. I came within an ace of losing it to the head waiter when he collided with me, too.

She was there all right, with a yellowish fur around her neck and heels you could have driven into a pine plank. She was up to the elbows in jangly brass and chrome, and when we got into a cab she threw herself on me with her mouth open. I don't know where I got the reflexes, but I threw my head down and cracked her in the cheekbone with my forehead, and when she squeaked indignantly I said I'd dropped the wallet again and she went about helping me find it quietly as you please. We went to a place and another place and an after-hours place, all her choice. They served her sherry in her whiskey-ponies and doubled all my orders, and tilted the checks something outrageous. Once I tipped a waiter eight dollars and she palmed the five. Once she wormed my leather notebook out of my breast pocket thinking it was the wallet, which by this time was safely tucked away in my knit shorts. She did get one enamel cuff link with a rhinestone in it, and my fountain pen. All in all it was quite a duel. I was loaded to the eyeballs with thiamin hydrochloride and caffeine citrate, but a most respectable amount of alcohol soaked through them, and it was all I could do to play it through. I made it, though, and blocked her at every turn until she had

202

no further choice but to take me home. She was furious and made only the barest attempts to hide it.

We got each other up the dim dawnlit stairs, shushing each other drunkenly, both much soberer than we acted, each promising what we expected not to deliver. She negotiated her lock successfully and waved me inside.

I hadn't expected it to be so neat. Or so cold. "I didn't leave that window open," she said complainingly. She crossed the room and closed it. She pulled her fur around her throat. "This is awful."

It was a long low room with three windows. At one end, covered by a venetian blind was a kitchenette. A door at one side of it was probably a bathroom.

She went to the venetian blind and raised it. "Have it warmed up in a jiffy," she said.

I looked at the kitchenette. "Hey," I said as she lit the little oven, "coffee. How's about coffee?"

"Oh, all right," she said glumly. "But talk quiet, huh?"

"Sh-h-h-h." I pushed my lips around with a forefinger. I circled the room. Cheap phonograph and records. Small screen TV. A big double studio couch. A bookcase with no books in it, just china dogs. It occurred to me that her unsubtle approach was probably not successful as often as she might wish.

But where was the thing I was looking for?

"Hey, I wanna powder my nose," I announced.

"In there," she said. "Can't you talk quiet?"

I went into the bathroom. It was tiny. There was a foreshortened tub with a circular frame over it from which hung a horribly cheerful shower curtain, with big red roses. I closed the door behind me and carefully opened the medicine chest. Just the usual. I closed it carefully so it wouldn't click. A built-in shelf held towels.

Must be a closet in the main room, I thought. Hatbox, trunk, suitcase, maybe. Where would I put a devil-doll if I were hexing someone?

I wouldn't hide it away, I answered myself. I don't know why, but I'd sort of have it out in the open somehow . . .

I opened the shower curtain and let it close. Round curtain, square tub.

"Yup!"

I pushed the whole round curtain back, and there in the corner, just at eye level, was a triangular shelf. Grouped on

203

it were four figurines, made apparently from kneaded wax. Three had wisps of hair fastened by candle-droppings. The fourth was hairless, but had slivers of a horny substance pressed into the ends of the arms. Fingernail parings.

I stood for a moment thinking. Then I picked up the hairless doll, turned to the door. I checked myself, flushed the toilet, took a towel, shook it out, dropped it over the edge of the tub. Then I reeled out. "Hey honey, look what I got, ain't it *cute?*"

"Shh!" she said. "Oh for crying out loud. Put that back, will you?"

"Well, what is it?"

"It's none of your business, that's what it is. Come on, put it back."

I wagged my finger at her. "You're not being nice to me," I complained.

She pulled some shreds of patience together with an obvious effort. "It's just some sort of toys I have around. Here."

I snatched it away. "All right, you don't wanna be nice!" I whipped my coat together and began to button it clumsily, still holding the figurine.

She sighed, rolled her eyes, and came to me. "Come on, Dadsy. Have a nice cup of coffee and let's not fight." She reached for the doll and I snatched it away again.

"You got to tell me," I pouted.

"It's pers'nal."

"I wanna be personal," I pointed out.

"Oh all right," she said. "I had a roommate one time, she used to make these things. She said you make one, and s'pose I decide I don't like you, I got something of yours, hair or toenails or something. Say your name is George. What is your name?"

"George," I said.

"All right, I call the doll George. Then I stick pins in it. That's all. Give it to me."

"Who's this one?"

"That's Al."

"Hal?"

"Al. I got one called Hal. He's in there. I hate him the most."

"Yeah, huh. Well, what happens to Al and George and all when you stick pins in 'em?"

"They're s'posed to get sick. Even die."

"Do they?"

"Nah," she said with immediate and complete candor. "I told you, it's just a game, sort of. If it worked believe me old Al would bleed to death. He runs the delicatessen." I handed her the doll, and she looked at it pensively. "I wish it did work, sometimes. Sometimes I almost believe in it. I stick 'em and they just *yell*."

"Introduce me," I demanded.

"What?"

"Introduce me," I said. I pulled her toward the bathroom. She made a small irritated "oh-h," and came along.

"This is Fritz and this is Bruno and—where's the other one?"

"What other one?"

"Maybe he fell behind the—down back of—" She knelt on the edge of the tub and leaned over to the wall, to peer behind it. She regained her feet, her face red from effort and anger. "What are you trying to pull? You kidding around or something?"

I spread my arms. "What you mean?"

"Come on," she said between her teeth. She felt my coat, my jacket. "You hid it some place."

"No I didn't. There was only four." I pointed. "Al and Fritz and Bruno and Hal. Which one's Hal?"

"That's Freddie. He give me twenny bucks and took twenny-three out of my purse, the dirty—. But Hal's gone. He was the best one of all. You *sure* you didn't hide him?" Then she thumped her forehead.

"The window!" she said, and ran into the other room. I was on my four bones peering under the tub when I understood what she meant. I took a last good look around and then followed her. She was standing by the window, shading her eyes and peering out. "What do you know. Imagine somebody would swipe a thing like that!"

A sick sense of loss was born in my solar plexus.

"Aw, forget it. I'll make another one for that Hal. But I'll never make another one that ugly," she added wistfully. "Come on, the coffee's—what's the matter? You sick?"

"Yeah," I said, "I'm sick."

"Of all the things to steal," she said from the kitchenette. "Who do you suppose would do such a thing?"

Suddenly I knew who would. I cracked my fist into my palm and laughed.

"What's the matter, you crazy?"

"Yes," I said. "You got a phone?"

"No. Where you going?"

"Out. Goodbye, Charity."

"Hey, now wait, honey. Just when I got coffee for you."

I snatched the door open. She caught my sleeve.

"You can't go away like this! How's about a little something for Charity?"

"You'll get yours when you make the rounds tomorrow, if you don't have a hangover from those sherry highballs," I said cheerfully. "And don't forget the five you swiped from the tip plate. Better watch out for that waiter, by the way. I think he saw you do it."

"You're not drunk!" she gasped.

"You're not a witch," I grinned. I blew her a kiss and ran out.

I shall always remember her like that, round-eyed, a little more astonished than she was resentful, the beloved dollar signs fading from her hot brown eyes, the pathetic, useless little twitch of her hips she summoned up as a last plea.

Ever try to find a phone booth at five A. M.? I half-trotted nine blocks before I found a cab, and I was on the Queens side of the Triboro Bridge before I found a gas station open.

I dialled. The phone said, "Hello?"

"Kelley!" I roared happily. "Why didn't you tell me? You'd 'a saved sixty bucks worth of the most dismal fun I ever—"

"This is Milton," said the telephone. "Hal just died."

My mouth was still open and I guess it just stayed that way. Anyway it was cold inside when I closed it. "I'll be right over."

"Better not," said Milton. His voice was shaking with incomplete control. "Unless you really want to . . . there's nothing you can do, and I'm going to be . . . busy."

"Where's Kelley?" I whispered.

"I don't know."

"Well," I said. "Call me."

I got back into my taxi and went home. I don't remember the trip.

Sometimes I think I dreamed I saw Kelley that morning.

A lot of alcohol and enough emotion to kill it, mixed with no sleep for thirty hours, makes for blackout. I came up out of it reluctantly, feeling that this was no kind of world to be aware of. Not today.

I lay looking at the bookcase. It was very quiet. I closed my eyes, turned over, burrowed into the pillow, opened my eyes again and saw Kelley sitting in the easy chair, poured out in his relaxed feline fashion, legs too long, arms too long, eyes too long and only partly open.

I didn't ask him how he got in because he was already in, and welcome. I didn't say anything because I didn't want to be the one to tell him about Hal. And besides I wasn't awake yet. I just lay there.

"Milton told me," he said. "It's all right."

I nodded.

Kelley said, "I read your story. I found some more and read them too. You got a lot of imagination."

He hung a cigarette on his lower lip and lit it. "Milton, he's got a lot of knowledge. Now, both of you think real good up to a point. Then too much knowledge presses him off to the no'theast. And too much imagination squeezes you off to the no'thwest."

He smoked a while.

"Me, I think straight through but it takes me a while."

I palmed my eyeballs. "I don't know what you're talking about."

"That's okay," he said quietly. "Look, I'm goin' after what killed Hal."

I closed my eyes and saw a vicious, pretty, empty little face. I said, "I was most of the night with Charity."

"Were you now."

"Kelley," I said, "if it's her you're after, forget it. She's a sleazy little tramp but she's also a little kid who never had a chance. She didn't kill Hal."

"I know she didn't. I don't feel about her one way or the other. I know what killed Hal, though, and I'm goin' after it the only way I know for sure."

"All right then," I said. I let my head dig back into the pillow. "What did kill him?"

"Milton told you about that doll Hal give her."

"He told me. There's nothing in that, Kelley. For a man to be a voodoo victim, he's got to believe that—"

"Yeh, yeh, yeh. Milton told me. For hours he told me."

"Well all right."

"You got imagination," Kelley said sleepily. "Now just imagine along with me a while. Milt tell you how some folks, if you point a gun at 'em and go bang, they drop dead, even if there was only blanks in the gun?"

"He didn't, but I read it somewhere. Same general idea."

"Now imagine all the shootings you ever heard of was like that, with blanks."

"Go ahead."

"You got a lot of evidence, a lot of experts, to prove about this believing business, ever' time anyone gets shot."

"Got it."

"Now imagine somebody shows up with live ammunition in his gun. Do you think those bullets going to give a damn who believes what?"

I didn't say anything.

"For a long time people been makin' dolls and stickin' pins in 'em. Wherever somebody believes it can happen, they get it. Now suppose somebody shows up with the doll all those dolls was copied from. The real one."

I lay still.

"You don't have to know nothin' about it," said Kelley lazily. "You don't have to be anybody special. You don't have to understand how it works. Nobody has to believe nothing. All you do, you just point it where you want it to work."

"Point it how?" I whispered.

He shrugged. "Call the doll by a name. Hate it, maybe."

"For God's sake, Kelley, you're crazy! Why, there can't be anything like that!"

"You eat a steak," Kelley said. "How's your gut know what to take and what to pass? Do *you* know?"

"Some people know."

"You don't. But your gut does. So there's lots of natural laws that are goin' to work whether anyone understands 'em or not. Lots of sailors take a trick at the wheel without knowin' how a steering engine works. Well, that's me. I know where I'm goin' and I know I'll get there. What do I care how does it work, or who believes what?"

"Fine, so what are you going to do?"

"Get what got Hal." His tone was just as lazy but his voice was very deep, and I knew when not to ask any more questions. Instead I said, with a certain amount of annoyance, "Why tell me?"

"Want you to do something for me."

"What?"

"Don't tell no one what I just said for a while. And keep something for me."

"What? And for how long?"

"You'll know."

I'd have risen up and roared at him if he had not chosen just that second to get up and drift out of the bedroom. "What gets me," he said quietly from the other room, "is I could have figured this out six months ago."

I fell asleep straining to hear him go out. He moves quieter than any big man I ever saw.

It was afternoon when I awoke. The doll was sitting on the mantelpiece glaring at me. Ugliest thing ever happened.

I saw Kelley at Hal's funeral. He and Milt and I had a somber drink afterward. We didn't talk about dolls. Far as I know Kelley shipped out right afterward. You assume that seamen do, when they drop out of sight. Milton was as busy as a doctor, which is very. I left the doll where it was for a week or two, wondering when Kelley was going to get around to his project. He'd probably call for it when he was ready. Meanwhile I respected his request and told no one about it. One day when some people were coming over I shoved it in the top shelf of the closet, and somehow it just got left there.

About a month afterward I began to notice the smell. I couldn't identify it right away; it was too faint; but whatever it was, I didn't like it. I traced it to the closet, and then to the doll. I took it down and sniffed it. My breath exploded out. It was that same smell a lot of people wish they could forget—what Milton called necrotic flesh. I came within an inch of pitching the filthy thing down the incinerator, but a promise is a promise. I put it down on the table, where it slumped repulsively. One of the legs was broken above the knee. I mean, it seemed to have two knee joints. And it was somehow puffy, sick-looking.

I had an old bell-jar somewhere, that once had a clock in it. I found it and a piece of inlaid linoleum, and put the doll under the jar at least so I could live with it.

I worked and saw people—dinner with Milton, once—and the days went by the way they do, and then one night it occurred to me to look at the doll again.

It was in pretty sorry shape. I'd tried to keep it fairly cool, but it seemed to be melting and running all over. For a moment I worried about what Kelley might say, and then I heartily damned Kelley and put the whole mess down in the cellar.

And I guess it was altogether two months after Hal's death that I wondered why I'd assumed Kelley would have to call for the little horror before he did what he had to do. He said he was going to get what got Hal, and he intimated that the doll was that something.

Well, that doll was being got, but good. I brought it up and put it under the light. It was still a figurine, but it was one unholy mess. "Attaboy, Kelley," I gloated. "Go get 'em, kid."

Milton called me up and asked me to meet him at Rudy's. He sounded pretty bad. We had the shortest drink yet.

He was sitting in the back booth chewing on the insides of his cheeks. His lips were gray and he slopped his drink when he lifted it.

"What in time happened to you?" I gasped.

He gave me a ghastly smile. "I'm famous," he said. I heard his glass chatter against his teeth. He said, "I called in so many consultants on Hal Kelley that I'm supposed to be an expert on that—on that . . . condition." He forced his glass back to the table with both hands and held it down. He tried to smile and I wished he wouldn't. He stopped trying and almost whimpered, "I can't nurse one of 'em like that again. I can't."

"You going to tell what happened?" I asked harshly. That works sometimes.

"Oh, oh yes. Well they brought in a . . . another one. At General. They called me in. Just like Hal. I mean *exactly* like Hal. Only I won't have to nurse this one, no I won't, I won't have to. She died six hours after she arrived."

"She?"

"You know what you'd have to do to someone to make them look like that?" he said shrilly. "You'd have to tie off parts so they mortified. You'd have to use a wood rasp, maybe; a club; filth to rub into the wounds. You'd have to break bones in a vise."

"All right, all right, but nobody—"

"And you'd have to do that for about two months, every day, every night." He rubbed his eyes. He drove his knuckles in so hard that I caught at his wrists. "I *know* nobody did it; did I say anyone did it?" he barked. "Nobody did anything to Hal, did they?"

"Drink up."

He didn't. He whispered, "She just said the same thing over

210

and over every time anyone talked to her. They'd say, 'What happened?' or 'Who did this to you?' or 'What's your name?' and she'd say. 'He called me Dolly.' That's all she'd say, just 'He called me Dolly'."

I got up. "Bye, Milt."

He looked stricken. "Don't go, will you, you just got—"

"I got to go," I said. I didn't look back. I had to get out and ask myself some questions. Think.

Who's guilty of murder, I asked myself, the one who pulls the trigger, or the gun?

I thought of a poor damn pretty, empty little face with greedy hot brown eyes, and what Kelley said, "I don't care about her one way or the other."

I thought, when she was twisting and breaking and sticking, how did it look to the doll? Bet she never even wondered about that.

I thought, action: A girl throws a fan at a man. Reaction: The man throws the girl at the fan. Action: A wheel sticks on a shaft. Reaction: Knock the shaft out of the wheel. Situation: We can't get inside. Resolution: Take the outside off it.

It's a way of thinking.

How do you kill a person? Use a doll.

How do you kill a doll?

Who's guilty, the one who pulls the trigger, or the gun?

"He called me Dolly."

"He called me Dolly."

"He called me Dolly."

When I got home the phone was ringing.

"Hi," said Kelley.

I said "It's all gone. The doll's all gone. Kelley," I said, "stay away from me."

"All right," said Kelley.